WAVES OF *Reason*

WAVES OF *Reason*

Restored

Part 5

Mary E. Hanks

www.maryehanks.com

Suzanne D. Williams Cover Design:

www.feelgoodromance.com

Cover photos: Jack Frog @ shutterstock.com

Visit Mary's website:

www.maryehanks.com

You can write Mary at

maryhanks@maryehanks.com.

For Ron

Thanks for being my big brother!

I admire your adventurous spirit.

.

For Jason

Here's to new chapters and happy adventures for us.

Always your girl.

"Come now, let us reason together,"

Isaiah 1:18

Basalt Bay Residents

Paisley Grant – Daughter of Paul and Penny Cedars

Judah Grant – Son of Edward and Bess Grant

Paige Cedars – Paisley's younger sister/mom to Piper

Peter Cedars – Paisley' older brother/fishing in Alaska

Paul Cedars – Paisley's dad/widower

Edward Grant – Mayor of Basalt Bay/Judah's dad

Bess Grant – Judah's mom/Edward's wife

Aunt Callie – Paisley's aunt/Paul's sister

Maggie Thomas – owner of Beachside Inn

Bert Jensen – owner of Bert's Fish Shack

Mia Till – receptionist at C-MER

Craig Masters – Judah's supervisor at C-MER

Mike Linfield – Judah's boss at C-MER

Lucy Carmichael – Paisley's high school friend

Brian Corbin – Sheriff's deputy

Kathleen Baker – newcomer to Basalt Bay

Bill Sagle – pastor

Geoffrey Carnegie – postmaster/local historian

Casey Clemons – floral shop owner

Patty Lawton – hardware store owner

Brad Keifer – fisherman/school chum of Peter's

James Weston – Paul's neighbor

Sal Donovan – souvenir shop owner

Fred Buckley – council member

Sue Taylor – council member

Penny Cedars – Paisley's mom/deceased

One

From the moment their hands touched over a basket of vanilla creamers in a hotel lobby in Las Vegas, Forest knew Paige Cedars was the woman for him. Sometimes it took only an instant for a man to recognize his destiny.

With a decade of investigative experience under his belt, Forest Harper controlled the urge to glower at Edward Grant, the man handcuffed to the table in the Basalt Bay interrogation room. He had to appear unbiased, as if he felt neutral regarding the case, just doing his job. Yeah, right. He despised this part of detective work. Staring into the face of a criminal, acting as if he didn't care what wrongs the guy had committed, drove him nuts.

Today, he was anything but impartial.

According to reports, Edward had physically injured and kidnapped his own daughter-in-law, Paisley Grant. And he threatened to harm a child in her sister Paige's care, which Forest was trying to get to the bottom of.

Thinking of Paige, the woman he'd been in love with for three years, being in potential danger shook his peace of mind to the core. It made him want to shake this rat until he got the answers he needed. Of course his own conscience wouldn't approve, and neither would the regional task-force director, Sheriff Morris, who contracted and deputized Forest to work on this case.

But how could he continue with the investigation as if the outcome didn't concern him? As if anything that happened to Paige Cedars didn't affect him, too? Should he recuse himself?

No way. Not after jumping at the chance to work in Basalt Bay. He had personal reasons for wanting to be here, near her, but he must stay focused on questioning the guilty man before him.

Steeling his features, Forest tapped the recording icon on his cell phone and eyeballed the sheet of questions on the table. "I hear you declined to have an attorney present during questioning. Is that true?"

"Innocent people don't need an attorney holding their hands. Unless she happens to be a real beauty." Edward grinned rakishly.

"What did you plan to do with Paisley Grant after you abducted her?" Forest asked in a monotone voice.

"Abducted." Edward snorted. "That the best you got, Detective? If so, let's adjourn this meeting due to faulty information."

Forest clenched his jaw, but he wanted to clench his fists, perhaps connect them with the ex-mayor's face. "Did you tie up Paisley? Put duct tape over her mouth?" How could any man treat a woman so vilely? Edward should be taken out to the woodshed and throttled.

Easy. Keep a cool façade.

"Sounds as if you've been watching too many cop shows. Next question."

With Edward's imperious attitude, the casual way his hands rested over the handcuff hook, and his crossed knees with one foot swaying, he could have been moderating a city council meeting—except for his attire. Instead of a three-piece suit, the prisoner's clothes were jailhouse orange with "Basalt Bay #106" embroidered in black across the chest.

"I'll remind you that you're accused of a serious crime." Forest leaned forward, his elbows pressing against the table. "Kidnapping is a felony in this state."

"As well it should be," Edward said in a milk-and-honey tone. "Why would I kidnap my daughter-in-law? Honestly, you've got the story wrong."

"So you deny the allegations?"

"Absolutely. Judah's missus and I get along *famously*."

This guy's smooth-talking lies riled Forest. Yesterday, he read Paisley's account of how Edward treated her contemptuously even before the kidnapping, and of his brutality when he subdued and tied her up. Now he claimed friendship with her? Unreal.

"What led to your abduction of Paisley?"

"You listen here." Edward rattled his chains. "That woman is troubled. Needs a psychiatric evaluation. Whatever she told you is false. I'm the mayor of Basalt Bay. Why would I abduct one of my citizens?"

"That's what I'm wondering. As mayor, you should have known better than to perpetrate a felony." As far as his ludicrous suggestion that Paisley was mentally unbalanced, Forest wouldn't even comment.

"Got proof of this so-called felony? I'm innocent until proven guilty, right?"

Forest felt that punch-in-the-gut sensation he got whenever he questioned some braggart who claimed innocence to get away with his crime. It made him want to buckle down twice as hard and make sure the guy got what was coming to him. "I've read the deputy's report and the eyewitnesses' accounts. There's plenty of proof of your guilt."

"Rumors. Too many liars in this town." Edward made a sucking sound between his teeth. "Check those supposed witnesses again. Some may tell a different story now."

"Meaning?"

"Question the deputy. I bet he'll recant his statement." Edward sneered. "Paige Cedars too. What will you do without any corroborating evidence?"

Why did he say Paige might go back on her testimony? If there was any coercion going on, Forest would dig up the truth.

"What were you doing at the art gallery the day Paisley found you there?"

Edward stared at the ceiling. "Taking a break from the job."

"Were you drinking alcohol?"

"A beer."

Forest skimmed through the paperwork. "According to Deputy Brian's report, seven empty, crushed beer cans littered the floor of the gallery."

"Paisley must have been thirsty." Edward chortled. "My son sure knows how to pick them."

Forest clamped his teeth together, keeping himself from saying something he might regret. Two years ago, he searched for and found Paisley in Chicago. For a brief time, he was in a serious relationship with her sister. He felt protective of both women, but he couldn't show his cards and expose his personal involvement.

"I take it you don't care for Judah's choice in women, huh?" Maybe he could find a chink in Edward's defenses.

"He doesn't listen to me. Never did. Always was a mama's boy."

"Did his choosing Paisley without your consent get under your skin?" Forest lowered his voice, trying to sound sympathetic. "Did it make you want to take revenge?"

"Uh-uh-uh." Edward squinted at him. "I see where you're going with this. Move on to the next question."

Too bad. For a second, Forest thought he was onto something. "On the day of Paisley's kidnapping, er, disappearance, what did you do after she stopped by the gallery?"

"Returned to City Hall. Mia Till will vouch for me, if you know what I mean." He exaggerated a sleazy wink.

"Mia Till." Forest jotted down the name. "Who is she to you?"

"She's my Girl Friday. A real looker, too."

Forest felt sorry for Mia Till, whoever she was.

"On the night of Paisley's disappearance, why were you fleeing to Portland?"

"There you go imagining things." Edward toyed with the lock attaching the handcuffs to the hook. "My favorite restaurant is there. No crime in that."

Right. "When you removed Paisley from the hospital in North Bend, what did you hope to achieve?"

"Can't a man take his daughter-in-law for a ride around town?" Edward shuffled his shoulders. "She needed fresh air. I was concerned about her."

Sure, he was.

"Do you call removing a patient's IV and dragging her through the hospital being concerned about her?"

"She wanted to get out of there. Didn't take much coaxing." Edward leaned his unshaven chin down and scratched his whiskers with his thumb. "You might as well stop questioning me. You aren't going to win."

"You want to bet?" was on Forest's tongue, but he didn't say it. In the reports, several people had mentioned Edward was manipulative and seemed delusional. That made sense now.

"Security camera footage at the hospital shows you propelling Paisley outside. If she wanted to go with you, why did she fight you?"

"Check your video again."

"Why?" Did someone tamper with it? "I'm sure what Deputy Brian said—"

"Deputy Brian is incompetent! If I didn't back his salary, promote him when he whined, he wouldn't have a job. Oh, I didn't mean—" Edward coughed hard.

"So, you're saying there have been underhanded dealings in the mayor's office?" Forest jotted down his words verbatim, even though he was recording the session, too. If anything went haywire in the case, he might get him on a technicality.

"Nothing like that. Meeting adjourned yet?"

"Have you ever pressured Deputy Brian or someone else into changing their eyewitness account?"

"Enough questions!" Edward shouted. "I demand a break!"

"Fine," Forest said calmly, even though he didn't get much from the deposed mayor. "We'll take a short recess." Pushing away from the table, he strode to the door and tapped on the glass for Brian, his temporary coworker, to let him out of the room.

Over the next couple of days, he'd be questioning others in town—Judah and Paisley Grant, Paul Cedars, Bess Grant, and Craig Masters, if the man who might have been Edward's accomplice could be located. He'd also speak with Mia Till, Edward's "Girl Friday."

And Paige. Unfortunately, interrogating her, when all he wanted to do was take her in his arms and promise her his undying love, wasn't something he looked forward to.

Two

Paige met Forest's gray-green gaze in the glow of candlelight, and shivers danced up her spine. Their clasped hands rested on an off-white tablecloth in a high-rise restaurant overlooking Las Vegas. Would he kiss her tonight?

Paige Cedars glided her paintbrush through several shades of acrylic paint on her palette—Ultramarine, Cadmium Red, Yellow Ochre, and Titanium White—and blended them together. Lightly, she swept the wet bristles above the horizon line of the canvas, deepening the hues of sunset. A touch of red in the center of the sky enhanced the focal point. A smidge of Prussian Blue mixed with white formed shadows beneath the clouds. A fan of yellow for the setting sun.

There.

Pleased, she picked up a clean paintbrush and swished it across the surface of the canvas, the brush dancing against her fingers as if it were an extension of herself.

She glanced at the wall clock—seven a.m. Piper, her two-year-old, would be waking up any minute. Per her normal routine, Paige had gotten up at five o'clock to focus on her art. A single mom needed to seek out moments in the day to nurture herself. Being an artist was who she'd always been, even as a child. It was her connection with the past, with Mom, and with whatever her future held. She could get lost in her art for hours.

Not everyone understood that about her. Mom had, but then she died, and Paige suffered the loss of the one person who really got her. Her sister, Paisley, didn't fathom how she felt about painting and photography. Forest probably wouldn't have, either. Although, for a short while, she thought he did. Just something else she misunderstood about him.

Goodness, she fell for the man so quickly. How had she, quiet, reserved Paige Cedars, let that happen? She didn't believe in love at first sight. Was a cynic when it came to the way some local girls fell in and out of romantic relationships. She pitied the poor guys who ambled into Basalt Bay and nosedived into Lucy Carmichael's or Mia Till's flirtatious traps.

Paige wasn't like that. Yet, foolishly, irrationally, she fell hard for Forest Harper during an art exposition she attended in Las Vegas three years ago. What a weak-willed ninny. So naïve. So in love. *Sigh.*

Never again. She was stronger now. She knew better than to allow a man past the brick wall she'd erected around her heart. At least, not until he proved himself trustworthy. Unlike Forest Harper ever had.

Ugh. Enough dwelling on the past and stirring up old feelings. That part of her life was over, and good riddance.

The only reason she gave in to so many thoughts about Forest recently was because she heard he was in Basalt Bay to investigate Edward Grant's kidnapping of Paisley. Knowing he was near, in her hometown, kept her heart pounding hard and her daydreams on high alert. But nothing good could come of daydreaming. Nothing good at all.

Plunging her brush into the paint-splotched Mason jar of water, she churned the cloudy liquid in a counter-clockwise motion as she'd seen her mother do a thousand times. Every time she cleaned her brush, she thought of Mom. Paige wiped her hands on a cloth and stepped back, observing her morning's work. Not bad.

Now, if she could figure out how to sell this nautical-themed piece without the benefit of her gallery, it would help pay the bills. Not that she only painted for provision, but since Piper came along, doing so figured into the equation. Besides, she'd rather make a living from her art than serving food at Bert's Fish Shack as Paisley planned to do after she recovered from her injuries. Selling her work would be more fulfilling to her than becoming a clerk at Lewis's Super like Bess Grant recently did, too. Although Judah's mom seemed to thrive in the grocery environment.

What would Forest think of her painting, if he saw it? Would he say her art had improved? But there she was wondering about him again. Why keep torturing herself?

He was a memory. A bad dream.

Although not all bad.

And therein lay the problem. Some of their romantic times together were swoon-worthy, golden moments to be taken out, remembered, and relished. *Relished?* Her cheeks burned. No going there. No reliving tender, unforgettable moments between them.

She trudged over to the sink and scrubbed her hands free of paint. If only her mind could be washed of the past as simply.

Ever since Judah told her three days ago that Forest would be assisting with the case, she hadn't stopped picturing her ex's sparkling gray-green eyes that sometimes hued to deep jade when he was feeling emotional or romantic. Nor could she forget the gentle way he used to smooth his fingers over her cheeks, gazing deeply into her eyes as if peering right into her heart. And the way he kissed her ... how could she ever forget that? She still dreamed of those kisses. Of him. The way he whispered he loved her.

And look how that turned out.

Groan.

Forest was a blip in her past. A mistake—except for Piper. She could never consider her sweet girl, the light of her life, a mistake, even if her father turned out to be a jerk.

She dropped several tubes into the plastic bucket of acrylics. Painting wasn't keeping her mind off Forest, so she'd better do something else—prepare Piper's breakfast, have another cup of coffee, scrub the house clean—until all thoughts of him disappeared.

Raising a daughter on her own had made her tougher and more independent. Maybe she had Forest to thank for that.

Because you left me alone and pregnant, I am who I am. Thanks a lot.

She rubbed the bristles of the brushes against a dry cloth, then set them in her paint supplies case. Even if she were chewing on injustices of the past, she wouldn't mistreat her paintbrushes. Carefully, she arranged each one in the tray so the bristles didn't get jammed together.

Was Forest as handsome as she remembered? Would his smile shoot tingling sensations all the way to her toes? Did he marry Elinore?

A sharp pain rippled through her chest. Why did she have to think of her? The other woman.

Three years ago, Forest left Paige because of his secrets.

Now, she hid from him because of hers.

For the last two days, she kept her doors locked, staying inside with the curtains drawn. Better safe than sorry. She didn't want to accidentally run into him at Lewis's Super or Bert's. She didn't want him seeing her with their daughter—the child she hadn't told him about yet—at the beach or in a public place. Even though she would tell him about Piper someday, she'd be the one to choose the setting and how it all played out.

If he hadn't left her, they would still be a family. Still madly in love, maybe.

A chill crept over her. Paige tugged on the cardigan she set across the back of the kitchen chair earlier. Cool fall weather was the cause of her shivers. Not because she might still be in love with Forest. If anything, she hated him. Resented him as much as she ever despised Edward Grant.

Yet, strangely, love and hate intermingled like white and black paint blending into gray. Three years, including nine months of pregnancy, should have scraped her heart clean of any tenderness she felt for the man. Should have.

Why didn't it? Because her heart hadn't healed? Maybe because her brain refused to let go of the sweet memories lingering, trapped, inside of her.

If she were tempted to fall for Forest Harper again—a highly improbable if—there was one foolproof protection she kept wrapped around her emotions like metal armor. She focused on it now, chewing on the words, letting the hurt swirl through her, engulfing her with … what? Bitterness?

On their last night together, with Forest falling asleep against her shoulder, he'd whispered three words that were hot-branded to her heart.

"*Sweet dreams, Elinore.*"

Three

Holding hands, talking and laughing, Paige stayed close to Forest as they strolled through the hotel lobby where her art exhibition was being held. How did they go from being strangers to a romantic relationship in three days?

Paige stacked building blocks with Piper on the carpet of the two-year-old's room, taking them higher and higher.

"Mow. Mow." Piper clapped her hands and danced around the tower.

A strong knocking at the back door stilled Paige's hands, her heart racing. Forest? Only family and friends used the back door. Did he remember that from his brief stay here?

She set the block on the stack and tried ignoring the knocking. Let him pound on the door all he wanted, she wasn't answering. Didn't want to talk to him. Wasn't ready for that discussion.

Shoving over the tower, Piper squealed, "I did it. *Mow. Mow.*" She clapped.

"Shhhh. Yes, you did it." Paige kept her voice quiet, not wanting the person at the door to hear.

"*Mow* blocks. *Biggew.*"

"Okay. Settle down."

Piper dropped onto her bottom and stacked a block over another one. "Mommy too?"

"Okay." Paige set a couple of blocks on top of Piper's.

The knock sounded again, louder this time. Whoever it was didn't appear to be going away.

Piper tipped her head. "Papa?" Her gray-green eyes reminded Paige so much of Forest's.

"I don't think it's Papa." She checked her cell. No calls or texts. Although, that didn't mean Dad hadn't stopped by. They often dropped by each other's house. Ever since his diabetic emergency six weeks ago, she kept closer tabs on him. But she hadn't seen him since they got back from North Bend two days ago. Maybe he was checking on them.

Should she sneak into the kitchen and peek around the curtain? What if it was Forest and he spotted her? Ugh. She was being silly. So what if he saw her? He might not recognize himself as Piper's dad, anyway. Although being a career detective, he'd surely notice the toddler's light hair, grayish eyes, and how her smile resembled his.

He deserves to know he has a daughter, too.

Yeah, yeah. She stuffed down the voice of guilt.

"*Pway* outside?" Piper jumped up and pranced in a circle. "Swing?"

"Not today. Let's clean up the blocks, then we'll read some stories." Paige tugged the empty plastic tub closer and tossed in one of the blocks. "Help me clean up, Piper."

"*Mow* blocks." Her voice turned whiny.

"I said—"

Her cell phone vibrated, and she checked the screen. Judah's name popped up.

Are you home?

Her brother-in-law was at the door? Not Forest. Thank goodness.

Yes. Sorry. Be right there, she typed in.

She scooped up Piper. "Uncle Judah's here."

"*Unca Dzudah!*" Piper bounced in Paige's arms.

"That's right." She scurried into the kitchen and peered around the edge of the curtain to make sure he came alone before opening the door. "Come in. Sorry I took so long to answer."

"No problem." Judah strode into the kitchen, grinning at Piper. "Hey, squirt."

"*Unca Dzudah!*"

He held out his hands and Piper nearly leaped out of Paige's arms and into his.

"Whoa. You're feisty this afternoon."

"No kidding." Paige self-consciously brushed her sweater where Piper spilled grape juice on her during lunch.

"*Hosie?*" Piper lunged up and down in Judah's arms.

"You want a horse ride?"

"*Hosie. Hosie.*"

"You got it." He galloped out of the kitchen and into the living room, bouncing Piper and making neighing sounds.

Paige followed them, chuckling as her brother-in-law galloped around the furniture, then down the hall. A minute later he stopped in front of her and, making a whinnying sound, set Piper on her feet. "There you go, squirt."

"*Mow. Mow.*" She lifted her arms and whined.

"Why don't you get some books to show me?" Paige intervened before her daughter started crying. Piper wasn't good at stopping an activity she enjoyed. Paige was proactively working on circumventing her outbursts, but sometimes a loud tantrum ensued. "Go get your books, Pipe."

"*Mow hosie.*" Her lower lip protruded. She stomped her foot. "*Hosie,* now."

"I'm all tuckered out." Judah blew out a breath.

"*Mow,*" she demanded, her face turning red.

"Piper"—Paige squatted down and looked her daughter in the eye—"choose two books and we'll look at them together while I visit with Uncle Judah."

"Books?" She sniffed and her lower lip wobbled.

"That's right. Get the horse book you like, okay?"

Piper wiped her eyes with both fists. "*Yike* books." She shuffled down the hall toward her room.

"Crisis averted. Thanks for making her day." Paige sat on the couch and swayed her hand toward the recliner. "Have a seat." What was Judah doing here? Bringing news of Forest?

"Sure thing." He dropped into the chair.

"How are things going? Is Paisley feeling better?" She almost forgot about her sister's injuries in the middle of hiding out from Forest. "Are things going okay?"

"She's getting better. Sitting on our veranda in the sunshine helps. I'm thankful for the mild fall weather." Judah sank deeper into the cushions. "I thank God that she's doing so well."

Yet, he wore a troubled expression. And he was here. Not that Paige minded him stopping by. He'd done that over the last couple of years since Piper came along. Although, she assumed he wouldn't be checking on them as much since he and Paisley renewed their vows. And ever since her personal conversation about him with Paisley, she'd felt a strain. Whether due to her imagination or her guilty conscience, she wasn't sure. Maybe her sister kept that conversation private, anyway.

"What's with the closed curtains?" Judah glanced toward the drawn floor-to-ceiling drapes. "And not answering the door?"

"Just staying home."

"Hiding?"

Annoyance zinged through her. Is that why he came over? To badger her about Forest? "What if I am? It's my prerogative whether or not I want to see him, isn't it?"

"Sure."

Piper danced back into the room, carrying two large picture books, and plopped them on the couch. She jostled up beside Paige.

"Good job, Pipe." She appreciated the distraction as her daughter snuggled beside her and opened the book to pictures of a bear family.

"Papa. Mama. Baby." Piper patted each character's picture.

"That's right." Avoiding Judah's gaze, Paige turned the pages slowly. Piper jabbered and pointed at objects in the book.

"Paige, look, I'm sorry." Judah cleared his throat. "I didn't mean to meddle or imply anything."

"No?" She cut him a glance.

"I'm concerned about you and Piper, that's all. I care for you both."

He looked so contrite all the fight drained out of her. Why was she taking out her frustration on him, anyway? He kindly stopped by, and here she was lashing out at him. And she *was* hiding.

"Is he still in town?" She kept her voice low.

"Yeah." Judah obviously knew who she meant. "He came by to question Paisley and me yesterday. Not a long session, since she tires easily. Even now, she's taking a nap. Forest's questions were pretty intense."

"He goes after what he wants, that's for sure." Paige felt the heat of a blush warm her cheeks. "You were right. I have been hiding."

"I shouldn't have said anything. Are you okay?"

If only she'd found someone like Judah for herself. Once, she thought she had. "Sure, I'm a tough cookie."

His wry expression said he doubted her. "I wanted to warn you that he mentioned needing to talk with you, also. He's pushing hard for answers."

Her heart lurched. "About what? Why does he want to see me?"

"He's interviewing people. Building his case against Edward." Judah gulped. Did he feel bad about his father being in jail? Or was he worried about her facing Forest? "He seems intent on finding out if anyone else was involved in the crime."

"Like?"

"You. Me. Any of us."

Tremors raced through her. Forest wanted to interrogate her? Here she was afraid of seeing him for personal reasons. Had he read her statement about the night of the kidnapping? What if he figured out who the minor was that Edward threatened? She didn't list Piper's name or say she was her daughter, but what if someone else did? The sensation of a hundred-pound weight pressing down on her shoulders got heavier.

"Is everything all right?"

She shook her head, not wanting to discuss anything about Forest. She'd kept it a secret for so long the words felt locked beneath her ribs, padlocked in an emotional dungeon.

"Is he—" Judah cringed. "Sorry, I shouldn't say anything."

"You might as well go ahead."

"You'll probably consider it none of my business. And, frankly, I agree."

His honesty surprised her. "I haven't told anyone he's her—" She nodded sideways at Piper. "You know, right?" When Paisley was in the hospital, Paige implied to Judah that she knew Forest. "D-A-D."

He nodded slowly.

Piper stared up at her with those Forest-esque eyes. Someday, she'd tell her daughter the truth. That her mama loved her daddy with her whole heart. That she thought they had something special. How could she have been so wrong?

Judah raked his fingers through his hair. "I saw the resemblance as soon as I met him."

"Did you? Every day I see him in her." She smiled at Piper, reassuring her in case the little girl felt any of her mom's tension. "Now isn't the time to discuss it, though."

"I understand." Judah leaned forward, elbows on his knees. "If you ever want to talk, come out to the cottage, okay? Paisley and I would love to hear your story. However much you want to share. Honestly, I just want what's best for you and the squirt, here."

She was thankful for Judah's and her dad's involvement in Piper's life. What would she have done without their caring and concern over the last few years?

"Thanks. Keeping it to myself has become a way of life. A way of protecting myself."

"A difficult one, I'm guessing." His eyes glimmered toward Piper.

"Sometimes."

Thankfully, he didn't push for answers the way Aunt Callie and a few others had done about her being a single mom. Still, it was difficult to be vulnerable about her past, about the choices she made.

She took a big breath, letting it out slowly. "At times, the magnitude of my deception chokes me. I will tell him, eventually."

"I'm sure you will. I'm sorry for your pain." He reached over and patted her hand where it rested on the couch arm. "Remember, God's grace covers our pasts, our hurts, everything. His love is beautiful and tender, and He gives it to us freely. All we have to do is accept it."

He'd told her these things many times before. Yet Paige struggled with the concept of a loving God caring for her. Still, Judah's comments about grace and mercy spoke to her heart. How could they not? She'd been taking Piper to Sunday School for over a year now, so she had listened to some of Pastor Sagle's sermons, too. But something always stopped her from accepting what he and Judah said about God's love and grace being enough.

"Like I said, if you ever want to talk—" He left the invitation open.

The room grew silent other than Piper's babbling.

"I should go, but I wanted to ask a favor." He stood. "Would it be possible for Piper to come out and spend some time with Paisley and me?"

"When?"

"Would this afternoon work?"

"Not if … he … is going to be there."

"He won't be." Judah spread out his hands. "Last I heard, he's doing paperwork at the deputy's office. I thought it might cheer up Paisley to spend some time looking at books with Piper."

"I don't know, Judah." She swallowed hard. "Bad timing."

"Okay. Another time. Whenever you feel comfortable."

"Thank you for understanding."

"No problem." He leaned down and kissed Piper's cheek. "Bye, squirt."

"Say goodbye to Uncle Judah."

"Bye-bye." Piper grinned.

"See you two later." He strode toward the kitchen. At the doorway, he paused. "We're here for you if you need anything. We're family. Don't hesitate to call on us, okay?"

"Okay." But she wouldn't. The fierce independence she developed over the last three years kept her from needing anyone.

Four

"Are you okay?" From his outdoor lounge chair next to Paisley's, Judah watched his wife, checking for signs of fatigue. Her eyes looked clearer than they had a few days ago. Her bruises were fading to yellow. The sores around her mouth were healing in the fall sunshine and fresh air. But she was supposed to be taking it easy—doctor's orders—and it seemed she kept trying to do anything but rest.

"That's the fifth time you've asked me how I'm doing in the last half hour." She shoved off the blanket he'd tucked around her. "I'm almost well, Judah. I know you're concerned but—" She grabbed the pillow from behind her back and bopped him with it.

"Hey. What's that for?"

"To show you I'm not an invalid. Lighten up."

"Okay, okay. You're not an invalid." He chuckled. "But you have to continue resting."

"I am, but I'm sick of it."

He liked Paisley's feisty side. It meant she must be feeling better. Still, she needed to relax until the week of bed rest ended, which meant five more days of R and R.

"I'm tired of sitting around doing nothing. However"— her tone changed, and her eyes sparkled—"I can't complain about the view." She looked him over and whistled.

"Oh, yeah?" Grinning, he let his gaze wander over her, too.

"What are you thinking about?" She ran her index finger around his wedding ring.

"Daydreaming about us taking our relationship to the next step."

"Mmm." She walked her fingers up his arm, dancing them in ticklish movements across his shoulder. "Sorry for all the waiting without a honeymoon, Mister Bridegroom."

Her whispered words caused a jolt to his heart. Leaning forward, he met her lips in a soft kiss, quelling the desire to push for more. While he was close to her, he stuffed the pillow behind her back again. Her gleaming eyes looked like she was still feeling mischievous.

"Now, be nice."

"I'm always nice."

"Sweetheart, I believe you are." Smoothing his fingers down her hairline, he swept back dark strands with the pads of his fingertips. He wanted to keep kissing her, but if he did it would be hard to put on the brakes. He planned to keep his promise to be patient and wait until she was completely ready for their honeymoon to begin.

He settled against the chair, watching the waves roll up their beach. Despite the peaceful scene, a troublesome image flashed through his thoughts. When he least expected it, he kept imagining Paisley lying in the hospital bed, pale and weak, injured, and emotionally broken. He glanced at her facial wounds that still looked sore, and thinking of what his father did to her, he wanted to weep.

"You know, one of these days you're going to look at me and not see me as some kid who got beat up in a school fight." Paisley huffed.

"What do you mean?"

"Stop acting like I'm battered and bruised. I'm not." She fake punched his arm, drawing his attention back to her instead of the darker place where his thoughts had drifted.

"We both know that wasn't any playground brawl." He brushed his fingers down the side of her face, avoiding the marks. "You were seriously injured, Pais."

"I know. But thank the Lord I'm doing so much better."

"I'm glad. And I do." He leaned his elbow on the armrest of his chair. "Tomorrow we start our counseling sessions with Pastor Sagle."

"You had to remind me."

"We probably need them now more than ever." A snapshot of her being tied up in the backseat of Craig's car came to mind and he tried to shake it off. "I promised the pastor we'd attend the three sessions we bailed on before our vow renewal. Maybe more."

"They'll probably help." She stuck out her tongue at him. "Teach us how to share dishwashing duties or something."

Judah chuckled. "I don't mind doing dishes."

"I know. Am I the luckiest girl in the world, or what?"

"I'm the lucky one." He stared into her dark gaze until the sound of a car door slamming drew his attention away.

A few seconds later, Forest Harper, wearing a dark baseball hat tugged low over his eyes, rounded the corner. "Here you two are. I knocked on the front door, but no one answered."

A shadow crossed Paisley's face like she wasn't happy to see the detective.

"Sorry I didn't hear you." Judah stood and shook the man's hand. "Welcome."

"Thanks. I hope I'm not intruding."

"Not at all." Although, Judah had assured Paige he wouldn't be here today. Good thing she said no about Piper coming out for a visit.

Why was Paisley frowning at their guest like that? Maybe she didn't appreciate the grilling Forest gave her yesterday. Judah figured he'd just been doing his job, hunting for answers.

"What brings you out this way?" he asked. "Did you think of another question?"

"One. Do you know where Paige is?"

"I saw her earlier today. Did you call her?"

"I did." Forest adjusted his hat. "And I went by her house, but no response. Although, she might have been there; her car was. Maybe she's avoiding me."

Perhaps, but Judah wouldn't give away anything about Paige's personal life.

"Why do you need to talk with her?" Paisley asked.

Her throat sounded dry, so Judah picked up a water bottle and handed it to her.

"Your abduction took place from her art gallery." Forest shrugged conclusively.

"So? My sister didn't know anything about Edward imprisoning me there."

"How can you be sure? In my experience, innocent people don't avoid being questioned."

So, Forest perceived Paige was hiding something? Judah inwardly chuckled at the irony, although not at his suspicions.

"Are you implying Paige knew of my kidnapping?" Paisley sounded indignant. "She's a private person, that's all. Just leave her alone." She took a long swallow of water.

"Sorry, I can't do that." Forest's voice deepened. "I'm not saying she's involved. In fact, I doubt she is, but I have to talk to her before I can wrap up the case."

Judah was aware of Forest and Paige's past. But did Forest assume Paisley knew?

"If you hear from her, please tell her I need to speak with her."

"Will do." Judah checked his watch. Half-past two. Paige was probably at home with Piper. If Forest couldn't leave town until he spoke with her about the case, she was prolonging his stay by hiding from him.

"Thanks. Talk to you guys later." Forest waved and strode out of sight.

Paisley pulled her blanket up to her chin. "There's something odd about that man."

"Why do you say that?" Judah dropped into the lounge chair he'd vacated and listened for Forest's car to exit the driveway.

"He questions everything. Stares at us as if we're the ones who did something wrong instead of Edward. It bugs me."

"He's paid to be suspicious."

She squinted at him. "Wait a sec. I recognize that look."

"What look?"

"The one you're wearing right now. You know something about him, don't you?"

Guilty thoughts reeled through Judah. Now, how was he going to be honest with his wife while honoring Paige's confidence?

Five

Forest linked his fingers with Paige's as they strolled around the hotel's outdoor waterfalls. She gazed into his eyes, her dark irises gleaming, and a breath caught in his throat. Was this how falling in love felt?

Forest parked his rental car, a white VW Jetta, down the block from Paige's house in the subdivision and sank low in his seat. Binoculars ready, he'd surveil her property for the rest of the day, all night, however long it took for her to come outside. He had plenty of stakeout experience from his last decade of detective work. Possessed enough patience to wait for a long time.

Was she hiding from him because of their past? Or was she involved in Edward's crimes against her sister like the ex-mayor implied? Not that Forest believed anything Edward said. But what did he mean about Paige changing her statement?

Surely, he was lying. There had to be an explanation for her not answering her door, too.

The sweet woman Forest had been in love with, was still in love with, would not harm anyone or be involved in any misconduct. Yet, he had to follow protocol and pursue the truth, regardless of his previous relationship with her. Even if it caused more problems between them? He sighed. Even then.

Lord, could You work things out for us? I want to trust You in everything. Help me find the truth yet walk in grace. And while You're working things out, could You speak to Paige's heart? Soften her feelings toward me. I'm so sorry for what happened between us in the past.

Having become a believer in Christ only five months ago, Forest was still new in his faith, walking in grace, and following the Lord. But every day, he was trying to remember to pray and cast his burdens, his doubts and struggles, his everything, on God.

His past still troubled him, too. In a recent sermon, he'd heard about sins being washed clean because of what Jesus did on the cross. That probably meant he shouldn't keep mulling them over, mentally chewing on them like a dog with a bone. Yet how could he break the habit? He had to face his past. Make amends, if he could, starting with talking to Paige. He sighed. More for him to pray about.

All along the block, he recognized the effects of the recent hurricanes. A downed tree lay partially chopped up in one yard. Plastic sheeting covered several homes' windows. Roofing materials were stacked on a few bare roofs. Paige's house looked normal, as much as he remembered from his short visit here three years ago. Apparently, her place didn't sustain major damage like others around town did.

Seeing her single-story house brought back fond memories of the days they spent together here. At least, before the phone call came that changed everything.

If he could alter one decision in his life, he'd never have left, never have broken Paige's heart, or his. However, when news of Elinore's near-deadly car accident came, it hit him hard. Guilt over how he ended things between them outweighed his new feelings of marital obligations. He hadn't meant for it to be a slap in Paige's face as if he didn't care for her. But how else might a new bride feel when her bridegroom of two weeks left without much explanation?

Wait. Was that movement in the carport?

Dropping the binoculars, Forest hunkered lower behind the steering wheel and picked up a road map. He held the large paper in front of his face, peering over the top. Paige speed-walked out of the carport and trotted past him without glancing his way. He heaved a breath. She looked amazing, even with a blue baseball cap tugged over her eyebrows, a bulging backpack flung over one shoulder, and dark sunglasses covering her eyes.

Paige. Here was the woman who filled his daydreams and night dreams. His heart pounded a drumbeat in his throat. He wanted to run after her, embrace her, and kiss her with every romantic impulse he subdued for three years. Fat chance she'd let that happen.

A picture of how she looked in her simple dark-gray dress, standing in front of him, her eyes shining at him in the wedding chapel in Vegas, came to mind. How they giggled in anticipation of their married night ahead, a life of loving each other just beginning, and sharing the high of doing something so secretive that no one in their real worlds knew about. He swallowed a bunch of times, having trouble getting the dryness out of his throat.

Even though they made a spur-of-the-moment decision to elope, he'd meant every word of his vows. In meeting Paige, his world flipped a switch from gray to multi-colored. That was Paige—full of life and beauty and color. When they split up, everything reverted to gray, drab, and lifeless for him.

He lost his purpose. Dove into more unfulfilling work. Passing time with meaningless tasks until he couldn't stand it anymore. Then the memo crossed his desk about a kidnapping in Basalt Bay. Of course, he couldn't let anyone else take the assignment.

Up ahead, Paige strode toward the trail he knew led to the beach.

With one hand, he fumbled with the door handle and zipped up his black coat to his chin with the other. Tugging his baseball cap low and donning dark sunglasses, he eased out of the car and shut the door with a soft click.

Replicating Paige's fast pace, he trailed her. A couple of times, he stepped off the sidewalk, playacting as if he were searching for something. Then he eased down the trail where she went, the sound of pounding waves drawing him forward. He peered around the last bush before the trail opened to the beach. There she was, trudging along the seashore toward the north side of town. Where was she hiking alone? Didn't she tell him she hated the sea?

He followed from a distance, wanting to observe her actions before speaking to her. What was the bulky object in her backpack? Did it have anything to do with Edward's claim of her recanting? What if he paid for her silence? Or threatened the minor again?

Forest groaned. Once his brain got hyper-focused on a piece of a crime puzzle, it was hard for him to let go of it.

He strode to the water's edge. Bending over, he grabbed a smooth rock. When Paige gazed back in his direction, he sidearm tossed the stone into the waves as if he weren't watching her.

A few minutes later, he leapfrogged over a chunk of driftwood and kept following her down the beach. What would she say when he caught up to her? What should he say? *I've missed you like I've been living with half a heart. I made a terrible mistake. Any chance you want to get married again?*

Yeah, right. For being a smart detective, he came up with some bogus ideas. But, man, seeing her back at her house for those few seconds undid him. Made him long for so many things he'd missed. Mainly, just having the privilege of being with her, holding her. He'd do anything to get that back.

Suddenly, a strong gust of wind hit him from behind, pushing him forward like a kick in the backside. He clutched his hat before it flew off.

Down the beach, Paige's hat became airborne like a kite flipping about in the wind. She chased it across the sand, almost reaching it, then it popped up as if not giving up the fight before diving into a tidal pool. Yelling at it—he couldn't understand what she said, although he chuckled at her vehemence—she scooped up the dripping hat, slapped the fabric against her hand, and shoved it into a side pocket of her backpack.

Even from here, her dark hair looked lovely. It was nice she kept it long. He'd loved her hair. Enjoyed strumming his fingers through it when he kissed her. When he— Ugh. Forbidden thoughts. Yet he couldn't stop thinking about that precious time with her. Didn't want to, either. *Lord, help me.*

Kicking at the wet muddy sand, he trudged forward, the dampness in his socks uncomfortable. How much farther was Paige hiking? Perhaps, to the old lighthouse in the distance. Too bad he didn't wear boots instead of the sponge-like loafers soaking his feet.

Not far ahead, she climbed up on a large, flat rock and was setting something up. A tripod? Oh, did she hike all this way to take photos? Now he felt foolish. Of course, the bulky items in her pack must have to do with photography. Nothing underhanded. Nothing having to do with Edward. Forest wanted to kick himself for the dishonorable thoughts he'd entertained about her based on something the ex-mayor said.

The graceful way her hands moved around the camera body, setting dials, adjusting the lens, reminded Forest of a dance. He recalled how her slim artist's hands had felt sliding into his. The two of them swaying to slow music. Kissing. Whispering flirtatious things in each other's ears. Man. Better rein in those thoughts. He yanked off his hat and ran his hand over his hair. Sighed.

Paige bent over, peering into the camera, caught up in what she was doing, and apparently didn't hear his approach. A mental image of her holding up a canvas painting, pointing out details to him, the way her dark eyes shone with delight, sent shivers through him. So many memories.

She glanced over her shoulder at him, her eyes widening. "What are you doing here?" Then grabbing her camera and tripod, she scrambled off the rock and took off running.

Not the reaction he hoped for.

"Paige, wait! I just want to talk with you." He sprinted around the boulder, his smooth soles skidding in the wet sand as he tried catching up with her.

Wearing rubber boots, she splashed right through a tidal pool, splattering the air with water droplets. She climbed on another rock and scurried over several low, wide layers of blackish boulders. Suddenly, as if skidding on ice, her boots slid. Her hands holding the photography equipment shot up, flailing. She made a squealing sound and disappeared over the other side.

"Paige!" Picturing her injured, maybe lying on the sand where she fell, Forest sped around the rocks. To his relief, he found her standing, dusting herself off. "Are you all right? I'm so sorry for startling you."

"I'm fine." She yanked off her sunglasses and glared at him.

"Anything I can do to help?"

"Walk away. You're good at that."

He gulped. Not knowing what to say, how to react to the pain her words caused, he bent over and picked up her tripod.

She snatched it from him. "Why are you here?"

His dreams of a possible happy reunion between them washed out to sea. "I'm working on Edward Grant's case."

"So I heard. I meant here. Why are you following me?"

"I was hoping we could talk." He kept his voice free of the emotional currents strumming through him. He wouldn't say anything about having suspected her of being involved with Edward's case, either.

"We have nothing to discuss."

"On the contrary, I'd say we have plenty to talk about. I've missed you, Paige."

Six

Heart hammering, Paige caught a whiff of Forest's musky deodorant as he placed his hands at her waist and pulled her to him. Before meeting him, she never knew how wonderful being held by a man could be.

Paige clenched her jaw, staring at the man who had vowed to cling to her for the rest of his life. The one who promised faithfulness and devotion, then rushed back to his ex the first chance he got. While part of her wanted to lash out, maybe to slug him, she felt strangely trapped in a time warp, staring into his moist gray-green gaze as if he'd just kissed her. Why was he looking at her so adoringly?

He missed her? Right.

Why was her heart beating so wretchedly fast? Like it might explode out of her chest. *Traitor.* Too much time had passed for such a reaction. Sure, she daydreamed of seeing

Forest again. Even journaled about her romantic feelings for him. But her strong reaction to him now was probably due to her secret about Piper. Not because of any amorous feelings she still had for the man.

She looped the camera strap over her neck. In jerky movements, she collapsed the tripod and tucked it and her sunglasses into her pack without mentioning anything personal like, "Oh, by the way, we have a daughter. And she looks just like you."

Hoping he'd take the hint and leave her alone, she turned and marched toward the lighthouse. She hiked out this far to photograph the decrepit relic of the past, and that's exactly what she intended to do.

With the tide coming in, she had to hurry, or else she'd be walking in deep beach grasses all the way back to town. Imagining wet strands brushing against her hands and legs like sticky spaghetti noodles, she shuddered.

Just ahead, in front of the lighthouse, white cascading bursts of sea-foam exploded into the air, startling her with their intensity and power as they hit the rocks. The turbulent seawater colliding with the land, even tearing up a plant growing between two chunks of basalt and submerging it into the waves, made her stomach twist in knots. Thanks to her mother's dire warnings—*Don't go near the waves or they'll grab you and drag you to your death*—she'd avoided being close to the sea for most of her life.

Lately, feeling bolder, she took more beach walks. But this, coming near the tumultuous swells, was far more daring than anything she'd ever done by the water.

Gritting her teeth, she was determined to get closer to her focal point and set up her tripod again. She'd take a few wide-angle shots, then some freestyle photos. She half climbed, half crawled onto a pile of wet boulders, being more cautious after her previous slip. Water pounded the stones, but the spray on the other side didn't reach her.

She glanced back at Forest, standing at the base of the rocks behind her. He wore a concerned look but didn't say anything as she withdrew the tripod from her backpack again. Maybe her sharp words had stymied him into not speaking to her at all.

If so, good. She didn't want to hear any of his lame excuses.

In fact, she'd like to forget about capturing the perfect shots of the lighthouse and go home. This was too close to the spray bursting in repetitions like a geyser over the basalt. Too near Forest. But if she left, she wouldn't get the lighthouse photos she wanted. Her hike out here, and the effort it took arranging a playdate for Piper with her neighbor's daughter, would have been in vain. She couldn't let that happen.

Keeping her balance on the precarious rock, she attached the camera to the tripod. The waning sunlight hit the top of the lighthouse, scattering the afternoon fog like glitter. She aimed the lens. A bit of fog still swirled at the top of the lighthouse.

"Great shot," Forest commented.

She didn't respond. *Focus.*

In her mind's eye, she pictured a cargo-carrying ship tossed about on a rough sea, barreling toward these rocks that would rip it to shreds, when suddenly a bright light lit up the night sky, leading the boat safely into Basalt Bay Harbor. Sometimes, creating a story in her mind helped her artwork come to life for her. Imagining the lighthouse being an object of safety gave her a sense of calm, too, if only momentarily.

She adjusted the F-stop manually. Any second the fog might return and hide the top of the lighthouse. She needed the right shot, the right lighting.

She stilled. *Wait for it.*

Staring into the viewfinder, she thought about the lighthouse being symbolic of a protector, like a mom safeguarding her child, the way she protected Piper. In the same way this lighthouse had directed ships to safety and well-being over the years, she wanted to guard and guide her daughter.

The last of the mist lifted off the top portion of the dome like a veil sliding off a bride. Perfect. She took a couple of wide-angle pictures, then unclipped the camera. Setting the dials, she took a dozen rapid-fire shots like a photographer at a modeling shoot. If these photos turned out as beautifully as she imagined, especially in a tri-cluster arrangement, they would make some tourists very happy.

Behind her, the roar of the surf grew louder, pounding the boulders. The air filled with white spray, coating her face and hair almost like snow. She spit out the salty taste. What was—?

"Paige!"

Forest's voice and the thundering blast of the sea warned her a second too late. A wall of water barreled over the rocks, smashed against her legs, bludgeoned her back, and swept her off her feet. Screaming, she clutched her camera to her belly as she shot through the air, propelled by the rush of seawater. Then she was falling. Toppling off the rocks. Her left side landed hard against the sand. Umph. She moaned as saltwater rushed over her body, over her face, but she tucked herself into a ball and nestled the camera against her middle.

As soon as the water abated, she sat up, hacking and coughing.

"Paige!" Forest knelt beside her, lifting her into his lap, cuddling her against his soaking wet chest. "Baby, are you okay? You scared me."

She'd scared herself.

His heart pounded strong beneath her ear. His arms engulfed her, making her feel safe, like one of those ships she'd imagined being guided to port. To him. But she was dazed. Soaked with seawater. If she were thinking clearly, she wouldn't be lying here limp in Forest's arms. She'd shove away from him. Tell him to stay away from her.

Instead, she watched as he swept wet hair off her face, his green eyes turning darker with some hidden emotion. "Can you hear me? Did you hurt yourself?"

Shivering, she extended her left leg. "Oww." Could she walk? She didn't want to be dependent on Forest to get home. She pressed her palms against his chest, sitting up and spitting grit and salt. Then crawled off his lap. Immediately chilled, she felt bereft of his warmth and strongly beating heart—things she lived just fine without for the last three years.

"My camera. It's worth—" On her knees, she swiped moisture off its face, checking for damage, groaning when she found sand sticking to the extended lens. "I can't believe that happened. My camera is irreplaceable to me."

"Can you walk?"

He didn't even seem concerned about her camera.

"Of course, I can walk," she snapped. She stood to prove it, but feeling a burning sensation in her side and thigh, she clenched her teeth. "I'm fine. Why don't you head back and finish the job you came to do?" Then he could leave town sooner.

"Paige—"

"If you think I need a hero, you're wrong. The days of me being a weak woman falling gaga over you are gone." A twinge of guilt rushed through her, but she didn't apologize.

He rolled his eyes toward the dark clouds. "I was going to offer to help you get back. Maybe carry something. Offer you my arm."

"I can manage on my own."

She hobbled around the rocks where water still pulsated over them, searching for her tripod, grimacing with each step. Forest silently searched too.

After a few minutes, she gave up the hunt. Her tripod must have been dragged out to sea. A disappointing loss considering her limited budget. Fortunately, the waves didn't sweep away her camera, the most expensive item in her photography equipment. She'd have to take special care in the sand removal, or else bring it to the city for cleaning. Nothing to be done about that now. Time to head home.

Chilled by her damp clothes and the sharp wind barreling across the water as if she were the target of its wrath, her mother's words taunted her. *Stay away from the sea. It will harm you in the end.* Maybe there was some truth to her warnings.

Not far ahead, the tide rolled in almost to the grass line. Now she had to do the thing she despised. She strode toward the wet grass, limping faster than she should have to stay ahead of Forest.

"I thought you didn't like the sea," his voice reached her from behind. "I was surprised to find you hiking this far alone."

"People change."

"Is there anything I can do to help? I mean with carrying your camera or backpack." He caught up with her and extended his arm. "You can lean on me if you want."

"I don't need your help. I'm fine on my own." Every other footfall, she winced.

"I can see that." Holding up both hands, he backed away again.

"You probably forgot I existed the day you left me," she tossed over her shoulder.

Now, why did she have to be so downright snippy?

"As I said, I've missed you," he said huskily. "I still need to ask you some questions about Edward's case, too."

She stiffened. "Didn't you read my report?"

"I did. But you want him to get what's coming to him for harming your sister, don't you?" Was there doubt in his voice?

"Of course."

"Then I must question you. Whether it makes you feel uncomfortable or not."

No doubt about it. Any questions Forest Harper asked would make her uncomfortable.

Seven

Paisley sat beside Judah, clutching his hand, as they faced Pastor Sagle on the other side of his desk for their first post-vow-renewal counseling session. The last time they were here, the pastor had asked her some embarrassing questions. Maybe that's why she felt weird about this meeting. But Judah insisted they not only follow through with marriage counseling but undergo trauma therapy in the aftermath of her kidnapping, too.

She didn't get it. What amount of talking about the crisis would help her stop thinking about what Edward did to her? However, when Judah said the sessions weren't just for her benefit, but for his too, how could she argue with that?

Only two days had passed since her release from the medical facility in North Bend. Since then, her health was slowly improving. Her face looked better, although scabs and scars remained. Mostly, she was impatient to walk on the beach again, check out the peninsula, and get to know her little niece. But no amount of impatience or complaining would help her improve physically or mentally, or help the time pass faster.

There was something else she felt impatient about, too. Her cheeks warmed with thoughts of her and Judah's delayed honeymoon.

"Paisley"—Pastor Sagle intruded into her thoughts—"I'm so glad you're doing better."

"Thank you. Me too. My face is still a little sore," she added in case he noticed her blushing.

"We're thankful she's on the road to recovery." Judah winked at her.

He was so sweet. If a magic elixir existed to help her heal quicker, she'd swallow it in big gulps. Not only was she in a hurry to feel more like herself, but she was eager to make love with her husband. *Sigh.*

"In this first session"—Pastor Sagle glanced back and forth between them—"let's just spend some time talking."

"Okay." Talking didn't sound so bad. Unless his idea of chatting meant bombarding her with embarrassing questions.

"Later, I have a questionnaire for each of you to fill out. Then we'll discuss your responses next time."

She expelled a breath. So far, so good.

"How have things been going with you two since you renewed your vows?" The pastor nodded at Judah as if expecting his reply first.

"Good. Excellent."

This week couldn't have been easy on Judah, especially with his father being hauled to jail, maybe staying there for a long time. Paisley leaned back against the chair, picturing Edward getting what he deserved—rotting in prison. However, that probably wasn't a very Christlike or grace-filled attitude.

"Paisley?"

"Um, er, what?"

"How do you feel since returning to live with Judah?"

It was a good thing these men couldn't read her thoughts. "Oh. We're doing good. I'm impatient to get on with our lives. Forget all the bad stuff that happened."

"No one expects you to forget." Pastor Sagle met her gaze with a kind look.

"But I want to." If she could stuff the rotten things she'd experienced deep down in her gut, or throw the whole emotional mess out to sea, she would in a heartbeat. Every time she thought of her hands being tied behind her back, lying in the dark closet, sobbing, picturing herself dying, and being petrified of Edward, her insides shook, and she felt close to a grandaddy panic attack. Her safest response was to not think about it.

She closed her eyelids. *Breathe.* Okay, so maybe she needed these counseling sessions more than she cared to admit.

"It's okay, Paisley." The pastor's soft voice penetrated her momentary panic.

Judah clutched her hand and gave a squeeze.

She opened her eyes. She was safe. Edward hadn't walked into the room. She wasn't locked in a small, dark space. "Sorry. I still freak out sometimes."

"No problem. What were you feeling just then?" Pastor Sagle leaned forward, his arms crossed on the desk.

"Trapped. Like my throat's too tight to catch a breath. The darkness is thick, feels drenched in evil. I hate dark spaces."

She shuddered. Then took slow breaths. Judah had suggested she recite Bible verses when she felt panicky. *Even though I walk through the valley of the shadow of death ...*

No thinking about shadows or dying today.

God is light; in him there is no darkness at all. Yes, much better. No darkness sounded safe.

Lord, please help me overcome these feelings of helplessness.

Judah rubbed his palm over her shoulders, his touch warm and comforting.

"Can we just talk about Judah and me this time? Not the kidnapping?" Paisley had thought being with Judah again, and becoming his wife, would remove the sting of Edward's horrendous actions toward her. So far, that hadn't happened. Even last night, she awakened in a cold sweat, feeling strangled by her sheets. Judah woke up, too, and prayed for her.

"For now, we can." Pastor Sagle smiled understandingly. "How about if you tell me how you two met?"

Oh, good. A safer topic.

Why was Judah snickering? He'd better not tell the pastor what he observed her doing at Maggie's Beachside Inn the summer she was sixteen. That was their secret.

"I spoke to Judah at Bert's when we first met," she burst out before he could tell his side of the story. "I was a server there."

"That's right. What did you think of him?" Pastor Sagle tipped his head, gazing at her.

"I thought he was cute. And a bit of a snob." She elbowed Judah.

"Hey!"

"It's true. He was the guy with a silver spoon sticking in his mouth."

He groaned. "I never thought of myself that way."

"You should have seen the way he used ketchup as if Bert had a never-ending supply." Paisley chuckled.

"Ketchup makes everything better."

"So you keep telling me."

"Judah, what did you think of Paisley?" The pastor directed them back to the topic.

Judah stroked his chin as if deep in thought. "That she was the most beautiful girl I ever saw. She took my breath away. Still takes my breath away."

"Aww." He still thought that even with the way her face looked? He was one in a million.

"Sassy and adventurous, she was fun to talk with." He drew in a long breath. "And she was too young for me."

"That's the truth." She'd still been in high school, so Judah, a man five years older than her and with the last name of Grant, wasn't fair game. "He was a rich kid, hanging onto his daddy's shirttails."

Judah laughed. "I don't think I ever did that."

"So you noticed the differences between you right off?" The pastor shrugged. "Makes sense."

"I couldn't forget her." Judah's gaze snagged hers and she melted a little inside. "Even while I was in my last semester of college, she was on my mind."

His intense look made butterflies dance in her stomach.

"Paisley?" Pastor Sagle prompted.

"Um. I was in my junior year of high school. Having problems at home and with the town." She smoothed her hands down her blue jeans, thinking of the black slacks she'd worn as a server at Bert's. "But I never forgot the cute guy who flirted with me. I looked forward to him coming into the diner again. Except, he vanished."

"Went to school, you mean."

"You were out of my league. I knew better than to pine for you."

"Come on."

"Aunt Callie told me the same thing."

Judah shook his head, his cheeks reddening.

Pastor Sagle cleared his throat. "Did those differences you both noticed impact your marriage later on?"

How sneakily he segued into a discussion about the past. Couldn't they avoid troublesome topics for one session? She enjoyed sharing the good parts about how she and Judah met. The beginning of their love story.

"I doubt our upbringing had much to do with our relationship's downfall." A crease deepened between Judah's eyebrows. "Ever since my college graduation, I've worked for a living. Never took monetary help from my father. He hasn't been involved in our lives much since we got married."

Not involved much? Edward might not have been physically present in their lives, but he was emotionally present. Judah's mother, Bess, was an amazing woman. But Judah grew up with Edward Grant—the scum of the earth—as a father. How could he not be influenced by him to some degree?

And what about herself? Paisley recently discovered some mysteries surrounding her mom and dad's courtship and married life. Wasn't she affected by her upbringing, too? Molded by her mother's stern, often unjust punishments? Affected by her father not standing up for her?

"Paisley, you look like you have something on your mind," Pastor Sagle said.

"It's nothing."

"You can say anything in these sessions. It's a safe ground for both of you."

She swallowed hard. "You may be correct that our upbringings affected our marriage, even when we didn't want them to, at least in the early days."

"Really?" Judah asked softly.

"Don't you think so?" She didn't want to offend him, but something compelled her to finish expressing herself. "You worked so hard, hyper-focused on C-MER as if you needed to prove something to yourself, or your—" She gulped instead of saying "dad." "But why bring up the old stuff? What good does it do?"

Pastor Sagle picked up a pen and rolled it between his fingers. "Talking things through can be an important part of your healing."

Paisley linked her hand around the crook of Judah's elbow. "Ever since I came back to Basalt, Judah has shown himself to be a kind man who would do anything to help me or to be there for me."

"I would." Judah sighed. "I'm sorry I wasn't there to protect you from my dad. I still struggle with that."

"I never blamed you." She blinked fast to absorb the liquid filling her eyes.

"There, now. We've made some progress." Pastor Sagle scooted back in his chair and tapped his pen against the calendar on his desk. "So, Judah, after you finished your schooling, what drew you to Paisley?"

"That's easy." He grinned at her. "When I came back from college and had an interview with C-MER, I stopped by Bert's to grab lunch. But I was secretly looking for my favorite server."

Paisley laughed, glad for the lighter turn in the conversation. "That's when I accidentally squirted a glob of ketchup on his shirt."

"Dead center on the white shirt I was wearing for my interview."

"Oh, my." Pastor Sagle rubbed his hand over the back of his neck. "What did you do?"

"I didn't have time to go home and change, and I didn't want to make this beautiful woman more embarrassed, either. So I finished my burger, wore my sports coat buttoned up, and went to C-MER as I was." Judah and Paisley exchanged grins. "Got the job even with ketchup smeared across my white shirt."

"You made me so nervous."

He kissed her cheek. "I thought you did it on purpose to flirt with me."

"I was humiliated to have made such a dreadful mistake to the mayor's son, no less."

"Did you care so much I was a Grant?"

"I cared that you sat in my diner stirring up trouble with my heart."

"That I believe." He tweaked her chin. "But you were the mischief-maker, stirring up all kinds of feelings within me."

He said it with such warmth, she gave him a spontaneous hug. Would have kissed him on the mouth if it weren't for the pastor watching them.

"Love you," she whispered against Judah's neck.

"Love you too, Pais."

They sat back, hands clasped.

Pastor Sagle beamed back and forth at them. "What a great beginning." He pointed toward a chair near the wall. "Now, Judah, take this questionnaire and sit over there." He handed him a printout and a pencil.

"Sure thing." He squeezed Paisley's hand before he strode to the chair.

"Here's yours." Pastor Sagle slid a matching page with a dozen questions and blank spaces across the desk to Paisley. After setting a pencil on top of the paper, he checked his watch. "You have twenty minutes."

Lots of time.

For her, it would be easier to write the answers than to discuss them out loud. Except, didn't Pastor Sagle say they'd have to talk about them next time? She already dreaded that.

Eight

Forest's lips brushed Paige's with such gentleness.
Did he recognize her inexperience in the art of
love? He smoothed his palms down her cheeks,
grinning. "I'm so glad we met."

Paige sat in the corner booth at the back of Bert's Fish Shack, drumming her fingers against the tabletop, her gaze locked on the front door. Any second Forest would saunter into the local hangout for their interview, and she must be ready. No smiling at him. No succumbing to his charms. She had it bad before she saw him yesterday. Now that he'd held her and acted so tender and caring on the beach, she was a goner unless she kept her emotions in check.

Sweet dreams, Elinore. Sweet dreams, Elinore, she repeated like a mantra.

Last night, she hardly slept. Tossing and turning, she replayed every word they said to each other. Every word she didn't say to him. Had he called her "baby?" Or did her romance-starved brain invent that memory? Groan.

A few minutes ago, when she entered the recently reopened diner, Bert greeted her enthusiastically. "Why, if it isn't Paige Cedars. How long has it been since you darkened these doors?"

She shrugged, going along with his teasing. "You've been closed for so long the locals are looking elsewhere for their favorite burgers and fries."

He grabbed the chest of his shirt. "Pains me to hear such talk."

"Just teasing." She patted his arm. "I'm glad you're open again, Bert. We missed you."

"Thank you for that. Where's the little one?"

Adrenaline shot through her. She glanced toward the door, making sure Forest wasn't within earshot. "Piper isn't with me today."

"She sure lights up a room." Bert greeted a dark-haired man entering the diner whom Paige didn't recognize. The guy didn't return the owner's acknowledgment. "Find a seat and one of the servers will take your order."

"Thanks, Bert." Paige limped to the back of the room.

As soon as she sat down at the table farthest from the door, embarrassment flooded her. Didn't local teenagers call this seat the kissing booth? Something about Bert not being able to see them from the register. What if Forest heard about that? What would he think of her choosing this spot for them to talk? Maybe she should pick a different table.

Before she could move, a familiar redhead sidled up to Paige's table and set a water glass down. "Bert says you always ask for water."

"Thanks, Lucy. I didn't know you work here."

"Just helping Bert and keeping a lookout for male tourists."
She fluttered her fingers toward the dark-haired guy who Paige
saw enter the diner. "Or someone like him. New in town.
Single." She sighed dreamily. "So, what are you having, or do
you need a few minutes?"

"Coffee and creamer, please." She wouldn't be able to
eat a thing with Forest at her table.

"No food?"

"Not this time. Someone else is—"

"Ohhh. Are you dating Craig Masters again?" Lucy leaned
in like they were best friends sharing secrets. "You two made
the cutest couple."

Forest dropped into the other seat, frowning.

For Pete's sake, did he hear Lucy's comment? A hot blush
rose from Paige's neck to her hairline.

"Well, hello." Lucy ogled him. "Are you the detective Mia
told me about?" She licked her pink glossy lips and giggled.
"You are yummy just like she said."

Ugh.

Forest lifted the menu tucked between the napkin dispenser
and the ketchup bottle and glanced at Paige. "Did you order
lunch?"

"Just coffee."

"I'll have coffee, too, then."

"Fine," Lucy muttered as if slighted by their minimal
choices and, perhaps, Forest's noninterest in her. Still, she
danced her eyebrows at him and sashayed toward another
table.

"So, what's Craig to you?"

His abrupt question brought Paige back to the reason for
this meeting.

"He's a friend." She wiped the condensation off her glass with her thumb. "Not that it's any of your business."

"You're right. Sorry. I appreciate your agreeing to meet me."

"Didn't have a choice, did I? Let's get this inquisition over with. I have things to do." Bills to pay. A daughter to raise. Responsibilities.

"Inquisition sounds a bit dramatic, don't you think?"

She shot him a glare.

He shuffled on his seat. The clanking of dishes and a cacophony of voices filling the room added to the tension at their table.

Lucy sauntered back with two coffee mugs filled with coffee. After setting them down, she dug into her apron and dropped individual creamers on the table in front of them. "Need anything else?" She leaned in and grinned at Forest. "My phone number, perhaps?"

Oh, brother.

"No, thanks. This is good." Forest lifted his mug and drank his coffee black, the way Paige remembered him liking it.

She opened a creamer and dumped the liquid into her coffee cup. Stirring, she let the spoon clatter against the ceramic mug as she waited for Lucy to walk away. Surely, Bert didn't approve of his servers being so flirtatious with the customers.

When Lucy finally moved on to the next table, Paige asked, "What did you need to ask me about?"

"I have some questions about the case." He withdrew a small tablet and a pen from his shirt pocket, apparently setting aside the personal issues between them.

"Shoot." She just wanted to get this over with.

He stared at her for a minute without saying anything. "How did you come upon the evidence you found in the gallery?" His voice changed like he altered it to a husky monotone for his detective role.

Focusing on the details surrounding Paisley's kidnapping a week ago, Paige answered his question. She imagined a lightbulb hanging over her head while she was being interrogated by some crotchety man like in old police shows she sometimes watched with Dad. That was safer than focusing on Forest's unique gray-green eyes or his handsome smile.

Although right now he wasn't smiling. Seemed hyperfocused on his questions. "Were you aware Edward Grant had been in the building that day?"

"No, I wasn't. Why would you ask that?"

"Gathering facts. Searching for more information than you wrote in your report." He leaned back against the bench and drank from his cup.

The way he eyed her made her squirm. She didn't want to be here. Was frustrated to be sitting across from her ex, discussing Edward Grant of all things.

"Look, Edward took over the loan, so he had rights to enter the gallery, even if I didn't want him there." She wrapped her hands around her warm mug.

"So, you're saying you had no idea he planned to harm your sister?"

"Of course, that's what I'm saying." A customer stared at her, so she lowered her voice. "Why are you asking me these stupid questions?"

She wanted to bolt out of the diner, or else slug Forest. She considered herself a nonviolent person, yet she kept having the urge to belt him one.

He scritch-scratched the pen across his pad of paper as if unaffected by the undercurrents at their table. "I'm sorry if this bugs you"—he didn't sound the least bit sorry—"but I have to find out the truth."

Was he implying she was lying? Her irritation level increased a notch.

She drained her cup dry then plunked it on the table. "I knew nothing of the mayor's plans, okay? I can't stand the guy."

"Then can you explain what you did after you found the evidence?" His voice sounded detached, emotionless, like he was questioning a stranger.

And that's what they were to each other. Strangers. Nothing else.

She sighed then answered him, but the words, *By the way, I had your baby,* a*nd she looks so much like you,* flashed through her thoughts. What would he say if she blurted that out? Would an iota of humanity seep back into his gaze? Of course, she'd never tell him about Piper in such an unkind way. She wanted him to be happy about having a daughter, even if he was furious with her for keeping their child a secret.

"Anything else, Detective?" Paige tried to sound as emotionless as he did.

"After you found the evidence, who did you talk to first?"

"Judah Grant."

"Why not Deputy Brian?"

"Judah's my brother-in-law. Why not?" She didn't attempt to hide the irritation in her tone. "Are we finished yet?"

"No, we're not finished." He gazed intently at her.

Did he mean this session wasn't over? Or that they weren't finished as a couple?

No. That was silly. She divorced the man. He signed the papers without opposition.

"Considering it was a kidnapping, shouldn't you have approached the deputy first?" His eyes glinted. "Or were you two—"

"Of course not." Her cheeks heated up. At the table across the aisle, Mr. and Mrs. Anderson, an elderly couple from her father's neighborhood, stared at her. She leaned toward Forest, keeping her voice low. "We didn't even know a crime transpired. Paisley left Judah before. Everyone thought she did it again." She cast an indignant glare at him. *He'd left her, too.*

A gray shadow crossed his face. Maybe he got her point. "Didn't Deputy Brian tell everyone in the search party to turn in any evidence to him?"

"I suppose."

A plate clattered in the background. Glasses clinked as if a busser scooped up too many dishes.

"Suppose or did?"

That spotlight-over-her-head feeling hit her again. "Okay, he did."

"Yet, you sought out Judah."

She didn't like his accusing tone. "He's Paisley's husband *and* my friend. I talked to him first. Big deal."

"Some might consider that withholding evidence."

A shiver raced over her. Is that what he thought? That she withheld evidence against Edward? How absurd. She pushed away from the table and jabbed her finger toward him. "Ask anyone on the beach that day if I was worried about my sister."

"Please, sit down. We aren't done."

"Oh, yes, we are."

"Please," he said tightly.

Teeth clenched, she lowered herself to the edge of the bench, but was ready to spring up again.

Lucy stopped at their table, coffee carafe in hand. "Everything okay here?" Glancing at Forest, she topped off both cups, tossed more creamers on the table, and leaned down near Paige. "Bert told me to check on you. Folks are whispering about what's going on back here in the kissing booth." She snickered.

Forest's eyebrows leaped halfway up his forehead.

"Tell him we're talking."

"Keep it down, will you?" Lucy scurried toward the new guy's table.

"The kissing booth, huh?" Forest grinned.

"Just drop it." She wouldn't smile. Wouldn't flirt. "Only love-sick teenagers call it that."

His grin faded. "Look, I asked Judah and Paisley these kinds of questions too. Nothing personal."

"It was personal when my sister went missing. When Edward threatened my—" She clamped her lips together. She'd almost blurted "my daughter."

"I read the notation about him threatening a minor. Who was it?"

Her heart thundered in her temples. "Someone I care about." She'd planned what to say if this question came up. "He threatened my peace of mind, too. If he went after Paisley, what would stop him from coming after me?"

"Valid point." He pinched the bridge of his nose. "Did you have any foreknowledge of Edward's intentions?"

"Why do you keep coming back to that?"

"I know you. It seems you're hiding something."

Hiding something?

"You and Judah, perhaps?"

"That's it." She thudded her fist against the table. The mugs and glasses clinked against each other. "You have no reason to ask me personal questions. You lost that right three years ago."

"This isn't about us."

"No?"

"Us?" Lucy sidled up beside Paige again, pointing at Forest. "Is he Pip—?"

"Shhhh." Paige jumped up, propelling the woman her sister used to call "Red" toward the center of the diner. "Don't say anything about Piper in front of him, please?"

"Is he her—?"

"Just leave it alone. I beg of you."

"Well, okay. Fine." Lucy wiped her hands on her apron. "Can you set me up with him?"

"No, I can't set you up with him."

"I don't see why not."

"I just … can't."

Lucy huffed and stomped off.

Taking a deep breath, Paige returned to the booth.

"What was that about?" Forest asked.

"Never mind." But there was something she had to tell him. "For the record, no one in this town knows about our marriage."

"Really?" His eyes widened.

"That's the way I'd like it to stay."

Nine

Paisley needed to take a walk, scrub some dishes, paint window trim, do anything to expend some pent-up energy. After her and Judah's counseling session last night, she struggled to fall asleep. Shuffling around so many times, she worried about waking up her husband, asleep at the edge of his side of the bed. Finally, she traipsed into the guest room and read until she got sleepy.

This morning, she did some light housekeeping, but Judah caught her working and reiterated the doctor's order about bed rest. Phooey. When would life get back to normal? Every time she saw herself in the mirror, she begged God to remove the scabs and scars. They were improving, but not fast enough to her liking.

"Judah, I'm going outside," she called toward the bedroom where he worked on his laptop.

"Okay. I'll be out to check on you in a few."

"You don't have to check on me. I'm fine." Grumbling, she grabbed her novel and headed out to her lounge chair.

At least the view of the sea in front of their cottage was delightful. She had a great place to rest. Shouldn't be complaining. And yet—

"Hello! Anybody home?" Aunt Callie called.

"In the back, Auntie!" Paisley hadn't even heard a car drive up. What was her aunt doing here? Was something wrong?

A minute later, Aunt Callie and Bess Grant shuffled around the corner of the house, arms linked, giggling. Something was suspicious about them right off. What were they up to?

"Hello, you guys. What's going on?"

"Paisley, dear, how are you?" Bess hurried over and kissed the top of her head.

"Okay, all things considered."

"You don't sound, or look, okay to me." Aunt Callie leaned down to peer at her. Leave it to her aunt to state her opinion brashly. "If I were a doctor, I would have made you stay in the hospital until those ugly sores healed properly."

"Now, Callie," Bess said.

Self-consciously, Paisley tugged her cowl neck sweater over her chin. "I'm doing fine, Auntie. Judah has been a good nurse." She swayed her hand toward two chairs by their makeshift table. "Have a seat."

Her mother-in-law retrieved a chair and set it in the shade for Aunt Callie.

"Thank you, Bess." Paisley's aunt sat down gingerly. "Ever since my accident at Pauly's, I haven't felt safe in outdoor furniture."

"These feel sturdy." Bess put another chair near Paisley and dropped into it. "Where's Judah? We knocked but—"

"He's probably on the phone. Job hunting." Paisley shuffled forward and called, "Judah, your mom's here."

Bess exchanged glances with Aunt Callie as if commenting without saying anything.

"What's going on? You both seem fired up about something."

"I confess we have a scheme up our sleeves." Bess chuckled.

"What kind of scheme? Don't keep me in suspense."

Judah came through the opening of the sliding glass door. "Mom. Callie. Good to see you."

Bess hugged him. "Got a minute, Son?"

"Sure." He dropped into the seat next to Paisley. "What's up?"

"Remember what I said about Kathleen and me possibly investing in a bigger place?" Bess grinned widely.

"Yeah."

"We found something." Aunt Callie clapped her hands and bobbed her head.

"Auntie, are you going in on this purchase, too?"

"I am. Isn't it exciting?" Her shoulders bunched up to her ears and her whole body seemed to shake with glee.

"What about your house? I thought you loved it."

"I do. But I'm not getting any younger." Aunt Callie's smile faded. "I've been lonely, Paisley Rose. It would be nice to share quarters and work on town projects with like-minded women." She withdrew a sales flier from her purse and fanned herself. "My, it's warm for mid-fall."

"So, Mom"—Judah settled deeper into his chair—"where is this place?"

"Not much farther south from here. Needs TLC, but with the three of us—"

"Or four," Aunt Callie cut in.

"That's right. With our group working together, and maybe with your help since you're out of work, we'll get it done." Bess raised an eyebrow toward Judah, a pleading expression on her face.

"Me? I'm not a carpenter. But I guess I can help. I'm trying to find a job too."

"I knew I could count on you." Bess nodded toward Aunt Callie as if they'd discussed his possible reaction. "Thank you."

"How much TLC are we talking about?" Judah asked. "Too much will mean a huge overhaul, plus a wad of cash. Be sure to have an inspection done first."

"Well, for better or for worse"—Bess clasped her hands together—"we put a low bid on it yesterday. And it's been accepted!"

"What? You should have talked to me about it first."

His stern-sounding words instantly doused the women's enthusiasm. They both frowned.

"Why would I have to talk to you first?" Bess asked.

"Last I knew we were adults." Crossing her arms, Aunt Callie glared at Judah.

"I didn't mean to imply you were required to talk to me." He sounded humbler, although his facial expression was as tight as his mom's. They'd been through so much. It would be a shame if this visit turned into an argument, or one that caused hurt feelings. "You might have mentioned such a huge step to me."

"I'm here now." Bess thrust out her hands, her short hair flipping in the wind. "Judah, I wanted to share our good news with you and Paisley. I'm not here seeking your permission. I love you, but I'm moving forward with my life. I'm making my own decisions, finally."

His shoulders sagged. "Sorry, Mom. Your news took me by surprise."

"I'm sure it did."

Paisley ran her palm over Judah's shoulder. "Congratulations from both of us! This must be such a thrilling step for you ladies."

Bess nodded, a soft smile replacing her frown. "It is exciting. All our plans and dreams are coming to pass in this new adventure."

Aunt Callie's glare intensified. Her makeshift fan flapped double-time.

"Auntie, will you be selling your house?" Paisley asked, concerned the woman might have something rude on her mind to say to Judah.

"Goes on the market day after tomorrow."

"That's fast. Do you need help packing up your things?"

"I do."

"You won't be able to help with that." Judah gave her a cross look.

"I have to start living again sometime." Paisley nudged his arm, trying to get him to ease up. "I could help with lighter tasks."

"I know you. You won't limit yourself to reduced chores."

She didn't want to argue with him in front of Bess and Aunt Callie, but she was going stir crazy staying at home. Her aunt needed help, and she was available and willing. "What if I promise to be careful?"

He bit his lip and didn't say anything. Maybe they could discuss it later.

"I'd appreciate your help, Paisley Rose"—Aunt Callie cast a squinty-eyed glare at Judah—"but if it's too much for you, don't worry about it. I'll ask Paige."

Paisley sighed.

"So, what do you think, Son?" Bess tipped her head toward him.

"I'm happy for you, honestly I am."

"But?" The word hung in the air like a gray cloud about to release monsoon rains.

"There's been so much change in our family." Judah let out a restrained groan. "Now you're plunging into a house purchase? Why buy a place when you haven't even finalized your divorce?"

Bess's facial coloring turned ashen. "All these changes must be unsettling for you. As for me, doing something on my own, making adult decisions, feels like I've been reborn. When you try something new, sometimes there's risk and you just have to go for it."

"She's right." Paisley nodded, hoping Judah wouldn't be insulted by her agreeing with Bess. "We want what's best for her, for them, right?"

"I wish you would have talked to me, that's all." Judah shrugged toward his mom.

They remained quiet for a few minutes.

Judah had gone through a lot since Paisley's return to Basalt—the aftermath of Hurricane Blaine, his father's abuse toward his mother, losing his job, then Edward kidnapping her. Hopefully, he wouldn't let anything stand in the way of being loving and graceful toward his mom who had always been supportive of their marriage.

Bess stood and wrapped her arms around Judah. "I can't wait to show you our project house. I want your help and opinion more than anyone's about how best to remodel it. But I understand and respect your feelings too."

"Thanks, Mom."

She returned to her seat.

"All of us are family here," Aunt Callie said in a gruff tone. "Family sticks together. Cheers when there's good news to be had." She lifted her chin as if daring anyone, particularly Judah, to disagree with her. "That's what should be happening right now. Not any fussy disgruntlement."

Ugh. How would Judah react to her aunt's outspoken statement?

After a pause, he clasped Paisley's hand. "You're right, and we are happy for you. We'll do anything we can to help."

"Thank you." Bess smiled at him, obviously relieved. "Since I'm paying cash, and the house is already empty, we can get started on renovations as soon as we sign the papers."

"Cash?" Judah asked. "Must have been a super low bid."

"I've had rainy-day money set aside for a while now."

"That's great. Which house are you talking about?"

"The old Peterson place near the cove." Bess pointed south.

"The Peterson—" Judah withdrew his hand from Paisley's and slapped his forehead. "That place is a disaster! It'll be a ton of work to fix."

"I know, but you and a crew can fix it, right?" Bess chuckled. "Callie, Kathleen, and I will do our share. We may be older, but we're determined to see this through."

"That's right." Aunt Callie nodded, still eyeing Judah like she had a beef to settle with him.

"I want to help too." Paisley pictured the Peterson place, an eyesore from the beach. "Hasn't it been abandoned for years?"

"Yep." Aunt Callie stuffed her flier in her handbag. "But we're going to transform it into a treasure."

Standing, Bess signaled the end of their visit. Aunt Callie pried herself out of her chair, huffing as if out of breath. Judah jumped up and offered her his hand, which Aunt Callie accepted. Maybe she wasn't as perturbed with him now.

"When would you like to see the place?" Bess patted Judah's arm affectionately.

"Whenever it's convenient for you."

Aunt Callie kissed Paisley's cheek. "I'm glad you're feeling better."

"Thank you, Auntie." Paisley stood and leaned into Judah as they watched the ladies walk around the corner of the house. "What do you think those two are up to?"

"What do you mean?"

"They were bubbly with excitement when they first got here, but Aunt Callie acted downright suspicious."

"I didn't notice."

Paisley chuckled. "That's because it takes a mischief-maker to know one."

Ten

Later that day, Judah sat in the small interrogation room at the jail, arms crossed, tapping his shoes against the floor. Mom sat beside him, clasping and unclasping her hands. Any second Deputy Brian would bring in Edward. The thought of seeing his dad for the first time since his incarceration four days ago, facing the man who had harmed his wife, gnawed at his gut and made him almost physically ill.

This afternoon, when Mom got a call from Deputy Brian saying Edward had to see her today, she phoned and begged Judah to come with her. He didn't blame her for not wanting to meet Edward alone, but he wasn't looking forward to it, either.

"I wish this was over already. Why did I agree to meet with him?" Mom's shoulders were hunched, her eyes pinched to narrow slits.

Judah patted her shoulder. "If he says anything rude, just walk out. I'll deal with him." He was itching to do that, anyway. *Lord, help me.* He knew he should be hunting for ways to show mercy and grace to his father, to somehow reach him with the truth of God's love and forgiveness. But he didn't have it in him yet.

Lord, how did you face brutal men and still have compassion for them? How can I ever look my father in the eye and not imagine him kicking my wife? Dragging her into his closet? Plotting to separate her from me forever?

"It's not a son's place to intervene on behalf of his mother." Mom took out a tissue and twisted it. "I'm sorry for putting you in this position."

"No problem. I'm here for you."

Lord, help us get through this.

Judah was only here to support Mom. Not to speak to Edward. He planned to hold his tongue, otherwise, a world of hurt was bound to come barreling out of his mouth, out of his heart, and he didn't know if he could stop himself once he got started.

The door creaked open, and Deputy Brian escorted Edward, his wrists in handcuffs, into the tiny room. Edward's haggard-looking eyes gleamed toward Mom. He didn't even glance at Judah.

Seeing his father wearing an orange jumpsuit, his wrists confined to cuffs, it felt like a rope tightened around Judah's neck, choking him. Was this how Paisley felt when she couldn't breathe?

Edward had done things worthy of a long prison sentence and would soon face a judge. Yet, conflicting emotions rose in Judah, catching him off guard. Shouldn't he be glad, relieved even, to see him this way? Instead, sadness filled him. Anger too.

"Bess," Edward spoke in a soft voice.

"Edward. How are you getting on?"

In answer, he rattled his chains.

Deputy Brian tugged Edward forward until he sat down, then secured the cuffs to a metal loop attached to the table. Edward's eyes moistened as he stared at his estranged wife. Was this moment tender for Mom, too? Or did she despise staring into the eyes of her abusive husband? Maybe she found some satisfaction in him being shackled. He'd hurt her also.

"Judah," Edward said coolly.

"Mayor." Judah didn't have the heart to call him "Dad" yet.

"You should have come alone, Bess. This conversation is just between us."

Hardly just them. Deputy Brian exited the room, but he stood on the other side of the window, observing. Was there a hidden speaker in the room?

"I asked Judah to come with me." Mom crossed her arms.

"Fine." Edward slumped in his chair.

"What did you want to see me about? I'm not staying long."

The prisoner's gaze bore down on Mom. Judah had the impulse to shield her, although Edward couldn't harm her, this time, restrained as he was.

"I heard you withdrew a large sum of money from our savings."

Mom flinched. "How would you know about that? The transaction was private."

Edward's sarcastic laughter echoed in the small room. "Never underestimate my power, even from a jail cell." He glared hard at her as if staring at a disobedient child. "Why did you take the funds without my approval, Bess? I need all the money in our accounts to cover my lawyer's fees."

"Your approval?" Mom uncrossed her arms and sat up taller, a steely glint in her eyes. "I took only my money. *My* mother's inheritance."

It was news to Judah that his grandmother had left money for her.

"You can't make that decision without me," Edward said condescendingly. "Put it back today."

Judah clenched his fists in his lap.

"I won't. The money my mother gave me is mine to do with as I please." Mom leaned forward over the table and Judah wanted to pull her back. "We're getting divorced, Edward. I'm making my own decisions."

"Not about our mutual funds."

Judah groaned. Edward's demands probably had nothing to do with the money. Just more manipulation.

Mom jabbed her finger toward Edward. "I let you use my mother's money to fund your financial dealings with the promise it would be available for me later. That time is now."

"I say when it's time. And divorce is off the table."

"How dare you!" Mom huffed. "You are no longer making decisions for me."

"Oh, yes, I am. What's yours is mine."

"Not anymore!" Mom stood swiftly.

Judah jumped to his feet beside her.

"Sit down!" Edward commanded. "Please"—his volume quieted, but not his sharp tone—"sit back down, Bess." His handcuffs clanked against the table.

When she did as Edward said, Judah groaned. Dropping onto the edge of his seat, he fought the urge to tell his father off. How dare he boss Mom around like she didn't have a brain! How dare he treat Paisley so horribly! A fire simmered in his chest, shooting adrenaline up and down his spine until the words on his tongue burst out, unrestrained. "How could you hurt my wife like you did? How could you kick her and tie her up and try to thrust her out of my life? Who do you think you are?"

"Be quiet. I'm not addressing you."

Judah wouldn't be silenced. "How could you injure the woman I love?"

"Judah," Mom cautioned.

"How could you have caused injuries to her b-body and her h-heart?" His voice broke as rage melted into a deep well of sorrow. Weeping seemed the only reasonable thing to do, but not in front of Edward. "You're my father. You're supposed to care for my welfare. Care for and love those whom I love."

Edward didn't meet his gaze.

"Are you even sorry for what you did to her or to Mom?" Judah slid his arm over his mother's shoulder. "Do you have any remorse for your wrongs?"

"I did what I did for the good of this family," Edward said with a snarl. "For the good of Basalt Bay. I'd do the same things again to get you to stop being a mama's boy and become the Grant you should have been all along."

Mom moaned.

Judah gritted his teeth. *Right.* Like Edward went to all these lengths to do him some big favor. To make him more of a man than he was. The nerve. The gall. Edward's justifications made him sick.

He swallowed down hot saliva. *Grace and mercy. Grace and mercy,* he reminded himself. But his frustrations weren't spent. "The good of this family, you say? What family do you even have left?"

"Show some respect!" Edward pounded his hands against the table in restrained movements. "I'm still your father."

Judah clenched his jaw to keep from saying something terribly rude, but he had another question. "And Craig's? Are you his father too?" It was time he had an answer about that.

"What lie is this?" Edward bellowed.

"I think we should go." Mom tugged on Judah's arm.

"Lie?" Judah glowered at his father. "You're the one who's good at lies. Lying to Mom and me. Lying to the whole town."

"Enough!" Edward jangled his handcuffs. "I need a favor. That, and the banking issue, are the only reasons I asked for this visit with your mother. Not you."

"You have a lot of nerve asking me for anything." Mom clutched her purse to her stomach.

"Tell Craig I need to see him immediately."

"I have no idea where he is," she said.

"He's not in Basalt Bay," Judah spoke up.

It was a good thing his possible half-brother was still on the lam. That way he couldn't be coerced into doing any more schemes for Edward.

"Believe me, I'm aware of that." Edward sneered. "I know everything that goes on in Basalt Bay. Metal bars won't stop me from running my town."

His town. Judah wanted to spit out the bad taste in his mouth.

"Do something right for once. Find Craig and tell him to keep his trap shut," Edward said gruffly, staring at Judah.

"I won't."

"When will you choose our family first?"

"Our family with you in it is finished." Judah leaped to his feet. "You think I'd accept you back into my life after what you did to Paisley?"

"You should never have married that—"

"Don't say one word against her, or so help me—" Judah thrust his index finger toward Edward's nose. "Not one word."

"Son, let's go." Mom tugged firmly on his arm, leading him to the door.

"We're not done here!" Edward pounded the table. "I'm still in charge! You'd better watch out. You can't stop a freight train once it's going full speed."

Eleven

Paige wanted to invite Forest up to her hotel room to visit, but she didn't want him thinking she was after a fling. Even though they met only a week ago, she longed for something lasting and real between them.

Paige was surprised to get her aunt's call for assistance in helping her pack up her house. Why was Aunt Callie selling her home and moving? She was too intrigued to decline. After arranging for Dad to watch Piper, Paige headed straight to her aunt's house.

"There you are, finally!" Aunt Callie said as she opened the door. She dragged Paige into the center of what looked like a packrat's den. Piles of stuff—coats, blankets, towels, books—had been thrown haphazardly over every piece of vintage furniture. Stacks of rubber tubs lined the wall by the couch. "Thank you for coming to help me sort and pack."

"Why are you moving, Auntie? And what are you going to do with all this stuff?" Paige told Dad she'd be gone an hour, two at the most, but this disaster might take a week to pack up.

"Follow me and I'll explain." Aunt Callie shuffled through the cluttered living room, leading the way to the kitchen. She waved her hand toward a pile of cardboard boxes near the back door. "Bess salvaged these boxes from Lewis's Super. You can start in here."

"Bess Grant?" Paige slipped out of her coat, hiding her slight limp from her fall yesterday. "Does she have something to do with you moving?"

"A few of us ladies decided to buy a house together."

"You did? When did all this happen?" She set her coat on the table.

"Signed papers today." Aunt Callie's grin widened. "I'm giddy with all I have to do." She flung wide several kitchen cupboards. The shelves were crammed full of dishes and plastic containers and lids. "Everything has to go. Have at it!" She turned toward the living room.

"Wait!"

"What do you need?" Aunt Callie paused.

"What am I supposed to do with all this stuff?" Paige waved her hands toward the cramped cupboards. "And why the rush? I mean, why are you selling this house? You've lived here, what, twenty years?"

"About that." Gazing at the clutter, Aunt Callie smiled fondly. "I've loved this home, but I'm embarking on a new journey with Bess and Kathleen. Look out world!"

"Are you certain?" This was happening way too fast. Her aunt packing up and moving on a whim? Spontaneity wasn't like her. Yet, here she stood grinning from ear to ear as if it were the best thing ever.

"Absolutely certain. Don't you worry. I've thought this through, and I'm ready for a new phase of life."

"Well, if you're sure, I'll help in any way I can." Although Paige still felt reluctant about her aunt's sudden choices. "Are you going to have a garage sale? Give it away, or what?" She glanced between the messy kitchen and living room. This would take a ton of work and time.

"A garage sale? Brilliant idea. That will help our cause."

"What cause?"

"Oh, never mind." Aunt Callie bustled out of the room. "Moving costs, you know."

Hmm. Was she hiding something? "Where are you moving to?" Paige followed her down the hallway.

"The old Peterson place."

"Isn't that house in terrible shape? I mean, it's a great location. But maybe it should be leveled."

"Young lady, you're talking about my future home. Needs some work, kind of like us old gals, that's all." Aunt Callie huffed. "Now, close your mouth, Paige. We have lots of work to do."

"Yes, ma'am." Still stymied, she shook her head. Her aunt was selling her house and moving into a broken-down relic at her age? She trudged back into the kitchen, surprised to hear Aunt Callie shuffling after her.

"See those cupboards I left open?"

"Yes."

"Box up all the dishes and plastic containers. With several of us moving in together, we don't need duplicate kitchenware. I will keep my grandmother's antique bowls."

"So I can box up everything but the antiques?"

"That's right." Aunt Callie strode back the way she came with almost a skip to her step.

When had Paige's matriarch aunt ever been so animated? Maybe moving was a healthy life choice for her, after all.

But all this work? Paige pulled up the sleeves of her Henley shirt, then took bowls and cups out of the cupboard. At least helping Aunt Callie would give her something to do other than sitting around her house thinking about Forest.

After a half hour, she'd packed several boxes and emptied quite a few shelves. The task wasn't difficult, just time-consuming.

What was Forest doing now? She imagined his glimmering gray-green eyes gazing at her. What did he think about their conversation at Bert's? Had he discovered anything new about the case? Ugh. There she was thinking about him again. Time for another distraction.

"Are you ready for a break yet?" Paige called. "Aunt Callie? Ready for some sweet tea?"

"I'm always ready for sweet tea, hon."

Chuckling, Paige found a pitcher of dark tea in the fridge. She poured the liquid into two old green Coca-Cola glasses she rescued from the discard pile. Then scrounging through a drawer, she grabbed packages of store-bought cookies and pretzels. After she retrieved a plate from a garage-sale box, she made a tray of snacks, put their glasses on it, and carried them down the hallway.

"Oh, my." At her aunt's bedroom doorway, she came to a stop. It appeared as if an explosion took place. "What happened in here?"

"You know the show where you pile every piece of clothing you own on the bed?" Aunt Callie spread her arms wide toward a gigantic mound of clothing. "Thought I'd try it."

"Is it working?"

"Beats me." Aunt Callie scooped clothes off two chairs near the window and tossed them onto the mound on the bed. "It's hard to eliminate a lifetime of stuff." She huffed and sat down.

"I bet." Paige handed her a glass.

"Bless you, child." The older woman guzzled her tea, then smacked her lips. "Just what I needed."

"I thought so." Paige dropped into the other chair and sipped her drink. "Please, tell me more about this new house."

"It needs work, lots of TLC, but it has so much potential." Aunt Callie grabbed a handful of pretzels. "That's why I have to sell this house so I can contribute to the remodeling expenses."

Paige decided to risk her aunt's wrath. "Maybe you should take a week and ponder these life changes. It's not too late to back out, is it?"

"Back out? Now you sound like Judah. What's to ponder?"

"Is the new place even livable?"

Aunt Callie guffawed. "Not at all."

"Then why are you doing this?" Paige tried to tone down her panic.

"Heavens. Haven't you ever leaped off a rock and plunged into the water?"

"Actually, no, I haven't."

Aunt Callie gawked at her. "Then you, my dear, have missed out on something spectacular."

"What do you mean?" Leaping off a rock and sinking into the sea sounded about as good as having a heart attack.

"When you plunge off a rock"—Aunt Callie's eyes sparkled—"you don't know if the water's going to be freezing, or if you might do a belly flop, or land on the bottom of the ocean."

"And that's supposed to be good?"

"It's exciting and adventurous. You get an amazing surge of life rushing through your veins." Aunt Callie chuckled. "Like anything is possible. Anything," she said dreamily.

Paige would never jump off a rock and plunge into the sea, especially with her mother's warnings playing through her mind. *The waves will grab you. Drag you to your death.* She cleared her throat. "Aunt Callie, what's gotten into you? I thought your things brought you comfort. Isn't that what you told me?"

"Certainly. But I'll enjoy the next house, too. My personal space will be smaller, so I have to minimize my belongings." She pointed at a monochromatic beach scene on the wall that Paige painted in high school. "That stays with me. Wouldn't part with your artwork for anything."

Warmth spread through Paige's heart. She was thankful for her aunt's involvement in her life, even if the woman's bossy side annoyed her sometimes.

"How's the kitchen coming along?" Aunt Callie slurped her tea to the last drop.

"Fine. You want it all boxed up, right?"

"All but Granny's bowls. Oh, and there's a mug I want to keep. *Best Aunt,* or something."

Paige groaned. She'd put the cracked cup in a box but was tempted to toss it in the trash. "I'll keep working in the kitchen, then."

"Thank you, sweetie."

Gathering the remnants of their snacks, Paige took one last look at the painting made from grays and whites, then sauntered back into the kitchen.

She sent a text to Dad. *Is Piper doing okay? This may take longer than I thought.*

She's fine.

Her father didn't articulate much in his texts, but he always answered her queries about Piper.

Thanks for helping with her.

Sure.

Now, if she could finish up the kitchen and pick up her daughter within three hours, maybe four—without Forest observing her leaving her dad's place with a child—that would be fantastic.

How long would she be able to avoid him?

Twelve

Paige enjoyed Forest asking about her art, and even inquiring about her mother who'd recently died. During breaks, they met at the coffee kiosk. Every time she saw him, she knew she was falling more in love with him.

The next morning, Paige tapped Piper's plate with five bites of pancakes left. "Finish your breakfast, kiddo."

"*Pway* sand?"

Ever since two days ago when Piper came home from playing at Necia's, Paige's friend from three houses down the block, she'd chattered about wanting to dig in the sand. Necia had arranged for a pile of sand to be delivered to her backyard for her daughter, Vi, and the girls enjoyed a fabulous time of digging.

"*Pwease*, sand?" Piper's eyes sparkled.

"Finish your breakfast. Then, maybe, we'll go to the beach."

Piper squealed and clapped.

Paige forked a pancake piece and put it into her daughter's mouth. Warm motherly feelings flooded her. Mornings were so delightful with this munchkin.

After breakfast and clean-up tasks were finished, Paige decided to take Piper to the beach. Why not? She'd let her play in the sand, then they'd come home and spend the rest of the day reading stories and playing with blocks. What were the chances of Forest being at the beach at the same time she was twice in a row, anyway?

She put on a sweatshirt and helped with Piper's coat, then they strolled toward the seashore. With her shovel in hand, Piper chattered about birds and rocks, dancing and frolicking down the woodsy trail.

As soon as the ocean came into view, she charged ahead, stumbling toward the water. Paige chased her, only slightly hindered by her gimpy leg, and got in front of her, hands extended. "Stay back, young lady. You are not getting wet today. You wanted to play in the sand, remember?"

"Sand." Piper waved her plastic shovel, her eyes glowing. "*Cwab*." Quickly distracted, she pointed at a small crab scuttling along the sand. Then, as if lured by the mud, she grabbed a fistful and hurled it into the sea, cackling. She kicked at more mud, sending flecks of dirt into the foaming waves.

"Come on." Paige clasped Piper's dirty hand, intervening before she charged toward the water again. She obviously didn't possess any of Paige's fears of the ocean. "Look, isn't that rock pretty?" She pointed at a peach-colored rock.

"*Pwetty*." Piper bent over, her fingers grabbing the stone and a wad of oozing mud along with it.

Paige reached out to keep her from getting dirtier than she already was, but stopped herself. Playing in the sand should be a part of a child's life near the sea, right? The healthy part Paige had been denied as a kid. Squatting down beside Piper, she picked up a handful of cool mud in her own hands, squishing it, surprised by the soft clay-like texture. "It's okay if you want to play in the mud and get dirty today."

Piper stared at her as if she'd grown horns.

"I mean it. Go ahead and play." Paige squeezed some more mud into an oval shape. "Hey, we could make things out of this. Sculptures."

Piper squished wet sand between both hands and laughed.

Thinking about the sculpting class she took in high school, Paige formed the glob of damp earth into a simple dog. She smoothed the nose and ears out with her fingers, making it as realistic as possible, then offered it to Piper. "How do you like this dog?"

"*Gog.*" Piper clasped the creature, her eyes glowing. "*Mow gog.*" She plopped down on her bottom in the sand and barked like a dog.

Paige sat next to her, laughing, relaxing, even with some moisture from the beach seeping into her jeans. She spent the better part of an hour creating a menagerie of animals.

Piper grabbed a cow shape and broke off its head. Then screamed.

"What's wrong, Pipe?"

"Moo-cow." She sobbed like it was the end of the world.

"Don't get so upset. Just shove it back together. It's okay."

Piper sniffled and hiccupped. Nodding, she set the animal on the sand and smashed the pieces together. Then wailed again. "*Mow* cow! *Mow* cow!" She held out the unrecognizable lump of clay to Paige.

"I'll fix it. No reason to cry." Remolding the animal a little differently than before, her cold fingers worked the clay. Were Piper's hands getting as chilled as hers? After she attached the tail and handed the sculpture back to Piper, she checked her hands. "Pretty soon, we'll have to head home and get you warm."

"No! Moo-cow." Piper dropped the cow next to the pig and scooted on her bottom farther away from Paige. "Moo. Moo."

"You can play for a few more minutes, then we'll go home and wash up."

"*Mow?*" Piper held up a chicken with a crooked beak.

"Okay. One more."

Who would have thought playing in the mud could be so enjoyable? And a free activity! Why hadn't she done this before? Good thing no one was watching her sitting on the sand, digging her fingers into fresh mud like she was the kid having a ton of fun. She pressed a glob together, envisioning a sea creature. A whale, maybe. She could create a whole bunch of sea creatures.

"So, what do we have here?"

Paige froze. Forest? Oh, no. She got distracted. Wasn't watching the beach. What now? Try to act normal? Would he see his likeness in Piper, who was now covered in dirt?

Heart hammering, Paige stood and faced him.

"Moo." Piper held out the cow to him.

Forest's eyes, so much like Piper's, gleamed in amusement. "Who's this, Paige?"

Thirteen

*Forest kissed Paige's cheek, not trusting himself
to do more than that, then strode to the elevator.
Glancing back, he saw her lift her delicate artist's
hand and shyly blow him a kiss. Man. He was
attracted to her.*

Forest went for a walk on the beach to mull over the case. Edward denying culpability for the kidnapping annoyed him. As did Craig Masters, the prime suspect as his accomplice— especially since Deputy Brian heard Edward urging Judah to tell Craig to keep his mouth shut—being in hiding. But Forest's interview with Mia Till, the most flirtatious woman he ever questioned, frustrated him to no end.

The call he made to Sheriff Morris, updating him on his progress, was stressful too. The sheriff wanted Forest's reports finished ASAP. But he was a thorough investigator. There were a plethora of reports to finalize. Missing pieces to solve. More data to analyze.

Even Sheriff Morris's question about the deputy's possible involvement could mean delays. *"Have you questioned Brian?"* Forest read his report and didn't find anything questionable. *"He was at the scene. Made the arrest. Don't leave any stone unturned."*

Right. But the deputy grew up in this small town. Folks seemed to trust him. Why throw suspicion on the only lawman in Basalt Bay, even if Edward insinuated that he could be bought? Considering it was the ex-mayor, a criminal and a man obviously lacking integrity, who said it, Forest doubted the accusation.

Then there was Paige, Judah, and Bess, who'd all met with Craig the night of Paisley's rescue. Of those three, why was Paige the only one who seemed suspicious to him? According to Bess's statement, she suggested twice that they contact Deputy Brian. Judah had been desperate to save his wife. Who could blame him for not following protocols? But Paige … why had Craig confided in her about Edward's plot?

Forest glanced down the seashore. A woman and a child sat on the beach near the water's edge. Was that Paige? Perfect timing. He'd been hoping for the chance to talk with her. Was she babysitting? He jogged over and asked about the kid.

Paige leaped up, glaring at him "You startled me."

"Sorry."

"Time to go," she told the little girl and dusted off her grimy-looking pants, her face turning crimson.

She was obviously upset, but why?

"Oink. Oink." The child pranced around him with a pig shape in her hands. "Oink."

He chuckled at her antics. "Those are cool farm animals you girls made."

"Mo—"

"Piper and I"—Paige cut into whatever the girl was about to say—"have been making animal sculptures. Now we have to leave."

Forest glanced back and forth between the child and the woman. A breath caught in his throat. Was this Paige's daughter? She didn't look anything like her. Where Paige had dark hair and deep-chocolate eyes, this child's coloring was blond and fair. Her irises almost looked ... what color were they? He leaned closer to see them.

Paige stepped right between him and the girl playing in the mud. "Time to go, Pipe." In one swoop, she picked up the kid and marched stiffly away from him.

What was that about? Couldn't they even have a casual conversation?

"Noooooo!" The girl screamed in a piercing howl. "Moo-cow. Moo-cow." She arched her back, her muddy hands extended his way as she cried and reached toward the creatures left behind.

"Don't leave on my account." His words were surely lost in the child's frantic screaming and the gust of air billowing in from the ocean. Here he hoped to talk with Paige. Get some things off his chest. That certainly wasn't happening now.

Paige marched farther up the beach, bouncing and shushing the kid. Another wailed followed.

Forest watched until they disappeared onto the trail that cut through the woods. Why was Paige so uncomfortable around him? He'd hurt her feelings, but this reeked of something more than a bad breakup. Did she hate him? A knife twisted in his chest. Why couldn't they talk about the past and try to find some resolution?

He glanced at the sculptures and an idea came to mind. Perhaps he could appease the child's unhappiness and show Paige he wasn't the ogre she seemed to think he was.

Removing his jacket, he knelt in the sand. Carefully, he set each barnyard creature—cow, pig, horse, chickens, ducks—on his coat. And a whale? He chuckled and placed the sea creature beside the others, imagining Paige's fingers touching each piece.

Her artistic flair was obvious in every snout, webbed foot, and eyeball. She went all out making these animals. He liked picturing her letting down her hair. Art in the mud? He smiled, thinking back to when they first met in Vegas, and she attended an art conference.

How differently things might have been if he stayed with her. But he couldn't turn back time. Couldn't undo the past, as much as he would if he could. But when he thought of her reaction to him a few minutes ago, her ice-queen glare piercing him, the way she rushed away from him with the kid as if he were poisonous, his insides hurt.

Jesus could heal their hearts, he knew that since he'd come to trust in Him. But how could Forest apologize and make amends with Paige before he left Basalt Bay if she wasn't even willing to have a discussion with him?

Fourteen

During a walk, Paige told Forest it would be fun to see the inside of a wedding chapel. What started out as a simple flirtation grew bigger in her mind. Paisley and Judah had eloped. What if Forest asked her to marry him in Las Vegas?

Paige stomped through the kitchen, then trudged back to her bedroom, before retracing her steps again. She'd changed Piper's clothes and settled her down in her room, but her nerves were taut. A tension headache shot pain up her neck and pounded in her temples. She kept moving, swinging her arms, then pausing and stretching to counteract the stress.

Forest had some nerve coming up to them on the beach without any warning like he did. Didn't she fear such a thing might happen? That's why she remained locked in the house for the last few days—where she should have stayed.

Did he notice how much Piper favored him? Did he see her gray-green eyes?

Groan.

She stomped down the hall again. Piper had finally stopped crying, but Paige could still hear her lamenting about the lost "moo-cow."

She'd race back to the beach and rescue the poor clay beasts from the tide if she could. They were nothing but disposable toys, but she hated disappointing her daughter. And she had enjoyed making the small sculptures. Until Forest showed up. Then she panicked and ran away with Piper wailing all the way to the house.

From now until he left town, she'd stay inside. Keep the curtains closed. How much longer would it take for him to get his precious evidence and leave?

Standing in front of the kitchen sink, she stared out the window toward the leaning swing set in the backyard. A hazard, thanks to hurricane winds. Piper still used it sometimes, but Paige had to watch her constantly for fear the whole structure might topple over. Maybe Judah could help her haul it to the dump one of these days.

A sound snagged her attention. Did someone tread down the porch steps? In quick strides, she reached the back door and flung it open. No one was there. But on the railing, lined up facing her, were the mud animals she left on the beach.

Oh, my. Forest must have done this.

She rushed over to the sculptures and fingered each one. Piper was going to be so excited.

"Pipe!" She ran into her daughter's room and picked her up. "I have something to show you." Back on the porch, she pointed at the creatures. "See the animals."

"Moo-cow!"

"That's right." She set Piper down and handed her the cow. "Be careful. It's still drying."

Paige placed the other animals on the porch floor. Piper dropped onto her knees, crawling around and making animal sounds.

Thank you, Forest.

She imagined him as she saw him a little while ago. His gray-green eyes shining at her, his hair blowing in the wind, his handsome smile that turned her insides to mush.

What did he think about Piper? Did he guess who she was?

Fifteen

"I've read over both of your responses to the question-naire." Pastor Sagle glanced at Paisley and Judah over the papers he held.

Paisley wiped her sweaty hands down her jeans. All day, she dreaded this second counseling session. Why was she so honest in the essay answers? She could have been vague and kept private thoughts private. She prayed her answers wouldn't cause a rift between her and Judah, especially when they were only three days from her one-week doctor's visit and, hopefully, a clean bill of health.

Judah's folded hands made him appear relaxed, but his knees bouncing up and down gave away his nervousness. He'd been distant ever since he and Bess visited Edward yesterday. Paisley leaned her head against his shoulder, initiating contact with him. Hardly a beat passed before his head rested against hers, too, and she sighed.

"Let's jump right in, shall we?" Pastor Sagle asked.

"Okay." Paisley sat up straighter.

"How would you describe your relationship with Judah's dad?" The pastor met her gaze.

"Edward? Oh. Um." Now, why did they have to talk about him first?

"Did he welcome you into the Grant family?"

"Hardly." That probably sounded rude. "Sorry."

"You can be candid here." Pastor Sagle set the papers down and crossed his hands on the desk.

It wouldn't do any good to ask for them not to talk about Judah's father, since Pastor Sagle seemed determined to dig up old stuff. Tear off the Band-Aid in one rip, and all that.

"Edward had it out for me even when I was a teenager, or so I thought."

Was the heat turned up too high? Her palms felt sweaty. Her throat dry. She gazed around the room. Water stains marked the ceiling. A painting of a dog was on the far wall. Judah fidgeted in the chair beside her. She focused on those things, not on the anxiety building within her.

"He and I ... never got along even before Judah and I ... became a couple."

"If that were true, then why do you suppose he felt the way he did?"

"Does it matter? He's going to ... prison." Her throat tightened. "He won't be involved in our lives anymore."

"Won't he?" Pastor Sagle tipped his head and stared at her.

"Oh. Well, I—"

Judah didn't meet her gaze.

A few awkward moments passed.

"He'll still be a part of your family because he's still a part of Judah's family, right?"

While Pastor Sagle spoke in a quiet, non-emotional sounding voice, his words punched her in the stomach. He was right. Edward would always be Judah's father. Even from prison, he'd be in their lives because Judah would probably visit him, then act sullen or disheartened like he did today. Whenever Edward got out of lockup, five or ten years down the road, he'd be free to do what he wanted. Cause more trouble. Drive wedges between her and Judah. Hurt her? The office was sweltering. She tugged at the neck of her sweater.

"You okay?" Judah stroked her arm.

"I didn't think about that." She swallowed over a choking sensation. "Him getting out ... still being ..." She coughed.

"What is it?"

"I fooled myself into believing it was over. But how can it ever be over?" She stared at her husband as anxiety wrapped around her like a boa constrictor, squeezing the air out of her lungs. "I'll always feel—"

"Shhhh. It's okay, Pais." Judah smoothed his palms over her shoulders, pulling her against his chest. "We're not going to live in fear, remember? We're trusting in Jesus, together. He's here with us, walking with us through whatever we face. He was with you during those painful experiences, too."

She focused on his words, his soft sweatshirt beneath her cheek, her inhaling and exhaling. She had been trying to lean on Jesus ever since she trusted in Him while she was tied up in Edward's closet. Her faith was growing. God's love was greater than her worries. Hadn't Judah told her so a dozen times? And yet? She sat up again. "What about you?"

"What do you mean?"

"You saw Edward yesterday. You've acted upset ever since."

He glanced at the pastor, then back at her. "I'm sorry for letting it stress me out."

She nodded. Sighed. "It's okay."

"Is it something you'd like to discuss?" Pastor Sagle asked.

"Another time, perhaps."

The pastor eyed him like he wanted to ask more questions. "You've both gone through a trauma." He nudged a tissue box across the desk. "You don't have to worry about what your future will be like, Paisley. You and Judah are building a bridge together."

"A bridge?"

"Yes, just imagine a viaduct of peace and hope spanning"— he spread out his hands—"from when you first met and married, to your separation and remarriage, and far into your future together. One by one, you're setting the foundation stones for the bridge."

She breathed slower, picturing Jesus being like a bridge for them, too.

"Do you remember the first time you met Mayor Grant?"

Why did he keep pushing her to talk about Edward? "Uh-huh. At a city council meeting I attended with my dad." She dug back into her memory. "He strutted around the room in his three-piece suit as if he owned the world."

Something her mother said came to mind. *That lousy mayor. Who does he think he is?* Things her father said came back too. *"Even Edward Grant has experienced losses. None of us are exempt."*

"There were conflicts, or offenses, between him and my dad when they were younger."

"Before Judah's and your elopement?"

"Yes, but what I know I learned from my aunt." She shrugged. "It's private, so I can't talk about it here."

Judah sighed, perhaps relieved for her not to discuss his family. In the hospital, she told him what Aunt Callie shared with her about their fathers going after the same woman when they were younger. How Edward, according to her aunt, had resented Paisley's dad ever since.

"I respect the privacy of all involved." Pastor Sagle stroked his chin. "You mentioned in your questionnaire that you felt inferior to the Grant family. Can you tell me about that?"

Judah glanced at her.

"I didn't feel that way because of Judah. It was how I perceived his father's disdain toward me and my family."

"I'm sorry, Pais." Judah swept a few strands of her hair back. "I never considered you inferior to me or my parents."

"Thank you. We eloped and our families were hurt. Your dad said some cruel things about me not being good enough for you. That even Misty Gale knew I wouldn't—" Now she needed a tissue. Grabbing one, she wiped beneath her eyes. Remembering the daughter they lost, and her father-in-law's spiteful words, hit her hard.

"He was wrong. So wrong." Judah hugged her comfortingly.

"I think we've found a stepping stone for that bridge I mentioned." Pastor Sagle grinned like he'd solved their problems.

She, on the other hand, felt the weight of the "stone" pressing down on her shoulders, dragging her into deeper emotional waters.

Sixteen

Paige approached Forest where he stood near the waterfall, and she knew if he were to ask her to be his wife, she'd say yes. Call her crazy, she'd fallen wildly in love with Forest Harper. Her life would never be the same.

The next morning, Paige received a cryptic text from an anonymous sender. *Meet me by the peninsula. Noon. Important. Your friend.*

Friend? Is that what Forest thought they were now? Had he gotten a new cell number? She didn't recognize the caller ID. What important thing did he need to discuss with her? Something about the case, no doubt. Unless he suspected Piper might be his daughter.

Uncertain whether she should go along with his mysterious invitation, she called Necia and arranged a playdate for their girls. She even put on a little lipstick and mascara, so she'd look her best.

After dropping off Piper, Paige hiked down to the beach. Pausing, hand over her eyes, she peered across the seashore to where a large machine with a crane-like arm picked up boulders from the peninsula and released them onto the sand. Caution tape, strung along by posts, created a border for the work zone. This must mean the removal phase of the peninsula's renovation had begun. How long would it take until the new dike was built? In the meantime, she'd keep Piper away from this area.

Forest wasn't anywhere on the beach.

"Paige!" a male voice—not his—called.

Heart thudding, she turned but didn't see anyone.

"Over here."

Some bushes swayed. She tensed. Nearly screamed.

What if Forest didn't text her? What if she made a terrible mistake and fell for a scam to meet a stranger on the beach?

Just then, a darkly dressed man stepped from the woods with his sweatshirt hood pulled tightly around his face. She backed up, keeping her distance. When the guy loosened the ties, revealing his face, she expelled a breath.

"Craig? What are you doing here?"

"Come and talk with me, will you?" He rocked his thumb toward a large chunk of driftwood. "I don't have much time."

"You sent me the text?"

"Yes."

Disappointment crashed through her. Forest wasn't the one who requested this meeting. Craig was the last person she expected to find here.

"Why are you back in Basalt Bay? What's with the new phone number?" She shuffled through the sand to reach him. "And hiding in the bushes?"

"It's a cheap phone I picked up. I don't want anyone to see me." He tugged his hood back on. "I need information. Knew I could trust you." He dropped onto the log and patted the spot next to him.

She sat down a couple feet from him. "What's going on? I mean, I'm glad you're okay. Alive."

"Thanks. Nice to see you too. Any news on Edward?"

She frowned. "He's in jail where he belongs, awaiting trial."

"Finagling to be released, no doubt." Craig scowled. "If Edward makes bail, or if he tricks the deputy into releasing him, he'll be out for revenge. You and I won't be safe."

"Do you think that might happen? Him getting released?"

"He'll fight to stay in charge of the town and take down anyone who stands in his way." His gaze locked on hers. "I mean anyone. Be careful, okay? Watch out for Piper."

"I will." As soon as they were done here, she'd hurry back to Necia's and take Piper home. "Thanks for the heads-up."

"There are some in town who have to do Edward's dirty work because he has a noose around their necks." Craig rubbed his palm beneath his Adam's apple as if he felt the burn of the rope.

"Who do you mean?"

"I'd rather not say."

"You?"

Was the mayor still calling the shots for Craig?

"Well, I—"

"What's going on here?" Forest charged toward them from the trail.

Paige stood. "Forest, why are you here?"

Craig jumped to his feet beside her.

"I could ask you the same thing." Forest's eyes glinted at her, then Craig. "I've been looking for you, Masters." He held out a badge. "I'm Detective Forest Harper."

"You told him we were meeting?" Craig glared at Paige.

"No, of course I didn't."

"I can't believe this."

Craig took off running toward the parking lot. Forest ran after him in close pursuit. On the other side of the crane, Craig lunged for his truck and dove inside. Forest grabbed the door handle, obviously trying to stop him from closing it. Craig gunned the vehicle, which forced Forest to let go. He flicked his hand up and down like he might have gotten it pinched in the truck door.

Paige was tempted to leave without even speaking to Forest, but he'd probably follow her home. She didn't want that. So she waited, kicking the toe of her shoe in the sand, taking some of her angst out on a shell.

"Why are you secretly meeting with Craig Masters?" he asked as soon as he was within earshot.

"Secretly?"

"Don't you realize he's a key player in the investigation?" Forest rubbed his hand and grimaced.

"Are you okay?"

"I'm fine." He stuffed his hands into his jacket pockets.

His sober expression reminded her of the day they argued three years ago. Remembering the way he left her, how he married her then fled at the first sign of trouble, her heart hardened a few notches. She didn't owe him an explanation.

Still, she didn't want him accusing her of being a part of Craig eluding him, either. "Craig helped my sister escape from Edward. He's been a friend to me."

"And—?"

What could she say so she didn't sound like she was intentionally meeting up with a criminal? "I received a text to meet someone here. Only, I didn't know it was Craig. In fact, I thought it might be you."

A smile spread across Forest's face. "You came to the beach expecting to find me here? To talk with me?"

"Y-yes," she sputtered. "Not because of any personal reason." She wouldn't admit that she put on lipstick and mascara because she thought it was him. "I figured you might need more information about the case."

"Oh." His grin faded. "Do you have more information?"

"Not really."

He sighed. "Is your leg any better?"

With his gentler tone of voice, she could almost imagine he cared.

"I'm not limping as much."

"That's good. Care to take a walk with me?"

"Why would I want to do that?" Her question came out snippy, but goodness, she'd avoided him for days.

"To talk."

About the case? Or did he want to ask more questions about Craig?

"I suppose we could sit down for a few minutes." She trudged back to the place where she and Craig had been sitting. She crossed her arms, trying to keep the chill she felt around Forest at bay. "Thank you for returning the clay creatures. That was you, right?"

"Sure was." He dropped down beside her. "You should stay away from Masters. I mean it."

Her hackles instantly caught fire. "What I do is none of your business, Forest Harper. Got it?"

"I've got it. But your friend could be thigh deep in this case. If he was acting alongside Edward—"

"Craig has proven himself helpful to me and my family." *Acting alongside Edward, my foot.* She scooted farther away on the log. "What else did you want to talk about?" Time to end this discussion.

"Us," he said quietly.

"There is no us." Paige shoved off the log. "We're done here."

"Please, let me explain." He stood and clasped her wrist gently.

She glared at his hand until he let go.

"For three years, I've waited to see you. To tell you"—he gulped—"that I still ... I still love you, Paige."

"Yeah, right."

"I'm serious."

His gaze seemed to caress her at the same time an electrical current zapped her senses. Stunned by her thundering heart and the heat infusing her face, she swallowed hard. She felt captured in a time capsule and sent back three years. Back to when she adored this man and truly believed he loved her.

"I do care for you."

Resentment and doubt sliced through her. "How can you say such things after you walked away so easily?" Which is exactly what she was going to do. "Never mind. I don't need to know the answer. I wish you the best in your case. Goodbye, Forest."

She stomped through the sand, chewing on his declaration. Was it love that kept him away for three years? Did his caring for her cause him to whisper his ex's name in the dead of night? She walked through the woods and tromped up the block.

Behind her, Forest's footsteps pounded the sidewalk. "Paige, wait. When are you going to stop running?"

She whirled around and pointed at him. "You want to talk about who ran? Who stayed away? Who didn't care enough—"

"I was stupid," he said huskily. His eyes flooded with moisture. "I'm so sorry for hurting you. For ruining the beautiful thing we had for such a short time."

His words, his tenderness, eased some of the tight knots in her chest. When he reached out and smoothed his hands whisper-soft down her arms, she didn't pull away as she should have.

"I'd do anything—*anything*—to make it up to you."

Another false promise? She stumbled backward, this time pulling away. Why didn't she stay in the house and keep her doors locked?

"Please, can we talk about it?"

"Look, it's over between us. Has been for a long time." Yet how could their relationship ever be over when there was Piper to consider? "Do what you came to Basalt to do, then leave, okay? I don't want to stir something up with you again."

Liar. Wasn't stirring something up with him exactly what she dreamed about last night? What she hoped for when she thought the text was from him. If she didn't want to stir something up, why was she disappointed when it wound up being Craig on the beach and not Forest?

His eyes closed for a moment. "I never got over you."

"No? What about Elinore?"

He flinched. "What do you mean?"

"Didn't you run back and marry her?"

"That's what you thought?" His voice sounded raw. "That I married her?"

"What else would I think when you didn't call or text? Why else wouldn't you have followed through with your promises? Your vows," she threw at him. When she realized she was jabbing his chest with her finger, she stepped back but didn't apologize.

"I stayed away because you told me to. And because of my wounded pride." He made a sharp whistling sound. "The divorce papers came, proving you gave up on us and moved on. I let you go. But so you know ... I've regretted my decision every day for three years."

Her angst deflated like a balloon releasing air. He regretted leaving her? Why did he wait this long to tell her?

Seventeen

Judah kissed Paisley's forehead as she settled down to take an afternoon nap and heard a car pull into the driveway. Not wanting her disturbed, he closed the bedroom door and strode outside.

"Judah." Deputy Brian approached him from his squad car.

"This is a surprise, Deputy."

The law enforcement officer faced the ocean. "Great view you have."

"Thanks. What brings you out this way?"

"I need you to come with me." The deputy's voice deepened authoritatively.

"What's this about? Did something happen to my dad?" Judah's thoughts leaped to imagining his father gripping his chest, suffering a heart attack in jail. The stressful lifestyle he led couldn't have been healthy.

"Edward's fine. Well, as fine as can be expected under the circumstances."

Why else would Deputy Brian summon him? His father's parting shot about the unstoppable freight train hit him. "What's Edward demanding of me now?"

"This is strictly City Council business. Your presence is requested." Deputy Brian's shoulders heaved. "Okay, honest truth? Your father railed at me until I agreed to drive out and haul you to City Hall to shut him up."

Judah chuckled. "That sounds more like it."

"Seriously, our city government is in trouble."

"Nothing I can do about that." He should have guessed Edward would try to twist his arm again. "My father's a force to be reckoned with, but I won't be coerced into taking his place as mayor. I've told him so."

"Not even as a temp?" Deputy Brian removed his sunglasses.

"Not even then."

"The council has been floundering ever since the unfortunate event with Mayor Grant took place." Using his shirttail, the deputy wiped his glasses.

"I still don't see how I can help."

"The crew began the removal phase of the dike, but everything's come to a dead stop. Negotiations broke down. Problems between Mike Linfield, C-MER, and the council." Deputy Brian cleared his throat. "A new guy's causing havoc too."

Maybe the new guy he referred to was Judah's or Craig's replacement. "What do you expect me to do?"

"Make the C-MER crew see reason. Become a liaison between them and the city." Deputy Brian shrugged. "Would it kill you to fill in as mayor?"

"Might," Judah said humorlessly. "Mike wouldn't listen to

me when I worked for him, so I doubt I'd have much influence. And no about the mayorship."

"I thought you believed in the Good Samaritan stuff."

"I do."

"You want what's best for Basalt Bay, don't you?"

"Uh-huh." Judah sensed a trap. "Did Edward tell you to make me feel guilty for not caring enough about the town?"

Deputy Brian's lack of a comeback was answer enough.

"I care what happens to our town. But I don't work for C-MER, City Hall, or Edward."

Lord, is any of this Your will? Judah paused to pray silently. Most likely, his recent attitude toward his father wasn't pleasing to the Lord. But he'd have to work on that and pray some more.

"For the good of Basalt Bay, will you accompany me to the council meeting?" Deputy Brian lifted his chin toward the squad car. "Talk to the members. They need direction on how to work with C-MER. And before you say it, yes, Edward's goading me about not doing my civic duty."

"You mean about me not doing mine?" Judah eyed the other man and for the first time felt sorry for the position Edward had put him in. "Okay, I'll talk to the council, but they won't like what I have to say."

"Whatever."

"I'll drive my own truck." Judah ran back into the house and checked on Paisley, who was sleeping soundly. He jotted a note, telling her where he was going, then grabbed his keys.

At City Hall, he strode toward the conference room with memories assailing him. The last time he was here, he barely persuaded the council to invest in the new dike. His success was short-lived when he got fired the next day.

"Judah, thank you for joining us." Sue Taylor gripped his hand. "I was afraid you wouldn't come."

He chuckled. If only she knew.

Fred Buckley shook his hand less enthusiastically. "Good to see you, Judah."

"Thanks."

A few others murmured greetings.

His gaze collided with Mia's.

"Why if it isn't Judah Grant." She batted her fake eyelashes at him.

"Mia."

"Aren't you looking comfy?" Her gaze traveled over his t-shirt and jeans a little too suggestively.

In three strides, he reached the far side of the table and sat down, focusing on the others around him.

"Let's get started, shall we?" Sue asked.

"I'll call the meeting to order," Mia announced as if reminding Sue that she was in charge.

Why was the C-MER receptionist directing these sessions, anyway? As Edward's protégé, she didn't hold an elected position. Someone should put her in her place. Not him, but someone.

"Since our new business is about old business, Judah has arrived just in time." Mia grinned and winked in his direction. "Who wants to explain to him why he's been invited?"

"I will." Sue lifted her hand. "Judah, you were the one who helped us realize the need for a new dike in the first place. But since that vote, we've had one problem after another with trying to move forward. Without leadership, we're flailing."

"I'd hardly call it flailing." Mia squinted at her.

Sue turned in her chair and faced Judah. "In the City Charter, it allows for a mayor to recommend his successor should he have to leave his post."

"Of course, that's you, Judah," Mia said in a gushing tone. "You and I already know how well we work together."

The possibility of working with her was reason enough for him not to accept the mayoral role.

"Mayor Grant had each of us dragged in to talk with him in jail," Sue said, "much like you were brought here."

"Now, Sue. Dragged?" Mia rolled her eyes. "Aren't you exaggerating?"

"As I said"—Sue's voice rose indignantly—"we were forced to speak with him so he could twist our arm and try to get us to do things his way."

Mia groaned.

Fred rubbed his chest like his breastbone hurt.

A palpable tension filled the room.

"With our lack of leadership"—Sue shot a glare toward Mia as if expecting her to interrupt—"and the mayor calling the shots from jail, this state of limbo has gone on long enough."

Mutterings resounded in the room.

"Maybe we should all simmer down." Mia's smile spread a smudge of red lipstick across her front teeth. "We're here to coax Judah into accepting our terms. Not to sling mud at our honorable mayor."

"I'm not slinging mud, nor would I call Edward honorable," Sue said in a clipped tone.

Bravo, Sue.

"Why not hold an emergency election?" Judah spoke up. "Choose a mayor who's voted into office by the people of Basalt Bay." He leaned his arms on the table and met the gazes of the appointed members. "The town needs a fresh start. Why not use this opportunity to make that happen?"

Mia gasped. "But, Judah, Edward expects you to fill his shoes until he gets out."

"Gets out? That could be years."

"You don't know that." She wagged her finger at him. "When Edward sets his mind to something, that's what will happen. He's more powerful than you think."

"Not this time. His punishment is out of his hands."

"What do you say, Judah?" Fred thumped the table with his knuckles. "Can we count on you to help us out in the interim? If the mayor has a longer stay in prison, we could reevaluate."

Judah smoothed his fingers over his rough chin. He hated to let down these people who'd selflessly given their time and dedication to the town. "I'm honored by the offer. However, I have no desire to be the mayor even on a short-term basis." Standing, he spread out his hands. "I'm sorry, but I can't accept. I wish you all the best. Have a good night." He strode to the door.

"Judah!" At Mia's piercing tone, he paused. "You must do what your father demands."

Must? Was she ordering him as if she were his father's spokesperson? Was this group deluded into imagining Edward was still in charge, even after the horrible crimes he'd done?

He met Mia's gaze and clenched his jaw, barely stopping himself from saying something defiant or unkind to her. *Grace and mercy.*

"Is there any way we can change your mind?" Sue asked. "We need a leader. Someone who appreciates our town and could work with C-MER on our behalf."

"That's right." Fred shoved his chair back and stood, huffing like it took a lot of energy. "You are our best option." He frowned at Mia.

"My decision stands." Judah couldn't exit City Hall fast enough.

"Judah?" Sue followed him out the front door. "Wait a sec."

"All right." He faced her slowly.

"Won't you reconsider? Our town needs you."

"Your best bet is to vote for a new mayor."

"We need someone now. Since the Charter allows Edward to choose his substitute, if you don't agree to do it, he says he'll pick Mia." Sue's grimace made it obvious how much she loathed that idea.

So did he. But most likely, Edward pushing for Mia to be his replacement was more about manipulating Judah to step up than a vote for the receptionist to fill his shoes. "Edward's criminal acts should preclude him from making any decision about the town."

"I agree, but he hasn't gone to trial yet. Until he's proven guilty—" She shrugged. "For whatever reason they let you go from C-MER, they were fools. You articulated the public concerns and the company's stance on the dike better than Mike Linfield, or the other fellow." She let out a strangled sounding breath. "If Mia is in charge of the council, even for a day, I will resign."

"That would be a loss for the town."

"Oh, Sue!" Mia trilled from the doorway of City Hall. "We need you back inside."

"Her majesty calls." Sue groaned.

"I'm sorry. If it would help—"

"Yes?"

"I could speak to Mike." He swallowed hard. Having a conversation with his previous manager, the one who fired him twice, wasn't on his wish list. "If it would help ease the burden—"

"Yes, it would. Thank you so much, Judah." She gripped his hand in a firm handshake.

As soon as he hopped into his truck, he moaned. Why did he volunteer to go back to C-MER?

Eighteen

On his way home, Judah parked behind Mom's vehicle on the road in front of the dilapidated Peterson place. A plethora of downed trees and piles of shingles made the driveway unusable. The property hadn't been cleaned up since Hurricanes Blaine and Addy hit, that much was obvious. He squinted toward the aging house, trying to look beyond the overgrown bushes and weeds to whatever potential his mother saw in the decrepit building. The gentle rumble of the ocean came from beyond the landscape, but he couldn't see it yet.

Mom skirted around the roots of a fallen tree and waved. "Judah, this way. We made a trail over here."

"Okay."

"Is that him?" He heard Callie's voice from the porch but couldn't see her due to the upended tree limbs.

"Yes, Judah's here," Mom called to her.

He meandered between bushes, shingles, and trash. When he reached her, Mom gave him a quick hug.

"Thanks for coming. It's a lot to take in, but Callie, Kathleen, and I have wonderful plans for the old place we've dubbed our project house." She patted his arm. "I can't wait for you to see it."

"Me too." Although, "project house" sounded ominous. When his foot broke through the first step on the porch, he groaned. Were the old boards even safe to walk on?

"Be careful. I forgot to warn you about the rotten wood." Mom's eyes glistened. "You're going to love the inside."

He gulped. If she expected him to love this monstrosity, he'd have to watch what he said. Why had she spent her mother's inheritance on such a risky investment? "How many bedrooms did you say it has?"

"Five. Six counting the attic. Can you believe it?"

"Wow." The eyesore was bigger than he thought. "You put *all* your money into this?"

"Now, let's not discuss money. Other than to say, yes, I made the initial investment. The other girls will pay for the renovations, including your salary if you're up to the task."

He could use an income for a few months while he applied for work outside of Basalt Bay.

"Please, keep an open mind."

"I'll try."

He'd noticed the windows on the front side of the house were busted. The horizontal wooden siding looked aged, broken, and was being taken over by moss. Was the sagging roof near collapsing, too?

Mom tugged on his arm, drawing him across the porch and past Callie.

"Hello," he said to his wife's aunt.

"Welcome to the project house," she said.

Inside the kitchen, he walked carefully across the mushy flooring, not wanting to step through any rotten boards as he did on the porch.

"Hello, Judah!" Kathleen smiled from behind the kitchen counter and swayed out her hands like Vanna White showing a game-winning prize. "Isn't it grand?"

"Hey," he said, not answering her query.

"Come look at the magnificent views." Mom led him around a pile of wet, broken Sheetrock. Then pointed through a dirty, busted window toward even more overgrown bushes and fallen trees in the back.

He still couldn't see the ocean.

"Beyond the scraggly mess is a perfect view of the sea." Mom stared at him, her eyes sparkling. "What do you think?"

Callie and Kathleen drew closer, gazes on him.

"Uh." He cleared his throat, still taking in the enormity of the task that would befall him if he accepted this project.

"Doesn't matter if he doesn't like it." Callie harrumphed. "We know there's beauty in the old girl."

"That we do," Kathleen added. "But it's okay if you don't see what we do, Judah. You will." She patted his arm and stepped closer to the window. "In my mind's eye, I envision a wide deck where we can have get-togethers. Maybe sit in the evenings chatting about the town, movies, art, or whatever."

"Mmhmm." Callie nodded, her plump folds creasing in her neck with each bob. "And barbecues. Do you know who's a great cook? Paige. We should ask her to cook for our"—she stared haughtily at Judah—"housewarming."

What was she going to say but didn't? Maybe Paisley was right about them being up to something.

"Let's finish the tour, shall we?" Mom tugged on his arm again.

He followed her into the kitchen with Kathleen and Callie whispering behind them.

"This room will need a complete modernizing." Mom patted the ugly green countertop. "Can you imagine the potential? Family dinners. Group gatherings. All of us sharing our lives here."

"I love to cook." Kathleen folded her hands. "We need plenty of room for all of us to work in here at the same time."

"That's right," Callie agreed.

Next, Mom showed him the first-floor bathroom, an antique setup from the sixties. Pink tub. Green Formica vanity. Torn and swollen linoleum. Sheetrock chunks had fallen from the ceiling. The water line from the storm surge was a foot up the wall. This room would need a major overhaul, too.

Callie claimed the bedroom next to the bathroom, explaining that traversing up and down the stairs in the middle of the night would never do.

Mom chattered about the building's potential and how it was a dream-come-true for all three ladies. As she walked up the creaking stairs, Judah tread lightly behind her, sensitive to the moaning sounds of old wood as Callie and Kathleen followed. Would the stairs hold all four of them?

At each of the bedrooms and the lone upstairs bathroom, the women gave him their ideas and plans for color choices and decorating tips for their individual spaces. They called one room a planning room. A folding table and chairs were already set up in the center. What kind of planning were they going to do here?

Judah crept up the rickety ship's ladder to the attic. The upper storage space would require a lot of junk removal and remodeling if they ever hoped to use it. Water stains speckled the floor where the roof had leaked. Lots of work everywhere.

When they finished the tour and stood outside, Mom nodded toward the rambling house. "What's the verdict?"

"I don't know what to say."

"Say you love it!" Kathleen laughed.

"His grim face says he hates it." Callie scowled.

"Not hates." He wouldn't say he felt eager to tackle the project, either. Mom called it a dream house. How she saw such positivity in the junk heap they just walked through remained a mystery. "It'll take a ton of work and money. You know that, right?"

"Yes."

"We're not idiots." Callie planted her thick fists on her hips.

Kathleen pulled up her sleeves. "None of us are afraid of hard work, but we need a leader to tell us what to do."

Twice in the same day, someone said they needed him to be a leader. A coincidence? A sign? Maybe something to ponder later.

"Please, Judah, will you help us?" Mom smiled warmly at him. "We'll pay for your time and expertise."

"Please?" Kathleen folded her hands in a begging pose.

Callie just stared at him, her eyebrows forming a V.

Glancing up at the weathered roof, he sighed. "I'm not a carpenter, but I'm willing to do what I can to lead this expedition."

The ladies clapped and cheered.

He stifled a groan. What had he gotten himself into? First, he volunteered to talk to Mike. Now, this?

Nineteen

Smitten, all Forest could think about, and dream about, was Paige Cedars. That had to be love. If he lost this connection with her, if he let her go, he might never experience something so wonderfully magical again.

Forest re-read Paige's eyewitness account of Craig coming to her house and telling her about Edward's possible abduction of Paisley. She'd written passionately about her concerns for a minor in her care. Forest knew when kids were involved in dangerous situations, people sometimes made rash, out-of-character decisions.

Did Paige go along with Craig's plan to rescue Paisley without contacting law enforcement because of possible harm to a child she was watching? Was it the same kid she was with on the beach? If only she had called the deputy, this suspicion about her involvement with Edward wouldn't exist. Other than that bit about the ex-mayor saying she might recant her statement, which Forest strongly doubted. Guilty people often blamed others in hopes of getting the spotlight off themselves. Was that what Edward had been doing?

Forest needed to speak with Paige again, but he couldn't confide any details about the case. Not even his concern that she might have known more than she was letting on. His urgency to pursue the truth, despite the awkwardness due to their past, might create even greater mistrust between them. He hated that but had to do his job.

Their shared past bound him to Paige, too. It made him more aware of her every nuance, every frown and smile. Those shiny chocolate-colored eyes peering into his undid him every time. Her soft gaze made him want to throw down his frustrations over what happened to separate them and beg her to take him back. If only he were that brave.

Even with all the unsettled emotions, he had to assure her that he'd never intentionally put her in harm's way, or drag her through a court case that might make her despise him more than she seemed to already. Surely, she knew he was only doing his job by digging for the truth—even if that made him her temporary enemy.

Over the last few days, he felt a burden on his soul, too. He'd been praying for the opportunity to explain to Paige how his heart had changed, how he wasn't the same insensitive clod who married her and then walked away. This is how she viewed him, right? Isn't that why he carried a weight of guilt? Although, since he accepted Christ, he was trying to commit that remorse to Him. Still, he wanted to make things right with his ex-wife.

Would she listen if he tried to explain? Would telling her about his faith journey make any difference in how she perceived him, or would she think he was making excuses? Justifying his previous actions. He groaned. He'd do anything to heal the breach between them. He apologized, but it would take more talking and sharing their hearts before they reached a place of true reconciliation.

Needing to see her, even for a ten-minute talk, he selected the Call icon on his phone and waited.

"Hello?"

"Paige? Forest, here."

"Oh." Disappointment oozed from her tone.

He steeled himself to not respond negatively. "Can you meet with me?"

"Why?"

"There's something I want to talk to you about. I'll be brief."

"Because it went so well last time?" Paige expelled a huffy-sounding breath.

"Please, I need to talk with you."

"About the case? Or so you can tell me how I shouldn't have been talking to Craig?"

"Just meet me where we did earlier, okay? It's ... personal."

Silence.

Then, "Fine. In one hour."

"Thanks."

For the next sixty minutes, he'd pray and contemplate what he could say to make things right with Paige, the woman he left but still couldn't get out of his mind.

Near the log on the beach where they last spoke, Forest paced back and forth. What should he say first? *Just don't say anything stupid.* Sighing, he kept pacing and praying.

Finally, Paige exited the trail, a hood encircling the scowl on her face.

"Thanks for coming." He swayed his hand toward the massive driftwood. "Care to sit?"

"I'm fine." She stopped six feet from him. "You said you'd be brief. Why did you want to see me?"

How would she react if he told her the truth? That he didn't want to live another day without her by his side? That since the day he signed the divorce papers, he felt like half a person, half a heart beating in his chest. Instead, he said, "I wanted to speak with you because we left things unsettled."

"What's new?" She kicked the toe of her dark tennis shoe against a broken shell.

The crumbling residue of calcium carbonate seemed symbolic of everything they'd gone through, all their brokenness, their unspoken yearnings. Well, his, anyway.

"There's something I've been hoping to tell you about." He breathed a silent prayer for God's help. "Five months ago I made a decision that changed my life."

"Oh?" She cut him a glance, then kept pressing her shoe against the shell.

"I was struggling to find purpose in my life. I felt weighed down about the choices I made. About you. About other things." He took a breath. "I didn't know what to do."

A softer expression crossed Paige's face. Maybe she could relate. If only he had the liberty to clasp her hands, put his arm over her shoulder—the thought of kissing her singed his brainwaves—but he'd lost the right to do any of those things. He needed to stay focused anyway.

"A friend of mine shared about his faith in Jesus and encouraged me to read the Bible." He didn't want to sound preachy. However, telling her the greatest thing that had happened in his life was important to him. "I accepted Jesus into my life, and He's changed me. Made me a better man. A more sincere one, I hope."

"And you're telling me this because—?"

Her disinterest stung, but he pushed on. "I want you to know I'm trying to be a more caring, grace-filled person. And to say again how sorry I am for how I left you before."

"And now?"

"I want to figure out how to make things right with you." He took a step closer, gauging her reaction. "If there's any way for us to find a way back to each other, I'd like that, too. A lot. I pray about reconciliation between us every day."

"Recon—" Her eyes widened, circles of chocolate in the middle of milky white. "I told you that part of our lives is finished."

"I know that's what you said."

"And what I meant." Her glare could have frozen a slug in place. She turned away, staring in the direction of where they hiked to the lighthouse. "How soon until you leave Basalt?"

Answering "never" probably wouldn't sit well. "As soon as my work here is finished."

"Good. Thanks for, uh, explaining the other stuff. I'm glad for you." She met his gaze for half an instant, then tramped up the trail out of sight.

Dropping onto the log, Forest bowed his head and spent a few minutes praying for her, and for a miracle that might bring peace between them. Right now, reconciliation seemed impossible. But he believed God was able to do anything.

Twenty

Paisley curled into Judah's arms on a blanket they were sitting on in the sand behind their cottage. Leaning against her husband, smelling his spicy masculine deodorant scent, she recalled the words he whispered to her the day of their vow renewal. *"Whenever you're ready for us to celebrate, alone, I'll be waiting and ready."* Imagining the intimacy he meant, shivers danced through her. *Deep blue sea in the morning!* Only two more days until her appointment with the doctor. Then let the romancing, and yes, the lovemaking, begin.

The wind gusted, and Judah's hair flipped about like beach grass. She smoothed her palm over his soft hair, his warm cheek, his scruffy chin, sending more shivers up her spine. They exchanged vows six days ago, which was a long time for Judah to wait for her to get well enough to sleep in his arms. Yet, he'd been so patient and kind.

"You okay?" He leaned back on his elbows, gazing up at her.

"I'm much better than okay."

"Oh, yeah?" His blue eyes seemed to light with a fire. "Glad to hear it." Slowly, he narrowed the gap between them, kissing her softly, then deepening the kiss. She melted into his embrace, leaning against his chest. Why did they have to wait for the doctor's approval, anyway?

"Paisley." He scooted back, clearing his throat. "Look, I, um, that's enough for now."

She wanted to laugh at his hesitancy. Instead, appreciating his caring attitude toward her, she whispered, "I love you."

"Love you too, Pais. More than I can express." He linked their pinkies like he did so many other times in the past. "I want more between us. I don't want any misunderstanding about that. But we should wait and make sure you're okay after the checkup."

"Why?" She dragged out the word like a petulant child.

He chuckled. "I'm glad you're looking forward to the next phase of our married lives, too." His brief kiss heated her lips again.

"Oh, I am." She sighed.

If they weren't starting their honeymoon tonight, they might need some ardor cooling. Maybe a few ice cubes dumped over their heads. She drew a heart over the back of his hand with her finger. "You said you love me more than you can express. It won't stop you from trying, though, right?" She winked, hoping he recognized her attempt at lightening the mood.

"I'll try to express my love to you, every day."

"Go ahead, then. I'm listening."

"You mean right now?"

"I do."

"Okay." Smiling, he stared up at the night sky as if hunting for ideas. "I love you more than all the clouds in the sky."

"That's nice. I love you more than the fish in the sea."

He brushed her already windblown hair back, gazing at her like he still had kissing on his mind. "I love you more than the sand on the whole Pacific Coast."

"Mmm. That's a good one. I love you more than the air we breathe."

His eyes sparkled. "I love you more than all the water filling all the oceans."

She grabbed some dry sand and tossed it at him. "How am I supposed to beat that?"

He laughed. "Don't beat it. Just enjoy it." Closing the gap between them, he took her gently in his arms and held her close, both facing the sea, side by side, sitting comfortably on the blanket.

"I like this," she whispered.

"I do too. Let's finish every day like this."

"Okay. It's a deal."

They stayed beside each other for several minutes, the breeze swirling around them, the taste of salt in the air, the rolling waves coming closer and closer to their feet.

"There's something I need to tell you."

"What is it?" She shuffled back to better see his face.

"Edward, via the council, is still pushing for me to become mayor. I politely refused."

"Oh." That was good, right? So why did he turn so serious, staring at the ocean, not meeting her gaze? "Who asked you about becoming mayor this time?"

"Sue Taylor. And Mia, speaking as Edward's assistant, I guess."

Mia. Paisley dug her heels in the sand. "When your dad mentioned about you stepping up and doing your duty, I figured he'd try to force you into taking his throne." She didn't attempt to hide her sour tone. "That's why I asked if you ever thought about being the mayor."

"I told him no, too. Doesn't matter who he gets to pressure me, I'm not interested." He grabbed a few stones and tossed them into the water. "I feel bad for Sue and the other council members, though. Especially considering Mia might become the interim mayor."

"How awful. Something should be done to get her kicked out of there." Kicked out of town, too. She felt the old angst toward the C-MER receptionist.

"I agree. She shouldn't be in office." Judah smoothed his arm over her shoulder. "Now, no getting upset, okay? We want you to have an A-plus report from the doctor. No stress between now and then."

"Talking about Edward and Mia always gets under my skin."

"Sorry." He kissed her forehead. Nothing like the kisses they shared before. Just mentioning Mia's name took care of that.

"Also, I stopped by my mom's house on the way home." He was obviously changing the subject. "It's a disaster. Reminded me of an awful renovation project on a house makeover show." A soft smile crossed his mouth. "But those women are crazy excited about it. They see so much possibility in the old house that I got inspired too."

"You mean you agreed to help them?" She stared into his baby blues.

"I may be sorry later but, yes, I did."

"That's amazing, Judah. I'm glad."

Not only was she proud of him for helping his mom, it meant she might never have to worry about him being out at sea during a storm, or about him agreeing to be the mayor, again.

Twenty-one

When Forest said, "I have to tell you something,"
Paige braced herself. Was he leaving? Was he
going to say it was over between them? How could
she ever prepare herself for their romantic interlude
to end?

Paige finished cleaning up her art supplies and stood back, perusing her morning's progress. Of the photos she took three days ago, she chose the shot she liked the best—the one of the lighthouse with fog swirling around the top—and enlarged it on her computer screen. Then she used the graphic as a guide to sketch out the basic shapes of the structure, rocks, and fomenting sea on her 18x24" canvas.

Something about the blues she used for the sky bothered her. Too purplish. Grayish undertones would have been better, more storm-like. Tomorrow she'd fix it.

A sound outside snagged her attention. Was someone on

the back porch? Forest wouldn't come to her house at seven in the morning, would he? Who else might it be? Craig? If it was him, she'd like the chance to apologize for what he obviously thought was a setup.

She strode to the door and peeked around the curtain. No one was on the porch. She opened the door, peering at the backyard. Everything looked the same.

As she started to close the door, a thin white envelope tucked into the crack of the doorframe caught her attention. Did Forest leave her a note?

Grabbing the envelope, she stepped back inside and tore it open. What might he have written to her? *"I love you." "You're the woman of my dreams." "I can't live without you."*

Now, why would he send her romantic notes when she treated him so coldly?

Instead of a sweet message, the words "Stay out of it or you'll be sorry!" leaped out at her in red block letters from a grungy sheet of paper. Who wrote this? Stay out of what? She slammed the door. With fumbling fingers, she fastened the deadbolt and ran to check on Piper. Thankfully, she was still in her bed, asleep.

Paige dashed to the front door and made sure the deadbolt was secure there, too. Then she hurried back into the kitchen, recalling Craig's words that if Edward got out of jail neither of them would be safe. Did this mean he escaped? Was someone else doing his dirty work?

She raked her fingers through her hair, pacing. Who left the envelope? Who would be so mean, so bold, as to try to frighten her like this?

Her phone vibrated. She tapped the screen.

You've been warned. Tell anyone and you'll be sorry.

What?

"Anonymous" was displayed as the sender. Anonymous as in Craig? Surely not.

Who is this? she typed.

No answer came back.

What should she do?

Call Forest? He was a detective. He'd know what to do. But she couldn't let him assume she needed him or that she was weak. Didn't she want him to view her as a strong, independent woman? Hadn't she told him she didn't need him to be her hero?

How about Judah? He was her go-to guy for the last couple of years, but she disliked causing trouble between her and Paisley by depending on her sister's husband. If she told Deputy Brian, Edward might find out, since he was in the Basalt Bay Jail. What if it was Craig warning her to stay out of his business?

Groan.

Piper's safety mattered the most to her. Maybe she should scoop her up and head for Dad's. Staying here alone might not be such a good idea right now.

A loud knocking at the front door made every muscle in her body tense. Another warning? She shuffled along the wall, staying in the hall close to Piper's room. If anyone tried breaking into her house, they'd have a fierce mama bear to deal with.

"Paige!" a male voice shouted. "It's Deputy Brian. I have to talk with you."

Deputy Brian? What a relief. Paige scurried to the front door and unlocked it. She would have thrown her arms around the lawman and hugged him, so thankful it wasn't a bad guy here to silence her. However, the officer's crossed arms and glare kept her from acting impulsively.

"I need you to come down to the station," he said gruffly.

"Why?" Was this the reason someone warned her to stay out of it? So she wouldn't talk to the deputy? "I'd rather not."

"There are questions we need you to answer."

We? "Can't you do that here?" She glanced up and down the street in case anyone was watching. If the person who left the envelope was spying on her, he might suspect her of informing the deputy about the warning.

"No. You may be implicated in Mayor Grant's case, so I need you to come to the station."

"Implicated?" Her heart thudded hard. "How is that possible?"

"Consider this an official inquiry." His eyes darkened.

"Is this because of Forest's findings?"

He didn't answer her question. "Where's your girl?"

"Sleeping."

"I'll wait while you take care of her."

Apparently, she didn't have a choice. But what about the warning? Here was a policeman at her door. The timing couldn't have been better. Should she keep the note to herself or risk telling him about it? She took a steadying breath. No one would try anything with a police car parked outside her house, right? "May I show you something first?"

He squinted at her. "Okay."

"It's back this way." She strode into the kitchen and picked up the red-lettered page, then met him in the living room. "Someone left this on my back door this morning."

He took hold of the paper. "See anyone?"

"No, I heard a sound. Whoever left it was gone when I opened the door." She pulled her cell from her pocket and held out the threatening text toward him. "This freaked me out, too."

"I can understand why. Mind if I send it to myself?"

"Be my guest." She handed the cell to him.

He tapped the screen, then passed it back to her. "Someone must think you'll go along with whatever you're told." He eyed her. "Is that the way it is?"

"No."

Taking his cell phone out of his pocket, he checked the screen, probably searching for the text he copied. "I'd say someone is guessing you're involved in Edward's case."

"Well, I'm not."

"Mooommmmmmy!"

Piper's high-pitched cry sent Paige scrambling for her room. "What's wrong, honey?" She scooped up her daughter and wrapped a blanket around her. "Good morning, pumpkin." Holding her close, she smelled her sweet scent of babyhood. Piper leaned her head on Paige's shoulder, whimpering. "It's okay, Pipe. Everything's going to be fine."

She grabbed a fresh set of clothes for her. When Paige entered the hallway, Deputy Brian stood there. Did he expect her to flee? Maybe to leap out the window with a two-year-old in her arms?

Piper glanced at the deputy and hid her face in Paige's neck, whining some more.

"It's okay, sweetie. This is Deputy Brian. A nice policeman. Our friend." Paige glared at him, warning him he'd better live up to those words.

She swept past him, dashing into the bathroom and closing the door. "Would you like to visit Papa?" she asked while putting on Piper's clothes. She had to tie her shoes twice, her fingers shook so badly.

"Mmm. Papa."

When Paige returned to the kitchen, holding Piper, the deputy followed her. She tugged out her cell phone.

"Who are you calling?"

"My dad to see if I can drop off Piper."

"Make it brief." He strode into the living room.

"Dad?" she said as soon as her father answered his phone and quickly explained what was happening. "Can you watch Piper? I'll drop her off in a few minutes."

"Sure. You want me to have a word with the deputy?"

"No, thanks. Help with Piper is all I need right now."

"You got it."

She made a piece of toast with jelly for Piper, trying to stay calm, but her thoughts churned. Implicated? How was she implicated in anything having to do with Edward?

"I'd prefer you rode with me," Deputy Brian said when Paige strode toward her own car.

Did he picture her as a flight risk? She didn't want anyone seeing her get into the police car. Wouldn't that set the rumor mill buzzing?

"Piper's child seat is in my car. Follow me if you want to." Although, she'd rather he didn't. All she needed was the neighbors spreading stories about her being in trouble with the law.

"But—"

"I'm not under arrest, am I?"

"Not yet," he said testily.

"Then I'll drive myself." She felt perturbed and testy herself. She settled Piper into the car seat, fastened the clasps, and shut the door. Sliding into the driver's seat, she started up the engine, her hands shaking around the steering wheel. How had things come to this?

Forest, if you caused this, so help me—

Twenty-two

Fearing that Forest might end things between them, Paige blurted out the words burning on her heart. "I love you." Then she kissed him fully, deeply, on the mouth before he could say anything else.

"Want some coffee?" Deputy Brian inquired as soon as Paige entered his office. "Not that it's any good."

Her gaze took in his paper-strewn desk, a bulletin board covered in printouts and mug shots, and a couple of doors, one probably leading to Edward's jail cell. "No, thank you. I've had enough caffeine." Although, holding a warm cup in her hands might stop them from shaking. She couldn't quell the apprehension running through her. "Can we just get this over with?"

"Fine." Deputy Brian poured himself a cup of dark coffee. "We'll talk in here." He grabbed a folder off his desk and strode toward a door with a glass window.

She followed him into a small, stark room with only a table and two chairs in it. A weird metal loop attached to the tabletop made her shudder. Being in this room where criminals were interrogated, like Edward Grant probably had been, made her heart pound like crazy. What was she doing here? She was a mom. An artist. Not a lawbreaker. The words in the text replayed in her mind. *Tell anyone, and you'll be sorry.* She told Deputy Brian. No one else knew that, right?

Dropping onto one chair, the deputy nodded for her to sit in the other one. "I thought of you as the smarter, less-into-mischief Cedars girl."

She'd thought so too. Sitting on the edge of the chair across from him, the metal handcuff thingy mocked her. She pictured her hands locked to it. Her pleading for a judge's mercy.

The deputy slurped his coffee and perused a couple of papers. Evidence against her? Something Forest had written? She glanced out the door's window. Where was he?

"No one else will be joining us."

"Oh?"

"Are you surprised Detective Harper isn't here?" He squinted at her. "Disappointed, perhaps?"

Was she that transparent? "The detective questioned me before. I thought he was the one who initiated this inquiry, that's all." Not exactly the full truth.

"He's preoccupied with other interviews." Deputy Brian flipped through several pages as if hunting for something.

So, Forest was too busy to be here, huh?

"Here we go." The deputy lifted a sheet of paper. "Tell me the details surrounding the evidence you found in the gallery."

Is that what this inquiry was about? Didn't she already explain about finding the cloth and duct tape to Forest? Besides, she wrote an official statement. Why waste Deputy Brian's and her time by questioning her about something he already knew?

"I told Forest—"

"Detective Harper?"

"Right." She'd have to be careful, or he might suspect them of being more than acquaintances.

"Just answer the question."

She sighed. "I went into my gallery—"

"Mayor Grant's gallery?"

"He and I were in the process of exchanging ownership."

"What were you looking for when you entered the building without the owner's permission?"

What was with him? Why was he so determined to go down this rabbit trail?

"Edward said I could rent the building. No reason why I couldn't be there."

"Did you pay rent? Sign a contract?"

"No. What does this have to do with him kidnapping Paisley?" She crossed her arms over the table, avoiding touching the handcuff clip. "We were searching for my sister. I would have gone into any unlocked store or business, without permission, to check if she were there." Her voice rose, probably sounding like a hothead, but she was tired of this. And hungry too.

Deputy Brian scrunched up his mouth like he was gnawing on his inner cheek. "After you entered the gallery, legally or not, what did you do next?"

"I looked for signs that Paisley might have been there."

"Then you ran straight to Judah Grant with the items you found?" His eyes gleamed accusingly. "The potential offender's son?"

"What? No. I—"

"You knew your sister's life was in danger, yet you didn't come to me?"

"I was distraught. Yes, I talked to Judah. Then we looked for you on the beach to tell you what I found."

He tapped the folder against the table's edge. "Were you hiding your knowledge of Mayor Grant's plans?"

"What knowledge?" Did Forest tell him she knew something? If he did, boy was she going to have words with him.

"If you withheld information from the police, namely me, it's a serious offense. Why weren't you in a hurry to bring the mayor to justice?" He glared at her like she was to blame for Edward's atrocities. "Were you in his debt? Did he force—"

"Listen, I didn't know anything about what he did to my sister. I told you about the evidence as soon as I found you." She stood, unable to sit still a second longer. "These accusations are unfounded and ridiculous!"

"Sit down. We're not done."

"When can I leave? You said I wasn't under arrest."

"Yet."

Her frustrations boiling to the surface, she blurted, "Maybe you're the one who's indebted to Mayor Grant. That makes more sense than me being involved. Everyone thinks you're in his pocket, anyway."

The deputy's jaw dropped. He scowled at her.

Uh-oh. That was harsh. She didn't want to be on Deputy Brian's bad side. But hadn't Judah and Craig both commented on his possible involvement in past nefarious dealings for the mayor?

"I've never heard you speak so passionately." He chin nodded toward the chair. "Guess you're more like Paisley than I realized."

She didn't know if that was a criticism or a compliment.

Begrudgingly, she lowered herself to the chair. Although she'd rather walk into the sea with waves pounding against her body than to continue answering his questions.

"That night when Masters showed up at your house to discuss the kidnapping, and you heard details—"

"Vague details."

"You knew enough to report the crime. Yet you didn't you call me." He studied her intently. "Why did you contact Judah instead?"

"I didn't contact him." Getting Craig into more trouble wasn't in her plans, but she wasn't taking anyone else's blame, either. "Judah called to ask if I'd cleaned up the mess in the gallery, which I hadn't."

"Another illegal entry."

She rolled her eyes at the redundant point. "Craig told me that Edward threatened Piper, whom I listed in my report as a minor. I don't want her involved in any of this."

The deputy didn't comment, so she continued. "Craig and Judah talked over a plan to rescue Paisley, and keep Piper safe, that's all."

"Still, you didn't call me. Looks to me like you withheld evidence." His voice rose. "No wonder someone's trying to warn you to back off. You did it once. Why not again?"

"Not true!"

"You conspired with the other two about hiding information, didn't you?"

"No, I did not!"

He stared at her intensely. "Then we need your help."

"What?" She blew out a breath. She wasn't being arrested? "What do you mean you need my help?"

"We want you to lure Craig Masters into our net." Deputy Brian cracked a smile.

"If I refuse?"

"I'll charge you with tampering with evidence, hindering prosecution—need I say more?"

"But you know I didn't do those things."

"I don't know any such thing. You concealed information." He shrugged conclusively.

"What would I have to do?" Not that she would help them. They couldn't force her into doing anything. But "tampering with evidence" and "concealing information" sounded bad.

"Invite Craig over. Have a chat. Ask him a question about the kidnapping. Easy as pie."

"Then what?" Paige couldn't believe the position he and Forest were putting her in.

"The detective and I will be watching from outside." He rubbed his hands together. "Then we'll nab the culprit."

"You have the culprit in custody already." She stood quickly. "Can I leave now?"

"I need your word you'll assist us. If you're as innocent as you want us to believe"—he snorted as if he doubted it—"I don't see why you wouldn't do as we ask."

Entrap Craig? Could she do that? She felt dirty even considering it.

Twenty-three

Forest had fallen for Paige in such a short time.
Her profession of love made him realize what he
had to say might crush her dreams. He felt terrible
about that. "Before we met, I was already engaged."

Forest peered through his binoculars from the driver's seat of the rental car he'd been using since he arrived at the Eugene airport six days ago. Brian sat in the passenger seat, munching peanuts, and slurping coffee. The sounds exaggerated in the otherwise silent car annoyed him. That was why he preferred running surveillance on his own.

Inside the single-story house, Paige scurried around the living room. Lighting a candle on the coffee table. Fluffing couch pillows. Even peering out the window toward him, although due to the darkness outside, she probably couldn't see him.

Tempted to wave at her, Forest kept his focus aimed through the binocular lenses. Too bad he went along with

Brian's suggestion to have Paige do this. If anything went wrong, if Craig became violent, or if he initiated something romantic, how could Forest sit here and watch as if he didn't care? He wouldn't, that's all there was to it. If anything happened, and he meant anything, he'd charge in there and protect Paige. If doing so hurt the investigation, so be it.

"Too bad she wouldn't wear a wire," Brian said around chomping his peanuts.

"Safer this way." Forest cleared his throat to disguise the way his voice went soft.

The deputy guffawed. "You don't have a thing for her, do you?"

Forest wouldn't answer that question. Wouldn't deny it either.

"Pity the man who falls for a Cedars girl. She'll break your heart and dump you in one fell swoop." Brian guzzled from his thermos.

What did he know about Paige and Paisley to have such a callous attitude toward them? Had one of the sisters been involved with him when they were younger?

Since Forest had something to address with the other man, this seemed like a good opportunity. "I read your report about Edward kidnapping Paisley."

"Yeah?" Brian tossed peanuts into his mouth and chomped.

"Edward says you'll change your story, too, same as Paige."

The deputy hacked and coughed like he was choking.

"Seems to think you'll do anything he says, including tampering with physical evidence."

"Well, he's up to his ears in bologna." Brian smacked the dashboard with his palm.

"He mentioned something about paying you more to keep you from whining, too."

"That's a lie!" Brian's face turned beet red. "He's a miserly, greedy mayor who only looks after himself. I had to beg for a raise. My salary increased by pennies." He mumbled an expletive.

Forest stared at his surveillance buddy, analyzing his reactions—immediate anger, terse expression, jerky movements, avoiding eye contact, coughing. "So, you weren't doing anything underhanded to help your old boss?"

"Look, just because I worked for him doesn't mean I approved of his actions."

"Good to know." If that were the case, Forest would report back to Sheriff Morris that while the deputy didn't have the most finesse on the job, his denial of culpability in Edward's claims seemed legit. "He must have been lying about you, Paige, the video, everything." He watched through his binoculars as Paige straightened the pictures on the mantle.

Hopefully, Craig would show up tonight. Once Paige gave them a predetermined signal—closing only one drape—Forest and Brian would charge into the house and bring Masters in for questioning. Most likely, arrest him on charges of being an accomplice.

Wait. Something was happening. Paige scurried to the back of the house and opened the door. Forest, preoccupied with watching the front door, must have missed Craig's approach from the other side. He cut a glance at Brian who now had his binoculars aimed at the large front window, too.

How long would it take before Paige shut the drape? She was supposed to ask Craig about the night of the kidnapping, then give the signal. That's when Forest and Brian would move for the door.

Craig entered the kitchen, giving Forest a view of their embrace, although it appeared non-romantic. But when they stepped out of sight, Forest groaned. Paige knew she had to stay within their line of sight. What was going on around that corner?

* * * *

"I'm glad you're okay." Paige hugged Craig, an overriding sense of guilt plaguing her. Why did she go along with Deputy Brian's scheme? Knowing he and Forest were outside watching her every move made her more edgy and guilt-ridden.

A week ago, Craig risked his safety to rescue Paisley. In doing so, he circumvented any harm coming to Piper. Now, Paige was repaying him with this entrapment?

She wrung her hands. "Want some coffee? Tea?"

"Coffee, thanks." He eyed her. Did he notice her nervousness?

She fixed two cups while Craig remained standing by the back door, his hand on the doorknob.

"What's this about? Do you have news for me?"

"Let's bring these into the living room and talk, hm?" She added two splashes of creamer and stirred before handing him a mug.

"Thanks." He sipped the drink. "You remember how I like it."

"Of course, I do." Subduing the nauseous feeling of remorse over what Deputy Brian had put her up to, she strolled into the other room and dropped onto the recliner. If Craig sat on the couch, the deputy and Forest would have a better view of him. Her back would be toward the front door and them. If she mouthed a warning to Craig, no one outside would be the wiser. Did she dare?

Craig set his coffee mug on the table, then strode to the window, peering outside. "I'd rather these weren't open." He yanked the drapes closed.

Uh-oh. What signal would closing both drapes send to the two guys observing from outside? They hadn't discussed alternate signs. Should she jump up and open the curtains again?

Acting tense, Craig stalked back across the room, swiveling to gaze down the hall, then checking the back door. Did he suspect her of being involved with the police? Surely, he didn't know, unless he was the one who sent her the warning note and text. Anxiety raced through her, manifesting in a throbbing headache and sweating palms. She wiped her hands down her skirt.

She had to stay focused. Piper was her main concern. And keeping herself out of jail.

I'm so sorry, Craig.

"You seem nervous." He sat on the edge of the couch and picked up his mug without bringing it to his mouth.

"Do I?" She needed to ask him about the messages before she mentioned the kidnapping like the deputy told her to do. "Did you, uh, send me a note this morning?"

"A note?"

"A warning to stay out of it."

"Stay out of what?" His eyebrows lifted. "What are you talking about?"

Okay, so if he didn't send the missive, who did?

"It's nothing."

"What's that rental car doing out front?" He gave her a dark look, probably still suspecting her of telling Forest about their meeting on the beach.

Suddenly, she couldn't go through with this. "You should get out of here, now." Leaping up, she pointed toward the back of the house. "I mean it. Hurry. Go! This is all my fault. I'm so sorry."

He stood. "What are you talking about?"

"You did a good thing for me by protecting Piper. We're friends, and this is a lousy way for me to repay you."

"What have you done?"

"They're forcing me to—"

The front door burst open. Deputy Brian charged into the room, gun extended. "Stay where you are, Masters!"

"Paige?" Craig leaped over the coffee table, scrambling through the kitchen, knocking over a chair on his way out the back door.

"Halt!" Deputy Brian shouted as he clomped through the house. "Craig Masters, stop right there!"

Paige covered her face, hating her part in trapping the man who'd kept Piper from being harmed by Edward. How could she have been talked into betraying a friend? All to save her own hide? She wanted to roar with frustration.

The deputy strode back into the room. "What spooked him? What did you say to him?"

"He saw the car in front. Recognized a setup. Who wouldn't?" The failed attempt at capturing Craig was as much Deputy Brian's fault as hers. "Where's Forest?"

"Detective Harper is chasing the perp." He pounded the air with his index finger. "For your sake, you'd better hope he catches him. You tipped him off, didn't you? Let's add obstructing justice to your list of crimes."

"No. I—" She clamped her mouth shut and inwardly plead the Fifth.

She wasn't telling him, or Forest, anything else about Craig.

Twenty-four

Paisley sat beside Judah, both facing Pastor Sagle for counseling session number three, the final step in their marital preparedness training. Would he expect them to return for trauma counseling too?

"Judah, maybe now is a good time to talk about your visit with your father. How did that go?" Pastor Sagle folded his hands over his stomach.

"I'm not comfortable discussing that yet." Judah's fingers clenched together, his knuckles white.

"The reason I mentioned it is with the things that happened between your father and Paisley, it might have an adverse effect on your marriage." Pastor Sagle swayed his hands toward them. "On your intimacy."

Now, why did he have to bring that up? She met Judah's glance and recognized his frustrated look. She linked their fingers, wanting to silently remind him they were in this together. The way he squeezed back, it seemed he was saying he remembered.

"About my question"—Pastor Sagle cleared his throat—"how did you feel when you saw your father for the first time since his incarceration?"

Judah sighed. "Rough, I won't lie."

"When you talked with him, were you angry?"

"Yes, of course. He harmed my wife. He's my father, but he's done terrible things. I haven't been able to let it go."

"I understand. Were you able to express your feelings to him?"

Judah made a choking sound. "Tried. Emotions aren't discussed with Edward. You stomach what he says, then you leave frustrated."

"And Paisley?"

She jerked to attention. "What?"

"Would you like the chance to face Edward and explain how you feel about him?" Pastor Sagle peered at her with what she interpreted as compassion mixed with curiosity.

"Not really. Detective Harper mentioned I might be asked to do that during the hearing in January, but I'd rather not." She wiped the back of her hand over her mouth, whisking away a sour taste. "I prefer to forget it ever happened. Get on with our lives."

"Me too," Judah agreed.

Pastor Sagle stroked his fingers over his scruffy chin. "If you go on pretending the kidnapping didn't happen, you'll be bringing more baggage into your marriage."

"We all have baggage," Judah said quietly.

"True." The pastor picked up a pen and tapped his desk. "That's why we're here. But the burden of despising Edward might fester into bitterness and unforgiveness. A crime was committed against you both. That must be faced, honestly, and openly. The sooner, the better."

What did he mean "against you both?" Edward kidnapped, kicked, gagged, nearly starved, and threatened to do away with her. While Judah—

Sniffling sounds reached her. Judah? He wiped his knuckles beneath his eyes, seemingly fighting his emotions. *Oh, Judah.* She rubbed her palm over his shoulders. "Are you okay?" Was talking about his dad too difficult for him?

"Sorry. I don't get why I'm emotional about it now."

"No reason to be sorry." Pastor Sagle pushed the Kleenex box forward. Judah snagged a tissue.

Paisley had been so focused on her needs, on her healing, she hadn't considered the struggle her husband might be going through. Silently, she prayed for him.

"You've been angry and hurt, devastated by the things Edward, the man you were supposed to be able to trust, did," Pastor Sagle said.

"Sometimes it hits me like a baseball bat in the face." Judah stuffed the tissue in his coat pocket.

What he said reminded Paisley of the bad attitudes she'd carried toward her mom, even after her death, and toward her father until she got the chance to talk with him. The bat-in-the-face feeling was part of her existence, a painful part, for the last three years.

"Your trust in your father, your security in his protection and leadership, even though you are an adult, has to have been shaken," Pastor Sagle said.

"Maybe." Judah was more composed now. "If anything, that was lost when I found out he abused my mother. I couldn't stomach it. Am still repulsed by it."

"I understand. Another tragedy in your family you must cope with."

"And from before."

"Before?"

"He tried to keep Paisley out of my life before we were married." He glanced at her sadly. "When she and I dated, he said bad things about her and the Cedars family. It was as if he carried a horrible grudge against them, yet I had no idea why."

"Is that why you eloped?"

The pastor's question wasn't asked pointedly, yet it dug at a tender, emotional place in Paisley.

"You declined to perform our ceremony, remember?" She gulped. "I don't mean to be rude, but it was your refusal that made us seek other means of getting married."

"Ah, yes, I remember." Pastor Sagle sighed. "I expected young couples to have their families' blessings. I'm sorry for my part in causing you pain."

His humble apology eased some of her remembered offense. She was trying to let go of the past, and that meant forgiving the role the pastor had played, too.

"Judah, this may be hard to hear. But what will it take for you to forgive your dad?"

"Is that what he expects? My forgiveness?" Judah asked hoarsely.

Paisley tensed.

"Don't we all need forgiveness and grace? Second chances?"

"Yeah, but he—" Judah clenched his lips, shaking his head. "He hurt my wife. Tried to keep her from me, again. He injured my mom. Tried to manipulate all of us."

"Our Lord suffered great wrongs, too." Glancing back and forth between them, Pastor Sagle's expression remained sober.

"Terrible atrocities. Yet he forgave everyone. He expects that of us also. Like the verse from Colossians says, 'Bear with each other and forgive whatever grievances you may have against one another. Forgive as the Lord forgave you.'"

The room went silent for a couple of minutes.

Paisley expelled a breath that felt like it came from deep inside of her. The pastor was right. They had to forgive others. But Edward? Ack.

Help me forgive, Lord. Rescue me from the bitterness that keeps swirling back into my heart. And Judah's too.

"It may take some time." Pastor Sagle jotted something on a 3X5 card. "More talking things through. It may take you facing Edward privately again."

Groaning, Judah covered his face with his hands.

"And it will take prayer." The pastor slid the card across the desk face down. "This is your homework assignment until our next session. I'm asking you to ponder this sincerely."

Apparently, he did expect them to come back. Paisley sighed. Yeah, they probably needed more time to talk things through.

Judah picked up the card and toyed with it between his fingers.

"I'm not taking his side, mind you, but I know your dad loves you." Pastor Sagle stood and shook Judah's hand. "I care for both of you. God bless you and your marriage to your bride." He shook Paisley's hand. "You have a healing bridge to cross. Remember we have a Great Physician who heals hearts and lives. He'll cross the bridge with you."

"Thank you." Judah stood and linked his fingers with Paisley's.

When they left the pastor's office, he passed her the card with the words *"Pray for Edward"* on it.

Pray for her father-in-law? How could she pray for the man she didn't even want to think about?

Twenty-five

"I've tried breaking off the engagement," Forest
explained. "Elinore's father has terminal cancer.
She begged me not to end it because of that."
Frowning, Paige asked, "You've been kissing me
while you're still engaged to her?"

Forest held his mug of coffee, glad for the warmth as he
sat at the counter at Bert's Fish Shack. The place buzzed with
early morning activity. The redheaded server—Lucy, according
to her nametag—stopped in front of him with a carafe of
steaming coffee, smiling widely. Any chance she knew where
Craig was?

"Ready for a refill?"

"Yes, please." He might have to sit here drinking coffee for
an hour to feel human again after chasing Craig through the
streets of Basalt Bay last night and coming up empty-handed.
He despised not doing his job well enough. "Do you know
Craig Masters?"

"Sure. Everyone knows him. In fact, see that dark-haired guy?" Lucy discreetly nodded toward a man reading a newspaper at a table near the bank of windows. "He asked about him a few minutes ago."

"That so?" Forest categorized the man—forties, dark eyes, full head of black hair, unshaven face, crisp white shirt and tie, business type. Why did he want information about Craig? "Where can I find him? Craig, I mean." He picked up the cup and sipped the strong brew.

"If I were to tell you, what would I get for my troubles?" Grinning, she whisked her tongue over her upper lip as if asking for a kiss.

Awkward.

"My humble thanks for helping with a case?"

"Hmm." She dropped the flirty façade. "Ready to order?"

"Yes. A short stack of pancakes, thanks." Although, the sugar spike alone might clog his arteries after so many hours of being on high alert. "Keep the coffee coming, too."

"Will do. Need anything else?" She arched an eyebrow before continuing down the breakfast bar refilling coffee cups.

Yeah, an answer about Craig.

Drinking his coffee, Forest wished things had turned out differently with Paige. Unfortunately, the tension humming between them might get worse if he hauled her in for questioning or, heaven forbid, if he had to detain her. His next slurp of coffee burned his tongue.

After last night's fiasco of not catching Craig, he and Brian went around and around, debating Paige's involvement. The deputy claimed she hindered their chance at prosecution by warning Craig of his impending discovery. Forest disagreed. Craig peered out the window before he closed the drapes. No doubt the fugitive saw the binoculars aimed at him before he took off running. However, if Forest didn't find the suspect today, Brian might seek charges against Paige. Forest couldn't let that happen.

He glanced out the window toward the choppy windblown sea. The nautical scene looked as wretched as he felt. He rubbed his hand over his hair, not caring about the messy look he portrayed.

The bell above the door jangled. He turned to look in case it was Craig.

Instead, Paul Cedars shuffled toward the breakfast counter, greeting people along the way. The older man wiped the sleeve of his jacket across his face as if the rain had pelted his cheeks. His wet hat was askew, and he quickly removed it.

"Morning, Paul!" The diner owner, Bert, smiled beneath his gray handle-bar mustache and tapped the counter two seats down from Forest.

Maybe this was his chance to ask Paige's father a few questions. During his interview, the man had been tight-lipped and grumpy. Would he be more open to talking in this relaxed setting?

Bert filled a mug and set it in front of Paul without the man asking for coffee. Must be a regular. "What'll it be this morning? Need a menu?"

"Nah. The usual."

"The usual coming right up." Bert sauntered back into the kitchen, saluting a man who entered the diner.

Forest glanced at the dark-haired guy near the windows again, curious what his reasons might be for asking Lucy about Craig. Was he connected to Edward?

Leaning across the empty chair, he spoke to Paul, "Good morning, sir."

"Oh, it's you." Paul squinted at him as if seeing something in him that he disliked. "Still pestering folks about getting the mayor off the hook? Blaming my daughter?" His voice rose loudly. A few customers stared in their direction.

Is that what people thought? That he wanted to get Edward Grant released? "It's not like that at all. I was hired to pursue the truth. Dig up details that might have been over-looked."

"The truth," Paul spat. "Hauling Paige in like she's a criminal part of that?"

"No. It's just—" He groaned, hating what still might happen to her. "I'm sorry, but I can't discuss an ongoing case with you."

Paul jabbed his index finger in the air. "My daughter had nothing to do with the mayor's abuse of her sister. If I were strong enough, I would have beaten the snot out of Edward myself. Was a time I could have." He stared hard into his coffee cup. "Wish I had. Then things might have been different."

"What did he do that's kept a bee buzzing in your hat, if you don't mind my asking?" Forest tried appearing nonchalant, drinking his coffee, watching the man who wasn't aware he'd been Forest's father-in-law. He felt bad about that secret.

"A woman. Always about a woman." Paul's voice drifted away. "But it's in the past. No good will come of digging it up. Leave Paige alone too. She has enough on her plate with—" Shaking his head, he turned away from Forest.

What did Paige have on her plate? Debt? Personal troubles? The loss of her gallery? Her involvement with Craig?

Forest's heart pounded harder. If only he could be honest with Paul and tell him he was doing everything he could so Paige wouldn't be implicated in the case. But that meant finding Craig and getting him to confess before the deputy took matters into his own hands.

He glanced toward the other side of the room again, but the dark-haired guy was gone. There went Forest's chance to question him. What would he have said anyway? *The flirtatious redheaded server mentioned you asked about a local suspect.* Yeah, that sounded real professional.

Bert set a plate of three pancakes in front of Forest. Then placed another plate with two over-easy eggs, two slices of crisp bacon, and toast in front of Paul. "Here you go. Enjoy."

"Feast for a king." Paul dug right into his breakfast.

Forest took several bites of delicious pancakes, savoring the sweet flavor. After a few minutes, he dared to intrude on the other man's solitude again. "When you mentioned Paige going through something, what did you mean?"

Paul didn't answer, just continued eating, his gaze on his plate.

"I care for your daughter, sir. Honestly, I do."

Paul snorted. "Is dragging her through an investigation what you call caring?" He took a big bite of toast. After he chewed and swallowed, he glared at Forest. "If you cared for her at all, you'd leave her alone."

Forest would like to reassure his ex-father-in-law, whom he never met before this trip, that he didn't want to cause Paige trouble. Far from it. He had hopes and dreams of beautiful things happening in their future.

Finishing his coffee, he set down the cup. Perhaps he'd try asking Paul one more thing. "Do you know of any bad feelings between the sisters? Possibly about Craig?" By the look of abhorrence turning the other man's face gray, Forest shouldn't have asked.

"Listen, Bub, siblings squabble. End of story." Paul slipped his dark-rimmed glasses up his nose. "Stop causing Paige difficulty. In fact, stay away from all of us." He slid his plate farther down the counter and moved to another seat.

Forest groaned. People in Basalt Bay sure didn't care for him questioning them. His prying into their affairs. He let out a long sigh. Could he blame them?

Twenty-six

Judah stepped into the foyer of C-MER where he'd worked for eleven years and had the urge to turn around and leave. Unfortunately, after the hurricanes hit, his career took a nosedive. Things transpired that had reeked of his father manipulating not only his life, but the lives of others—Craig, Mike, Mia, and who knew who else? All of that left a gnawing ache in his chest. He didn't want to be here now. But he promised Sue, so he'd see this through.

The last time Judah entered the C-MER building, he was hauled out by security after he barged in during Paisley's abduction, demanding to talk to Craig. How vastly different ten days changed a person's perspective.

"Why, Judah, is that you?" Mia's heels click-clacked across the open space as she headed toward him, grinning. "What are you doing here?"

"I sent Mike an email. He's expecting me." Tension rippled across his shoulders. With Mia's flirtatious behavior, he always felt like he had to be on guard around her. Doubly so, today.

He was here on a covert mission for a member of the town council, and he didn't want her knowing about it.

"I didn't know you were coming."

Just what he hoped.

At least she didn't act blatantly flirtatious with him this time. And her business-style suit with its modest length looked more professional than her usual attire.

"I'll find out if he's ready for you. Want some coffee?"

"No thanks." He straightened his sports coat.

A man with black hair, probably in his early-forties, entered the front door and strode past Judah, his gaze fastened to his cell screen. Was this the guy Deputy Brian mentioned?

Mia met the dark-haired man on her way back from Mike's office. "Good morning, C.L." She flashed a bright white smile in his direction. "Have a good weekend?"

"Not really." He walked into the office previously used by Craig, then Judah for a short while, and shut the door.

Mia shrugged. "Mike says come on back. Have you met our newest employee?"

"No, I haven't."

"He's the brooding type. Rumor has it he's from head-quarters." She giggled. "And single."

"Hmm."

"Have you given any more thought to my suggestion?" She linked her hand around his elbow, keeping stride with him as they walked. "I'd leave my job in a flash to be your assistant."

He pulled his arm away from her. Mia being his assistant? No, thanks. He rapped on his old boss's door and waited.

"Come in," Mike called.

Taking a deep breath, Judah opened the door and stepped into the office.

"Judah, good to see you." Mike shook his hand. "No hard feelings, I hope."

"No, sir." He'd committed any feelings of injustices to the Lord. Didn't want to hold grudges in his heart.

"Found work yet?" Mike ran his hand over a roll of blueprints. "We've missed your input with the coastal surveys."

"Thanks. The daily boat trips were my favorite part of the job."

In the following silence, the awkwardness of Judah's abrupt firing settled between them.

"So, what's this about?" Mike tapped his watch, not inviting him to have a seat. "I have another meeting, so—"

"Right." Judah quickly explained Sue's concerns. "What's the problem between the City Council's and C-MER's goals for the peninsula?" He kept his tone as respectful as possible. "I'm sure both entities want what's best for the safety of the community."

"Sure, sure." Mike's face turned ruddy. "However, the mayor's still keeping a tight leash on everyone. Budgets are limited. Tensions are at an all-time high."

"How's it possible for Edward to have any say when he's in jail, and will probably be incarcerated for a long while?"

Mike chuckled as if embarrassed. "Look, he's your father, and I've had my share of run-ins with him, but the man's got powerful allies. Many in Basalt Bay look up to him. Are still, how shall I say, protecting his best interests."

Protecting, huh? Edward was manipulating people from jail? A familiar knot formed in Judah's chest. "What does he have to do with the work on the peninsula? The council voted to move forward with the project."

"Talk with him." Mike patted Judah's shoulder. "For now, everything's at a standstill."

"What about the safety of the citizens? The tourists?"

Mike escorted him to the door. "Don't worry. We'll get this sorted out in good time." He stopped suddenly. "If you were acting mayor, this conversation would have a much different outcome."

Ugh. Now someone else was pressuring him to follow in his father's footsteps?

"I said I'd talk with you—"

"And so you have." Mike shook his hand. "Goodbye, Judah."

Disappointed over the brief meeting and how little he had to report back to Sue, he strode across the room. As he passed the receptionist's area, expecting to find Mia at her desk, the new guy—C.L.?—rummaged through her desk drawer, fingering some files.

Judah stopped mid-stride, curious what the guy was doing at Mia's desk.

C.L. met his gaze with a serious expression, almost a glare. Then, raking his fingers through his hair, tramped back to his office and slammed the door.

Judah left his old work place feeling unsettled over his conversation with Mike, but relieved to be done with C-MER. Unfortunately, he hadn't helped with the peninsula at all.

Twenty-seven

Paige listened as Forest explained, "I'm not in love with Elinore the way a man loves a future wife." His gray-green eyes darkened. "I want to be with you, Paige." She wanted that too, dreamed of it, but was he over Elinore?

Can we meet at two o'clock?

Paige sat at her kitchen table texting Craig. Meeting in public might be risky. What if Forest planted a tracking device on her phone? That was possible, right? Not wanting to put Craig in the detective's crosshairs, and needing to protect herself, too, she sent him a cryptic message.

Where the sun shines brightest.

He'd understand. She set the cell phone on the table and waited for a response. None came.

Surely Craig recalled the time they walked out to Baker's Point. That day they took Piper for a walk along the beach to the south of town where locals used to go for proposals, picnics, and gatherings before the hurricane smashed the gazebo.

Craig had been so sweet, making her think there might be a chance of a long-term relationship with him. He loved Piper, and she adored him. Craig raised Paige's hand to his lips and kissed her knuckles. "Because of you, this place will always be where the sun shines brightest."

What if he received her text and thought she meant she wanted to restart their relationship? Of course, she didn't. But she had to talk with him and explain how badly she felt about setting him up for the sting.

While she didn't want him thrown in jail, she didn't want to go there, either. Didn't Deputy Brian imply that's what the result might be if Craig escaped? What would happen to Piper if Paige got whisked off to the slammer?

Maybe she should talk to Judah and Paisley. Ask them to be her daughter's guardians if anything happened to her. Piper loved Judah. She'd have a happy life with them. Tears flooded Paige's eyes. She shook herself. She was not going to prison or taking the rap for Mayor Grant's, or any of Craig's, suspicious activities.

Jumping up, she dashed into Piper's room to get her up from her nap and prepared for a walk. A warm sweater, rubber boots, and a toy shovel should be sufficient for an hour at the seashore.

A little past two, Paige sat on a flat rock at Baker's Point, watching Piper prance along the beach, hurling mud into the sea. A couple of times, she acted as if she were about to charge into the water, but Paige called to her and, thankfully, she stopped.

After checking her cell phone for the sixth time, she

groaned. Craig probably wanted to avoid the risk of meeting her. Maybe her trek out to the Point had been for nothing.

She turned to face the breeze, enjoying the wind skimming her cheeks, and the musty scent of saltwater filling her nose, although she couldn't really relax. She didn't like being this close to the incoming tide, but she had to stay near enough to watch Piper and keep her from charging into the sea. Her daughter's fearlessness, even at two, amazed her.

With the rumbling sound of waves creating tension up her neck, the warning text she received yesterday taunted her. *"Tell anyone and you'll be sorry."* Sorry, how? What did the person intend to do to her? So far, she mentioned it only to Deputy Brian and Craig. Did the deputy tell Forest? What would he say about someone threatening her?

Her thoughts replayed what Forest said about becoming a man of faith and trying to be a more caring person. Change was good. But did he think that erased what he did in leaving her? That because he said he'd changed, she should forget what transpired between them?

A sound snagged her attention. A car door? The beach grasses swayed along the cliff leading to the parking lot. A creepy sensation skittered over her skin. Was someone watching her from those tall grasses? Or was she being paranoid because of the warning? Heart thudding hard, she scanned the beach in both directions. Other than a few seagulls, she and Piper appeared to be alone.

"Mommy, *pway?*" Piper lifted a handful of sand.

"Not now, sweetie."

Piper flung the dirt into the water. Bending over, her bottom up, she scooped more sand with both hands, flinging it again and again, then cackling.

Paige chuckled too. When she was a little girl, did she ever go to the beach with her father and play like this? He'd brought her and Paisley to the ice cream shop near City Beach. But when anyone suggested playing in the water, or even beach walking, she cried and hid in her bedroom. Terrible things happened at the seashore—hadn't her mother told her so? Another chill skittered up her neck. Maybe she should take Piper by the hand and head back the way they came.

"Paige!"

She swiveled around. Craig was walking toward her from the south side. Waving at him, relief flooded her. No one had been watching her. Just her imagination. She didn't run to meet him, couldn't leave Piper unattended, but she scooted off the rock and waited for him.

The wind suddenly felt stronger, almost pushing her backward. Paige rushed over to Piper and wrapped her arms around her, steadying her lest she get swept into the waves. Piper whimpered and reached toward her shovel on the ground as if not caring at all about the harsh winds.

"*Mow* sand."

"Okay. Just stay away from the water."

A few minutes later, Craig embraced her in a brief hug then squatted down and hugged Piper. "Hey, Pipe."

"*Cag. Cag.*" She patted his face with her dirty hand.

He chuckled, not seeming to mind. "I'm glad you're both okay." He stood, tucking his hands into his jacket. "What's going on? Anyone follow you?" His voice turned gruff. Did he imagine she might have set him up again?

"We walked. No one knows we're here." She glanced at the high grasses, double-checking. "I wanted to say I'm sorry about setting up the other meeting."

"Why did you? I thought we were friends."

"We are. I didn't have any choice. Well, the only option was unacceptable." She watched Piper playing in the sand with her shovel. "I would never choose to cause you difficulty. But they think I'm involved in Edward's crimes against Paisley. That I knew something about it." She tucked her hair behind her ears to keep the wind from blowing it in her face. "The deputy may still throw me in jail alongside Edward."

"That's ridiculous."

"I know, but it's what he said. That's why I wanted to meet privately. To ask—"

"What?"

"Did you … um … did you know what Edward planned to do with Paisley beforehand?"

He groaned. "I can't believe you'd think that of me." He strode to the edge of the surf, staring out to sea, his back toward her. "You know me better than that," he tossed over his shoulder.

She thought she did. "I'm sorry for betraying our friendship. I don't want to go to jail or be away from Piper."

"You won't." Scuffing his boot against the sand, he made ditches the tide quickly filled. "Look, I knew something shady was going down. Something illegal I shouldn't have agreed to participate in, no matter what Edward held over my head. But I'd never harm—"

"Hold it right there!"

Forest?

"Put your hands up where I can see them." He held a gun aimed at the sand, but he was striding straight for Craig.

"What are you doing here?" How dare he invade her privacy like this!

"Paige?" Craig's anguish-filled expression cut her to the quick.

"I didn't tell him about our meeting. Honestly, I didn't."

"Mommy!" Piper screamed. "Mommy!"

Paige scooped her up. "There, there, it's okay, honey."

Oh. Piper called her "Mommy." Forest must have heard. Paige met his bewildered gaze.

"Mommy?"

So this was how he'd find out. *Yes, I'm her mommy*, and *you're her*—

But then, he was patting down Craig, checking for weapons. Paige shouldn't have texted him. Shouldn't have put him at risk again.

"Craig Masters," Forest said sternly, "you're under arrest as an accomplice in the kidnapping of Paisley Grant. By the authority conferred on me by the Coastal Police Department …" He read him his Miranda Rights.

Craig's gaze collided with hers. "Why?"

"I didn't do this. I'm so sorry."

His silent accusation of betrayal would surely haunt her dreams.

Forest gave her a long look before dragging Craig through the grassy hillside toward the parking lot. It must have been his car she heard earlier. How long had he been watching them? If only she'd been more aware. Warned Craig.

Still holding Piper, Paige's gaze followed the men until they reached the top of the sandy cliff. Craig's hands were cuffed behind his back, and Forest propelled him forward. Before they went out of sight, both men gazed back at her with injured looks of blame and disbelief.

Twenty-eight

*Even with the concern for her father's illness,
Forest had to break things off with Elinore. A
phone call would have to suffice. Would she finally
accept the finality of him ending their engagement?*

At the police station, Forest took Craig through the paces
of getting his mugshot, filling out paperwork, and taking his
statement—which wasn't much. Despite the man declining his
right to an attorney, he wasn't being cooperative. Didn't answer
Forest's questions, muttered snide remarks, which meant this
might be a long, drawn-out interrogation.

In the tiny room Forest used for interviews throughout
the week, he and Craig sat opposite each other. "When did you
meet Paige Cedars?"

"What's it to you?"

"I'd like you to answer the questions truthfully."

"And I'd like a million dollars." Craig squinted back at him like a belligerent teenager. "What does Paige have to do with anything?"

"I plan to find out if she was an accomplice, also." He despised even suggesting she might be involved in Edward's crimes.

"If you implicate her, you're pathetic." Craig shook his head.

So, they agreed on something. Forest pictured Paige with the little girl and the sand sculptures. The same kid who called her "Mommy" today. Did she have a child … with Craig? If that were true, if she loved this man—

"Tell me, Masters, what kind of a relationship do you have with Paige?" He peered at the handcuffed man. "Boyfriend? Spouse?"

"You're just fishing, aren't you?"

More than Forest cared to admit. "Are you two romantically involved?" His shoulders tightened. He swallowed more times than was necessary.

"We're friends. So what?"

"Is the child yours?" Forest gritted his teeth.

"That's none of your business." A shadow crossed Craig's features.

"Everything you're privy to about this case is mine to discover." Forest pointed his pen at him. "We can do this the hard way or the easy way. Tell me what you know, or we'll spread this discussion over as many days as it takes for me to wring the truth from you. Is the child yours?"

"Of course, she's mine." Craig shuffled back in his seat. "Any man would be proud to call Piper his kid. She's a hoot."

The air rushed from Forest's lungs. After things ended between him and Paige, she must have gone straight back to

Basalt to be with Craig. Was he an old boyfriend? Her high school sweetheart?

A flaming arrow burned in Forest's chest. He needed a break, a breather, lest he drown in misery with the realization of this man—this jerk—having been involved with Paige, the woman he still loved. He stood, raking his hand through his hair.

"What's wrong?" Craig taunted. "You have a personal interest in our girl Paige?"

Forest braced both hands against the table. "What I need are answers. How close are you with her? Close enough to divulge Edward's secrets? Is she as involved in this case as you are?" Saying the words made him feel sick.

Craig stared at him with a mocking grin on his face, but kept his mouth shut.

Forest groaned. This interrogation might be dead in the water, and he didn't know if anything Craig told him so far was the truth. His guess that this process might take a long time was correct.

Picking up his legal pad, he peered down at the prisoner. "Did Paige have any foreknowledge of the events on the night you rescued Paisley from Edward?"

"You mean before I told her what was happening?"

"That's right. Did you inform her that her sister was being abducted by Edward?"

"You do go around in circles, Detective. Must be dizzying." Craig stared intensely at Forest. "What's Paige's and my relationship to you?"

"If you're close, you may have told her private information. Maybe what you and Edward planned to do with Paisley?" Forest's voice rose out of frustration.

"What?" Craig banged on the table with the heels of his hands. "That's crazy talk!"

"Is it?" Forest shoved away from the table. He could use a cup of coffee or a short walk. This investigation was too personal. Too close to his heart to remain emotionally detached.

Maybe he should recuse himself. In fact, it might be time to get out of the criminal business altogether. Live an ordinary life. That used to sound boring. Now, a normal night's sleep sounded great. A family life, too, if only he had a family.

"Paige didn't know anything about Edward capturing Paisley," Craig spoke in a hushed tone. "I told her what I assumed was going down. She's innocent."

His admission after not saying anything worthwhile surprised Forest. It relieved some of his dread. Not that the man's statement was entirely reliable. But Forest was glad to hear him say Paige was innocent.

"She's the most honorable woman I know. Raising a little girl by herself. Even when folks in town badmouthed her about being a single mom, she lifted her chin and did her best."

"Why didn't you marry her, then, if you're so proud of being the girl's father?" Forest didn't try to hide his sharp tone.

Craig shook his head and stared at the wall. "Sometimes things just don't pan out the way you think they might."

Wasn't that the truth? Forest sighed.

Twenty-nine

Paige held a tiny, gift-wrapped box from Forest in her palm. Staring into his twinkling eyes, she tore off the paper. When a velvet ring box toppled onto her palm, he dropped to his knee in front of her. "Will you marry me, Paige?"

Paige traipsed across her living room and kitchen and back again for the tenth time since returning from her terminated meeting with Craig. All the way home, she felt nervous like someone might be watching her. Thoughts of the warning note, who might have sent it, and who might be following her, combined with her agitation about Forest taking Craig into custody, made her jumpy at every sound, every shadow.

Why had she texted Craig to meet her? He got caught because of her. This time she was to blame. Would he resent her forever?

What could she do to help him? She couldn't stay here as if everything were okay and do nothing. If she barged into the deputy's office and defended Craig, would Forest listen to her?

What would she say? That he'd been honorable and helpful with Paisley's rescue, therefore they should trust him? Even she knew he had a past, although not the extent of it.

Why did Forest have to arrest Craig in front of her and Piper like that? She stomped across the room again. He probably handcuffed him to that horrible metal piece. What if Craig told him about Piper?

Groan.

But then, Forest probably figured it out when Piper called her Mommy. Did he see the resemblance between him and her?

What she needed to do was talk to someone and get this horrible angst off her chest. Who would understand how confused and miserable she felt about Craig? How guilt-laden she was about keeping Forest from finding out about his daughter?

Wouldn't Judah want to hear what happened to Craig, especially if it turned out they were brothers? Okay, so she'd go by Judah and Paisley's and tell them about Craig, maybe even about her and Forest, then she'd figure out what to do next.

Back in the kitchen, she stuffed a few things into Piper's backpack. If Forest were monitoring her texts, she didn't want him seeing any information about her visit, so she wouldn't warn Paisley she was coming. She pulled her cell phone out of her back pocket, tapped the settings icon, and disabled the GPS app. No sense making it easy for him to spy on her, if he was.

At Judah and Paisley's cottage, she scooped Piper out of her car seat and scurried toward the patio where she imagined her sister was recuperating.

Judah nearly ran into her as she barreled around the house. "Paige." He thrust out his hands to stop her from colliding with him. "I heard a car and came to check."

"Hey. Sorry I didn't call."

"No problem." He leaned toward Piper, hands out in invitation. "Hey, squirt."

"*Unca Dzuda.*" She leaped into his arms, pointing at the ocean. "*Watoo. Watoo.*"

"No water," Paige told her. "No getting muddy and wet again."

"I'm so glad you came." Paisley waved from her lounge chair. "Hi, Piper!"

"Say hi to Auntie Paisley," Paige instructed her daughter.

Piper giggled and patted Judah's face, not acknowledging Paisley.

Instead of pushing the issue, Paige hurried over and gave her sister a hug. "Sorry I haven't visited before now."

"That's okay. As you can see, I'm a lazy sluggard this week." She laughed. "Judah insists I follow the doctor's orders until tomorrow's appointment. Sit down and visit with me."

"Thanks." Paige dropped into a recycled-looking kitchen chair. "How are you doing?"

"So much better."

"That's great news."

"Yeah, hopefully, the doctor declares me fit for normal married life. Don't you agree, Judah?" Grinning widely, Paisley winked at him.

"Oh, yeah. Right." His cheeks flushed as he set Piper down on the sand.

Paige, getting her sister's unspoken message to her husband, felt a moment's embarrassment, but she shrugged it off. Her sister and brother-in-law only renewed their vows a week ago. They deserved to enjoy the marital joys Edward almost thwarted.

"*Watoo.*" Piper reached her arms toward the ocean.

"Look at the rocks." Paige jumped up and redirected her daughter to play with some rocks and sand. Too bad she forgot her shovel this time.

"What a sweet girl." Paisley grinned. "Hey, Piper, come over and talk with me."

Piper lunged against Paige's knees.

"She's shy around strangers."

"That's okay. She seems to love Judah."

"Yeah, she does." Paige glanced appreciatively at her brother-in-law. "He's been a blessing to us in the absence of a father figure." Hopefully, Paisley didn't take that wrong. Paige wanted so badly to keep the lines of communication open between them. "Dad helped too. And even Craig."

"That's wonderful, Paige."

Judah sat down in the lounge chair next to Paisley. "What brings you out here? We're glad you came, but did something happen?"

"Sort of."

Thinking Piper might play by herself for a few minutes, Paige sat back down and quickly explained about Craig meeting her at Baker's Point and the ensuing arrest.

"Man, that's too bad." Judah grimaced. "It was bound to happen, since he's done some questionable things, but still."

"Yeah, I feel horrible it was my fault he got caught."

"It might not have had anything to do with you." Judah met her gaze. "Forest is churning the waters in this case. Maybe he found out something about Craig."

"Maybe." Paige knew better. But she wasn't supposed to talk with anyone about the setup she'd been involved in.

"How did Forest know where you were meeting Craig?" Paisley asked.

"That's what I'd like to know. Perhaps he's stalking me." Paige swiveled to check the beach behind her.

"Craig being in jail is a bummer." Judah stroked Paisley's arm on the chair rest. "If he hadn't stuck out his neck to help us, I don't know how I would have found you."

"That's what I was thinking." Paisley shook her head. "Craig isn't my favorite person. In fact, not long ago I was terrified of him, but I'm grateful he aided in my rescue. Otherwise, Edward may have gotten away with hurting me worse."

"I hate to think of that." Judah sighed.

"Me too."

Paige watched Piper shuffling sand from one hand to the other and had similar thoughts of gratitude about Craig keeping her daughter safe.

Now for the other reason she came here. "I, um, have something else I'd like to tell you guys. Something that's sort of hard for me to admit." She swallowed with difficulty. "Judah has already guessed this, but I wanted you both to know ... Forest and I ... well, we have a romantic history together." She glanced at her sister, then met Judah's sympathetic gaze.

"History, as in—?" Paisley lifted an eyebrow.

"We met in Las Vegas three years ago. Mom had died. You were gone. Peter too." Paige dreaded exposing the vulnerable parts of her past. Was tempted to skip over some facts. "I was attending an art exposition. Forest was doing detective-type training. I was feeling lost, to put it mildly. We hit it off. Love at first sight, if you believe in that sort of thing."

"I do." Paisley patted Judah's hand. "Are you saying he's Piper's—"

"Yes."

"Oh, I thought Craig—"

"No, he isn't. Although he's terrific with Piper. For a short time, I thought I might have cared for him, but he wasn't over someone. Same as me." Old wounds she didn't want to get into.

Paisley nodded as if she understood.

"Has Forest met Piper?" Judah asked.

Just then, Piper carried a rock over to him and placed it in his hand. "*Wock.*"

"Best rock ever, squirt."

"I like rocks, too." Paisley held out her hand.

Leaning around Judah, Piper stared inquisitively at her. Then she bolted back over to Paige and buried her face in her lap.

"Give her some time. She'll get used to you." She nudged Piper from her hiding position. "Go get more rocks for Uncle Judah, okay?"

"*Yike wocks.*"

"I know you do. Hand a rock to Uncle Judah, and he'll give it to Auntie Paisley." She pointed at the rock pile. "Go get one."

Piper pranced back to the pile of stones, jabbering.

"He's seen her, but he doesn't know about her being his. He might have guessed, but I haven't told him." Paige glanced at her sibling, dreading any condemnation she might see.

Paisley smiled back at her. "Honestly, I'm so proud of you for raising her on your own—being a single mom. For becoming a stronger person despite the hardships you've faced. You even started your own business. That's amazing."

If they were standing, Paige would have hugged her fiercely. "Thank you." Relief filled her that her sister was being so understanding. Yet what she still had to say tugged on her emotions. "Also, I want you to know what Forest and I experienced wasn't just a one-night stand."

"You don't have to explain anything to us." Paisley pushed off her chair, shuffled over to Paige, and wrapped her arms around her. "I love you, little sister. I love Piper, too. I can't wait to spend more time with her."

Paisley's arms and words comforted Paige. She sniffed. Swallowed back tender feelings. No sentimentality. She needed to express the truth and be done with it. Although, she knew she was far from being done with it.

Piper's singsong voice talking about *"wocks"* and *"Unca Dzuda"* saved Paige from caving in to tears. The two-year-old danced over to Judah and handed him her treasures. *"Wocks."*

"Thank you. Shall we give these to Auntie Paisley?"

"Peezee?"

"That's right." Judah waved for Paisley to come closer.

She hurried back and sat down on the edge of her lounger. "May I have a rock, Piper?" Paisley held out her hand, smiling.

Piper stared at her as if trying to figure out if she were worthy of her precious stones.

"This is Auntie Paisley." Judah handed her a rock.

"Oh, isn't this nice." Turning the stone over in her hand, Paisley oohed and aahed.

"Peezee wock." Piper shuffled back to the rock pile.

"Sounds like that's going to be your name." Paige chuckled.

"Peezee. I like it." Paisley tapped the rock she held against the one in Judah's hand.

"Are you going to tell Forest?" His question brought them back to the discussion.

"Maybe she doesn't want to talk about that with us." Paisley nudged his arm, sending him a warning look.

"Sorry. I didn't mean to be insensitive."

"No, it's okay. I wanted to discuss what happened with Craig, but I need to share about my past, too. The short answer is yes, but I don't know when." A breeze brushed against Paige's face, flapping hair over her mouth. She whisked it out of the way. "Part of me is still steamed about Forest's actions—from today and three years ago."

"If you don't mind my saying so"—Judah's face darkened, whether from embarrassment or concern he might overstep, she was unsure—"if I was the father, I'd want to know. No matter the circumstances."

"Yeah, but it's complicated." Paige's face heated up. "Forest and I were married briefly."

"What?" Paisley lunged to her feet again.

Judah's jaw dropped.

"It's true." Paige thought of the wedding ring hidden in a box in her bedroom closet. "My fairytale marriage lasted a whole two weeks, then crashed and burned."

Thirty

*Forest waited for Paige's answer to his proposal.
She stared at the ring, then gazed at him with
moisture in her eyes. "I want to say yes." He
wanted her to say yes, too. "But if you're still
engaged to Elinore, I can't."*

Needing a break, Forest left Craig in Deputy Brian's care, and headed south for a drive along the coast. Fresh air, and a fresh perspective, sounded good.

Not far ahead of his Jetta, a gray vehicle resembling Paige's was heading south, too. By the driver's long dark hair and medium stature, it might be her. The closer he got to the car, the more certain he was that it was Paige. Where was she going? Out to Judah and Paisley's?

If she pulled into a beach turnout, maybe he'd try talking with her again. She probably wouldn't be happy to see him after the way he crashed the tête-à-tête between her and Craig earlier. What was she thinking cavorting with Edward's accomplice? Didn't she realize how much trouble she could get into?

The gray car slowed down and pulled into Judah's driveway just like he thought Paige might do. He drove on to the next pullout where he could use his binoculars, if necessary.

He wasn't on official duty, but who could blame him for being curious about Paige and her little girl? Craig's daughter, if the prisoner had been truthful about that. How soon after Paige and Forest broke up did she get together with the other man? Was her relationship with Craig the reason she filed for divorce so quickly?

He groaned. Anger and jealousy twisted together, knotting up in his throat, threatening to choke him.

Ever since coming to Basalt Bay, ever since Paige and some of the others acted secretive about her life, his suspicions had been on high alert. This must be the reason for the secrecy. She had a child with Craig. Yet on her police report, she used her maiden name, so she must not have married him. Still, they seemed close.

Setting the binoculars down on the passenger seat, he rubbed his hand across his forehead. Craig saying the girl was his kid hurt worse than anything Forest had experienced in years. If he were being honest, he'd secretly hoped the child was his. But that couldn't be the case. Paige would have contacted him with the news.

The girl's blond hair, more like his than Craig's, was a curiosity. Even Paige had dark hair. In fact, the child somewhat resembled his twin nephews, Tommy and Taylor. He gulped. What if Piper was his kid? He exhaled sharply. No way. Paige wouldn't be so cruel as to withhold that kind of information from him. She wasn't that angry with him, was she?

In coming to Basalt Bay, he'd hoped there might be something meaningful left between them, some spark of love or romance to resurrect. Maybe her association with Craig was at the crux of the matter. Maybe she was in love with him.

Forest imagined the blond pixie in Paige's arms. Her light-colored eyes so much like his. That's right. Her eye color! Could she be his daughter? Obviously, she could be. But was she? He had to find out.

Thrusting open the door, he jumped out of the vehicle.

As he stomped down the sandy cliff, trudging through high beach grasses toward the patio where Paige, Piper, Paisley, and Judah were gathered, questions nagged at him. Were they all in on this secret? What if Paige was pregnant when he left and didn't tell him? Kept it from him all these years?

Paige wasn't a conniving person. But look at her relationship with Craig. Even meeting privately with him this afternoon, after last night's disastrous sting, seemed fishy.

If Paige had kept fatherhood from him, if she perpetrated the ultimate lie, that was a personal affront he couldn't tolerate. However, if it wasn't true, if he was making a giant thing out of nothing, he might be about to make the biggest blunder of his life.

Thirty-one

Still on his knee, Forest assured Paige that he'd ended things with Elinore on the phone. "It's over. All I want is you. Will you marry me, baby?" Smiling, barely containing her happiness, she whispered, "Yes."

"Sweetie, we have to leave," Paige called to Piper who was still playing in the sand. "Tell Uncle Judah and Auntie Paisley goodbye."

"No. *Wocks.*"

"Come here."

"No!" Piper screeched, her face turning bright red.

Too bad her tantrum was going to happen in front of Paisley and Judah.

Piper stomped through the sand, heading straight toward the water. "*Waaatooooo.*"

"Piper, stop!" Paige trounced after her. "Young lady, stop

right there." At the water's edge, she scooped her up. Piper flailed her arms and screamed in high-pitched shrieks.

"Anything I can do to help?"

Paige froze. Forest? What was he—

Jostling Piper, who was still busting out ear-piercing wails, Paige faced him. "Why are you—" Piper's screams overrode her words. Just as well, shocked as she was to see him.

"Mind if I give it a try?" He held out his hands, a tight expression on his face.

"I don't think that's a good idea." Was he offering to help because he suspected she was his? Did Craig say something?

"I'm a pro with my sister's kids." Forest met Paige's gaze over Piper's blond head. "May I try?"

She'd wondered what it would be like to tell him what a precious girl their two weeks living as husband and wife had created. Apparently, she was about to find out.

"Piper," Paige spoke over her sobbing. "This is Forest." She maneuvered her daughter away from tangling her fingers in Paige's hair. Piper drew in a shaky breath, hiccupping. "He's a ... a friend of Mommy's." She stole a glance at him.

Eyebrows high, his eyes widened.

Piper stared at him, sniffling, her eyes teary and red. "*Watoooo?*"

"I enjoy the water also." Forest drew her out of Paige's arms before she could object, and marched down the beach with their daughter, chatting and pointing at things as if he knew exactly what to do with an upset child. What did he say? His sister had kids who he played with?

Piper reached out her hands toward the water as if she were going to dive into it.

"Watch out!" Paige yelled. "She moves fast."

"I've got this." Forest secured Piper with both arms and bounced her as he trotted down the seashore. Strangely, Piper stopped crying. She even giggled in between hiccupping. Forest squatted and picked up a rock, handing it to her. Then, from the safety of his arms, she thrust it into the sea, making a splash and laughing.

Apprehension segued to hope as Paige watched father and daughter together for the first time. She blinked fast to stop tears. How long had she dreaded and dreamed of this day?

Forest picked up more rocks. Turning with Piper in his arms, he met Paige's gaze. A spark flashed between them. He knew, didn't he? Paige's heart flitted into her throat. Today was judgment day.

"Watoo. Watoo."

Forest handed Piper the rocks and stepped right into a wave, the lower portion of his jeans getting soaked. "Go ahead, princess. Throw them in the water."

Princess. Paige liked that endearment for their daughter.

Piper tossed the rocks one by one.

"That a girl."

Paige swallowed down a behemoth gulp of emotion. Piper looked like she always belonged in her daddy's arms. Nearly matching hair, although he was grayer than he was three years ago, and matching eyes, Piper was so much like him. Anyone could probably see that.

"We should go, Piper," she called, not wanting the others to witness her confession to Forest. It was something she needed to do privately.

Judah jogged to the water's edge. "How about if I take Piper for a couple of minutes? Give you two a chance to talk. It's up to you." He stared at Paige with concern in his gaze.

"Sure, that would be great. Thanks, Judah."

Clapping, he ran toward Forest and held out his hands toward Piper. "Hey, squirt, how about a horse ride up the beach?"

"*Hosie. Hosie.*" Piper reached for Judah.

Forest passed her to him, a reluctant expression crossing his features.

"*Hosie.*" Piper patted Judah's face.

"You got it." He galloped down the seashore to the squeals of a delighted two-year-old.

"Why didn't you tell me?" Forest demanded as soon as he crossed the beach to Paige. "How could you conceal you had a child with me? She is my daughter, right?"

"Yes, she is yours ... our daughter."

He expelled a loud breath. "I can't believe you did this to me."

"I didn't do it to you."

"No? What would you call it? Withholding vital information from a father?" Forest, obviously enraged and shocked, thrust his index finger in Judah and Piper's direction. "You have a daughter on your own and don't give me a chance to have a part in her life? You don't even tell me?"

She wanted to ask him where all that grace was that he mentioned two days ago, but she didn't. Whatever he was feeling, she deserved his anger.

"You never came back." Her voice came out small and inadequate to express how deeply she felt. "You left me alone so you could chase after someone else. Thought more of your job than you did of being devoted to your wife." There, she finally got the courage to say the words penned up inside of her for three years. "You were all caught up in your own life, so I let you go."

"Must have been easy. Here I thought you loved me." He sounded wounded, his eyes moist.

She'd guessed he would be mad at her, but this hurt, or devastation, took her by surprise. She kept Piper a secret for her own self-preservation, knowing one day she'd tell Forest everything. But his anguish struck a raw chord in her spirit now.

Maybe she had done this to him. Payback for his abandonment. Yet, in exposing her secret, in observing Forest's heartbreak, she felt no satisfaction … no revenge, although she hated to think she ever wanted that.

"All this time I've been a father and didn't know." He shook his head. "How could you?"

"I'm—" What, wretchedly sorry? Disappointed in herself? If turning back time were possible, she'd think more about what Forest might feel on this day when he discovered the truth before doing the same thing again. Hindsight was always better, but no one had the luxury of it beforehand.

"What about Craig?" He said the man's name harshly.

"What about him?"

"He said"—Forest kicked his wet shoe against a clump of sand and more grit stuck to it—"that he's her father."

What a laugh. Although, the moment was too ripe with tension and pain for humor.

"He's aware that he's not her dad."

"You never dated? Never—" Forest's glare could have melted snow. Is that how he got criminals to confess their wrongdoings?

"Craig's and my relationship is none of your concern." He'd been out of her life too long for any of that nonsense. "He loves Piper, and she loves him. Much like she adores Judah." Turning, she watched her brother-in-law carrying Piper on his shoulders far down the beach. Looked like he was giving her plenty of time to talk to Forest. *Hurry back, Judah.*

"Why didn't you tell me you were pregnant?" He tucked his hands in the back pockets of his jeans and gazed toward open waters like he didn't even want to look at her.

"Would it have made any difference?" The crux of the matter three years ago wasn't as important now. "If I called and told you I carried your child, you might have felt duty-bound to quit your job and come to me." She shrugged, the heat of the words she still had to say burning through her. "I'd never have known if you came back only out of obligation."

"How about honor and integrity?"

He didn't say love.

"I didn't want you showing up on my doorstep out of some misplaced sense of honor, either. It had to be"—she swallowed hard—"love or nothing." She chose nothing.

Forest groaned and turned west, his gaze following Judah and Piper. "Had I known, nothing would have stopped me from being here for you. And her." He raised his hand and shielded his eyes. "This. Your not telling me about her is unbelievable. What you stole from me is so unfair."

"I'm sorry." What else could she say? It would take time for him to process. "I thought you went back to Elinore. You loved her."

"I didn't. And you were wrong about us."

Did he mean him and Elinore, or him and Paige? Not that it mattered now.

"I have to go and think things through, but before I leave town, we need to talk." His voice turned harsh. "Work out custody details."

"Custody?" Panic raced up and down her spine like an ice cube running over her skin. She hadn't contemplated a custody dispute as the outcome of this reveal.

"You didn't imagine I'd waltz out of town as if Piper wasn't a part of my life, as if you haven't kept her from me, did you?" He glared at her with a sharp glint. Then he strode down the beach.

Why didn't she just stay in her house and hide until he left town like she planned to do in the first place?

Thirty-two

Forest loved Paige and wanted to be with her for the rest of his life. They were in Vegas, the Marriage Capital of the World. So with over fifty wedding chapels to choose from, why should they wait?

Trudging back to his rental car, Forest moaned with frustration and disillusionment. Sure, he guessed Piper might be his child. But this? Being told outright the small girl was his flesh and blood? That Paige kept this secret from him because she assumed he married Elinore? Outrageous!

How unreasonable it was for her to make that assumption, that decision. For her not to have, at least, attempted to contact him and share the good news felt like she committed a crime against his emotions, his life.

Who else shared in this tyranny? Judah? Forest aided him in finding his wife. In fact, Judah was the first one who spoke to him about grace and faith being a real part of his life. Yet, he never said anything to him about Paige. Perhaps, his previous brother-in-law didn't even know Forest was Piper's father. He should give him the benefit of the doubt, he supposed.

He ran both hands over his hair and groaned. How could Paige have knifed him in the back like this? She had divorce papers delivered to him, so she knew how to get ahold of him. Could have called or texted him. No skirting the truth about that.

She'd stolen Piper's infancy and much of her toddlerhood from his life as if she were a thief stealing a priceless gem. How could she live with herself? Well, he'd do something. He wouldn't fight for full custody, repaying her with what she did to him, but he'd figure out something. He knew people in law enforcement. A few lawyers. He'd do something.

A fire burned in him, and by the depth of his irritation, he probably shouldn't be driving. But he had to get back to the deputy's office and finish Craig's interrogation. Maybe question Edward again. Even with this disturbing news and how awful he felt, he had a case to finalize.

How much did Craig know about Piper's parentage? Is that why he blasted Forest with sarcasm and rude answers earlier? Another groan rumbled through him.

He turned back for one last look at the scene below. Judah galloped along the shoreline toward Paige with Piper on his shoulders. He looked like the father Forest wished he'd had the chance to be. Envy and resentment dueled in him, causing an ache in his chest unrivaled by any heartburn he ever experienced. Guilt too.

He wasn't completely innocent. Three years ago, he didn't return to Basalt Bay as he should have. He didn't push to work things out with Paige, just accepted the inevitable result of their brief marriage and divorce. Had even thought of it as a mistake. But had he known ... man, if he knew he had a daughter ... things would have been different. Was anything more important than being there for his own kid?

For his wife, too. The thought coursed through him like an invader chinking away at the foundations of his inner peace. He'd made his share of blunders. Ever since coming to Basalt Bay, he intended to make things right with Paige. But then he got caught up with the case. Trying to figure out Paige's involvement with Craig. Now that he felt worse than ever toward her, what was he supposed to do? How could there ever be peace between them again?

Thirty-three

Paige held Forest's hand as they walked after dinner. "When shall we get married?" When he took her in his arms and whispered, "Tonight?" against her mouth, her heart nearly pounded out of her ribcage. Tonight?

The day after telling Forest about Piper, Paige sat beside Aunt Callie in her overcrowded living room, surrounded by a wall of boxes and junk, trying to explain Forest's and her past. Earlier, she told Dad, who patted her shoulder but didn't say much. Typical of him. She couldn't tell if he was disappointed in his youngest child or if he'd already figured it out.

"Tell me again"—Aunt Callie peered at her—"why didn't the man do the honorable thing and marry you?"

Maybe she explained too quickly. "Forest and I did get married, Auntie."

"Then you divorced him?" Her voice zoomed to the ceiling. "Kept the child a secret from him?"

"Yes. And, yes." Groan. Telling her family members, one by one, was tough. She even wrote a letter to Peter in Alaska marked "General Delivery" and explained. Who knew if her brother would receive it? She'd written to him like that before and he never answered. But she felt better for having unloaded her burden of secrets.

"I don't know what you were thinking." Aunt Callie seemed to be gearing up to deliver advice. "The man deserved to hear the truth from you. It was your responsibility to tell him, Paige. To tell your family the truth." She held up a hand. "Even if I say he's a cad for not pursuing you properly and marrying you where I could attend, a father has a right to know he has a child."

"I know. I know."

"What's with you and your sister not letting your family take part in your weddings?" Aunt Callie tossed out her hand, thwacking it against a cardboard box, and grimaced. "Why act like you weren't married, and not telling me you were?"

"I wasn't trying to hurt you by getting married in Vegas. Honest. It was spontaneous and romantic and ... perfect."

"If it was so perfect, what happened?"

"Two weeks of unforgettable bliss, then real life caved in on us like an avalanche. We discovered we didn't know each other at all."

"Who does, dear? It takes time, sometimes years, to adjust to living with another person, or so I've been told." Aunt Callie shuffled in her seat. "Doesn't mean you throw it all in the trash."

Paige was ready to be finished with this conversation. "Anything I can help with before I go?"

"Certainly. I can use all the help I can get." Aunt Callie swallowed a couple of times. "Obviously, you're done talking about Forest, while I'm still adjusting. Tell me again why he left you alone, pregnant."

If only the past were easier to explain. But how could it be when it was buried beneath so many layers?

"We fought. He didn't know of my pregnancy. Neither did I, at the time."

"Poor man. I think—"

"I wanted you to hear this from me," Paige cut in before Aunt Callie went on another tangent. "I'm sorry for any of this that hurt you. I'm trying to make things right."

"Oh, honey." Aunt Callie struggled to a standing position and drew Paige into her arms. "We're family. I'm always here for you, no matter what, even if I don't understand your decisions."

"Thank you, Auntie."

"Come with me. I have a pile of clothes to sort." She shuffled toward the spare bedroom.

Paige followed her aunt into the messy room. She fingered an antique dress dangling over the edge of the guest-room bed. "What's this?"

"A costume from my youthful days."

"It's nice to imagine you wearing this when you were young and carefree."

"I was a party-goer back when parties were innocent affairs where people met and danced the jive, or what have you." A soft smile crossing her mouth, Aunt Callie stared toward the window as if recalling a fond memory. "Me and ... well, never mind about that."

Her and who? A young romance?

"Our family has a history of making terrible mistakes when it comes to relationships. Just ask your father." Aunt Callie patted Paige's cheek. "Any chance you can make things right with your fellow?"

"I don't know."

Was there anything she could do to mend their past?

Thirty-four

"Do you promise to love and cherish this woman for as long as you live?" Gazing into Paige's dark eyes in the tiny wedding chapel surrounded by artificial flowers, Forest whispered, "I do."

Forest felt cut to the quick by yesterday's revelation. He was a dad for what, two years, without knowing? What kind of a cruel trick was that? Here he thought Paige might still have tender feelings for him. How could he have been so wrong?

He needed to finish up the case and leave Basalt Bay ASAP. Only, didn't he make that mistake before? Leaving abruptly? Not talking things through?

His groan turned into a cry for God's help and wisdom. His mercy. In all Forest's raging and hurling mental accusations against Paige, he almost forgot to consider his walk with the Lord. Harboring bitterness and resentment was wrong. What might God's will be in all this? It was hard to see any good coming out of Paige's deception.

Three years ago, Forest made lifelong vows to her, and she to him. He'd fully intended to keep those vows. But things happened, they divorced, broke their promises. Surely God didn't intend for him to pursue Paige and marry her again. Not after what she did.

But before he knew Piper existed, before he discovered what Paige kept from him, hadn't he hoped for that very thing? That by his coming to Basalt Bay there might be a slim chance they could find their way back to each other? Back to marriage, even?

Something hurt so deeply in his chest. The betrayal and lies invaded his spirit like cancer. How could he ever be free to forgive Paige for keeping their daughter from him?

Like I forgave you, whispered through his thoughts.

Moaning, he strode to the coffeepot in the deputy's office and poured himself a cup of thick-looking dark black coffee. Smelled acidic. He sipped the strong brew. Tasted the bite. His system needed the jolt, so he forced himself to drink it despite the bitterness that mirrored his feelings.

As soon as his investigation ended, he'd finish writing his plethora of reports, then head back to Portland. Since being in this coastal town, he'd received a couple of requests for his services from other agencies in the Pacific Northwest. Coos Bay. Spokane. Even Seattle. That was his life, traveling from city to city, from one job to another.

Is that how he wanted his life to continue? Rarely being home. Spending too many hours on the road. Living in cheap motels. Now that he knew of his daughter, he seriously had to question that lifestyle.

Back in Vegas after they married, he asked Paige to join him on the road. It didn't matter where they lived as long as they were together, right? But she said her life was in Basalt Bay, that she wanted to open an art gallery here. What of his job? His aspirations? Old resentments churned inside him. Bleeding wounds made fresh by the secrets she kept.

Back then, if he'd given up his job and lived here with her, what would his life have been like as Piper's dad? As Paige's husband? A longing for what might have been filled him. The things he missed out on stirred in his mind—taking part in Paige's pregnancy and delivery, holding their infant daughter, watching her grow for the last two years, providing for them. He could have been happy here. Would have adjusted. Maybe he and Paige could have figured out how to compromise between his job and her dreams. Maybe even still be married. In love.

A groan roared through him. He had to focus on his tasks. With about a day's work left, two at the most, he had a decision to make. Would he fight Paige for custody? Rake her over the coals in court? He didn't want that, not really. But he wouldn't disappear as if being a father lacked importance to him, either.

An hour later, after staring numbly at a mound of paperwork spread across the table in the investigation room, his head pounded with a migraine. His last interview with Craig was another epic failure. Forest stormed out of the room, twice, with excuses that he needed coffee or had to find something. But even he knew that had more to do with his mixed-up emotions toward Paige, and her possible relationship with Craig, than anything to do with the prisoner refusing to answer his questions.

He tapped a pen against the form he'd been attempting to fill out for the last thirty minutes. How many times had he read the same question? A note written in Brian's handwriting snagged his attention. He picked up the crumpled sheet of paper. "Paige Cedars reported she received a threatening note."

"What?" Paige had received a threat and didn't tell him? Why didn't Brian inform him of this? What kind of threat? He continued reading the sloppily written missive describing a text Paige received. Did the deputy discover who sent it?

Forest shoved away from the table and strode from the room. Ten minutes later, he stood at Paige's front door, fist poised to knock.

"You break that girl's heart again and I'll break your nose."

Forest spun around. Callie Cedars stood on the sidewalk, hands on hips, glaring at him with a piercing scowl.

"Miss Cedars, it's not my intention to hurt your niece. Never was." He stepped off the cement slab forming the porch and faced the daunting woman.

"You have an odd way of showing it." Her index finger jabbed the air. "If you care anything for the little girl, you'll be the daddy she needs and let this strife between you and Paige go. I've had my share of secret offenses that settle between folks like glue, building strongholds, keeping hearts apart for decades."

"Ma'am, I'm the one who's been kept in the dark. The secret-keeping is Paige's doing."

"Excuse me. I must have the facts wrong." Callie peered at him like he was from outer space. "Aren't you the man who asked my niece to marry him in a clandestine manner, then left her?"

Forest toed the grass.

"Well, aren't you?"

"You're partly right. Leaving like that wasn't my best decision."

"I should say not. Want some advice?"

"Not really." He came over here not only to inquire about the threat but to have it out with Paige. She was to blame. She—

"When two people vow to stay together until they die, especially when these promises are made without the accountability of family present"—Callie shot him a puckered grimace—"then one of them walks away after a tiff—"

"She threw her purse at my head! Told me to leave and never come back."

"That so?" Callie chuckled. "Didn't know she had it in her."

"Me either. Now, look, I'm here to talk to Paige. This is between her and me."

"If anyone needs to 'look,' it's you, kiddo. We take care of our own here." Callie wagged her finger at him. "I'm part of this family, and I'm staying put until I'm sure my niece is safe with you."

How dare she accuse him of being untrustworthy!

"I assure you I'm esteemed by my colleagues. I'm a trusted member of—"

Callie hooted. "I don't suppose those colleagues know you married Paige and left her with a child to raise on her own."

"Miss Cedars—"

"If you plan to stir up something with my niece, it better be kind and forgiving, or get lost. You did that once, go ahead and do it again."

Embarrassment, rage, and guilt swept through Forest.

"Do you still love her?"

Her softer-spoken question stole his breath away. Stole any rebuttal from his lips too.

Paige yanked open the door. "What's going on out here? Aunt Callie?" She glanced back and forth between them. "Forest, did you need something?"

"We're just getting acquainted." Callie gave him a tight grin.

He swallowed a groan.

Paige stepped onto the porch. "Aunt Callie, thank you for checking on me. But I thought you were heading back to your place."

"I'm staying right—"

"Auntie, please."

"Fine." Callie stormed down the sidewalk but shot daggers at Forest over her shoulder for half a block.

"Sorry about that." Paige's gaze followed her aunt. "Whatever our problems are, you don't deserve to have my family ganging up on you."

"Thanks. Although, I'd say the whole town is in your corner."

"If so, that would be a nice change." She sighed. "Now, what's this about?"

"I figure we have things that need to be said privately."

"So, you're deciding the time and place?" A tic twitched in her eyelid.

"Why not? For three years, you've decided what we weren't going to discuss." Man, he didn't mean for the hurt in his chest to barrel out in a fiery attack on her.

"Everything okay here, Paige?" A mid-twenties redheaded

woman pushing a stroller with a toddler who looked to be about Piper's age passed by, eyeing him suspiciously.

"Yes. Thank you, Necia." Paige waved. "How's Vi?"

"Feisty as usual. Bring Piper over whenever you want. The girls have so much fun playing together."

"Thanks, will do."

The woman gave Forest another once over, frowning.

"You want to come in, so the neighbors don't wonder why an angry man is at my door?" Paige's tight voice let him know just what she thought of him coming into her house.

Thirty-five

On his wedding day, Forest had no doubts. He would love Paige forever. What they had found together was truly special.

Forest followed Paige into the dimly lit living room.

She pulled open the long curtains, allowing light in. "Piper will be waking up from her nap soon. We can tell her, if you like."

"Tell her I'm her long-lost dad who just found out about her?" He felt a check in his spirit. A reminder of the still small voice telling him to forgive, to show mercy. He hadn't been acting in grace or showing the love of God in his words or tone lately.

Sorry, Lord. Help me to find Your love and goodness in all this.

"I didn't mean to sound snide." He dropped onto the couch cushion. "Before we talk about Piper, I saw something about a threat you received. Can you tell me about that?"

"Why do you care?" Paige sat stiffly on the edge of the recliner.

"No matter how undone I am about us having a child and not knowing about her, I want you both to be safe."

Paige stared at him for about twenty seconds. Then sighed. "Thanks for that. As you've probably guessed, I'm still upset about Craig's arrest."

"I'm sorry you had to see that." Forest gulped.

"I don't believe he's guilty of kidnapping Paisley, being an accomplice, whatever. You're wrong about that. He would never hurt her!"

Her impassioned speech made it obvious how much she cared for the other man.

"Sorry. I can't comment on an ongoing case."

A look of disgust crossed her face. Then she sighed.

"Deputy Brian came by the house right after I received the warnings—a note left on my back door and a text. That's when I told him about them." She twisted her hands together in her lap. "It's been two days and Deputy Brian hasn't contacted me, so it's probably nothing."

"Still troubles me."

"Me too. Also, I've felt watched."

"Watched?"

"Could be my imagination, or nerves, but I've felt eyeballs peering at me. Sound weird?"

Their gazes met, hers looking wary of him.

"Not r-really." The words didn't come out of his mouth right. Callie's question about whether he loved Paige replayed in his mind. Did he? Even after she withheld essential information from him? Wasn't unconditional love like that? Continuing to be kind, grace-filled, and yes, loving, no matter what the other person did. "If you ever feel unsafe or are threatened again, please call me, or the deputy."

Her eyes pulsed as if she were surprised to hear him being nice.

"Despite the twist in our relationship, I care about you, Paige."

Her eyes moistened. The warmer expression on her face, and her soft, rosy lips, stirred his senses. He had to stop staring at those lips. His hope for a happy outcome with her was gone, wasn't it?

"When I discovered I was pregnant"—her voice sounded almost melodic—"keeping the information to myself felt like the right choice, even if it's reprehensible to you now. I thought you went back to Elinore. Honestly, I did. I felt so alone. Used. Forsaken." She sighed. "I faced the greatest challenge of my life—motherhood—by myself." A tender smile crossed those lips he couldn't peel his gaze away from. "I wouldn't change being a mom for anything. That's the best part of our two weeks together."

Warmth spread through him, invading the icy coldness surrounding his chest walls. All this time, he blamed her, resenting the choices she made to end things between them as if he hadn't had any part of the decision. Yet, he had. In not coming back, in stubbornly nursing his pride and not talking to her, he proclaimed loud and clear that he agreed with her decision to separate. Seconding the motion that they made a big mistake by getting married in Vegas. Like her, he'd never again resent their time together because of Piper.

And because ... he still loved Paige. He did, didn't he?

"I didn't return to Elinore." He smoothed his palm over the arm of the couch. "Whatever it looked like, whatever you assumed, she and I were finished. Never started, really. The thing with her father's illness kept me hanging around, but I should have explained that better to you." A measure of his previous anger returned, igniting in his veins. "But you went psycho. Wouldn't listen to reason. Threw things at me."

"Did my brief reaction to the news you were leaving me justify you giving up on us?"

"You're the one who had divorce papers delivered. Not me." He nearly howled, thrusting his hands through his hair that was already sticking up on end. "I would have come back. I just needed more time." The self-righteous words tasted vile. More time? He'd taken too long as it was.

"How was I to know? You didn't tell me you still wanted us to be together. Didn't contact me."

"No, I didn't," he admitted. "But you should have come clean with me."

"And so should you." She slapped her hands against her knees. "You convinced me to marry you. Like marrying Forest Harper secretly in Vegas was the greatest adventure in the world. Silly me. I thought you were in love with me and wanted us to be together."

Her face reddened, but thankfully she didn't cry. He couldn't handle a woman's tears.

"I was serious about us. Confused too. But I loved you, Paige, more than I've ever loved anyone." Although hard to say now, he meant it. He wanted to add that he still loved her, still dreamed about her, but he had to forgive her before uttering those words. "When did you find out you were pregnant? Before or after you filed for divorce?"

She stood and glared at him like he didn't have any right to ask.

He stood also, adjusting his position so the coffee table separated them. "Come on, Paige, I deserve to know the truth."

"After, okay? But not by much," she said in a quieter tone. "And I'm a good mom. I've taken great care of Piper."

"I'm sure you have." That she might not be a good mom, or hadn't taken care of their daughter, never crossed his mind.

"If you try a smear campaign to get custody, it won't work. Everyone in Basalt knows Piper comes first with me."

"That wouldn't be an issue."

"Okay. Well, then, good." She dropped back into the recliner, folding her hands. "I wanted to tell you about her. I never meant for it to take this long."

He lowered himself to the edge of the couch just as Piper danced into the room. Paige leaped up and embraced her. Forest gulped at the tender scene.

"Piper"—Paige turned the child to face him—"do you remember Forest?"

Piper buried her face in Paige's shoulder.

"We'll be right back." Paige left the room, carrying Piper into the kitchen.

Quiet noises reached him—Paige telling Piper to get a book and show him; the water running; Piper frolicking down the hallway. Paige returned and set a glass of water on the coffee table in front of him.

"Thanks." He took a long swallow. "What now?"

"You can spend time with our daughter, if you want to." Paige sat down. "She's shy around strangers. But you've met her, so she's going to show you her books."

"Okay."

"You might start by relaxing. Try not to scare her off."

"Fine." He scooted back against the couch cushion, letting out a slow breath.

Piper walked on tiptoe into the room, carrying a book that seemed too large for her to hold.

"Sit by Forest and show him the baby bear."

Piper climbed up on the couch beside him, somehow juggling the book too.

"Good job, Piper," Paige said encouragingly. "Show Forest the bear family."

When he drove over here, he hadn't expected this. Paige letting him hang out with Piper was a pleasant surprise. So was seeing Paige looking more relaxed around him.

"Baby." Piper held the book open to a colorful page with tattered edges. "Mama. Papa."

"What's the baby bear doing?" Forest asked.

"Walk, walk, walk," Piper chanted.

"The bears are going for a walk. That's good." He clasped her hand. "Do you like to take walks?"

Piper pulled away from him, bouncing on the cushion. "Walk. Walk." Her voice got louder.

"Pipe," Paige said quietly, "show Forest who comes to the bear's house."

Piper stopped bouncing and turned the pages roughly like she couldn't get to the requested page fast enough.

Forest had read this story to his nephews. He remembered a girl showing up at the bears' house and eating their oatmeal. Although, he wondered why a young girl was out in the woods alone, especially in a kids' book.

Piper smacked her hands against the photo of a blond girl with a bright blue cape.

"Who is she?"

"*Gwoopy-wooos.*"

He read the text. "Goldilocks?"

"*Gwoopy-wooos.*" Piper clapped.

The questions, the excitement over each picture, and her cackling continued until they finished the book.

"*Mow. Mow.*" She pushed it toward him.

"You want us to look at it again?"

"Welcome to my world." Paige chuckled. "This can go on for hours, reading the same book, rehashing the same questions, cheering all over again."

This version of Paige—her smiling at him and acting relaxed—reminded him of the woman he fell in love with. He thought of something. "It must have taken a lot of courage and faith in yourself to raise a child alone."

"Thank you." By her wide eyes, his gentle words surprised her. They surprised him too.

Spending time with Piper must be at the helm of his fickle emotions. Part of him wanted to take Paige in his arms and beg her to accept him back. To let him be part of this family. The family he always wanted. But the wounded pride stuck in his craw had to be reckoned with first.

Paige stood. "Piper, would you like a snack?"

"Snack. Snack." She clapped.

Paige held out her hand toward the blond cherub and drew her into the kitchen. "Come with us, if you like," she said over her shoulder.

"Sure. Thanks." He followed and sat down in a chair next to where Paige set Piper on a booster seat. Paige sliced an apple and dropped several slices in front of Piper.

"Want anything? Tea? Soda?"

"No, I'm good." He watched his daughter—still couldn't get over the wonder of that—munching the fruit and jabbering, recognizing a little of his nephews' personalities in her. He could sit here watching her all day and not tire of it. *He* had a child. *He* was a dad.

If anyone peeked in the window, they might assume they were a perfect little family, the three of them. If only that were the case.

Thirty-six

Inviting Forest into her hotel room as newlyweds was a dream come true. Hadn't Paige longed for a romance of her own? They were going to be the most-in-love couple in the world. Nothing would ever part them.

Paige watched Piper giggling at Forest and his eyes shining with moisture. Even though she was still annoyed with his legal actions toward Craig yesterday, and she hoped he was wrong about Craig's involvement in the crime, Forest's tender expression took her breath away. Should she explain to Piper that this man, who looked so much like her, was her father? Could a two-year-old grasp such a leap from having no father to embracing this true-life "Papa bear?"

He laughed at something Piper said and their voices blended beautifully. A sweet, gentle feeling tugged at Paige.

"*Mow* books?"

"Not now." She helped Piper safely descend from the booster seat. "How about if we play ball in the backyard?"

"Ball. Ball." Piper danced around Forest, who stood too. She patted his leg. "*Pway?*"

"Sure. I can do that."

"Come on, Piper." Paige helped her get her coat on.

"Anything I can do?" Stuffing his hands in the back pockets of his jeans, Forest looked uncomfortable, yet seemed determined to be helpful.

"Why don't you grab the beach ball in the living room?"

"Okay." He strolled into the other room.

Putting on a sweatshirt, she zipped it up, then walked Piper onto the porch and helped her get down the steps. Piper scurried over to the swing set. Leaning her stomach over the seat, she swayed back and forth, her feet remaining on the ground.

What was taking Forest so long?

Paige peeked in the door without turning her back to Piper. "Forest, are you having trouble finding it?"

"Be right there," he called.

A few minutes later he crossed the porch, holding the pink beach ball, his eyes filled with moisture again. "I was checking out the pictures on the mantle. Trying to catch up."

"Right." A sword's tip turned in her gut. Would she have to endure guilty feelings for the rest of her life about her decision not to contact him?

Piper squealed, obviously noticing Forest had her ball. "Mine." She tackled him around the knees. "*Pway?*"

"Absolutely." He stepped a couple of feet away from her. "Hold out your hands. Ready?"

He tossed the ball gently, and Paige helped Piper catch it. Then Piper hurled the ball catawampus. Paige snickered as Forest scrambled to the fence to retrieve it.

"She has a good arm." A little pride in his voice?

"Yep. She just needs to learn the art of catching."

"Maybe I can help with that." He leaned over like a pitcher, his knee bent. "Ready?"

"*Weady.*" Piper thrust out her arms.

They played until Piper tired of the game, then she begged Forest to push her on the swing. He complied and everything went great until she slipped off the seat, landing on the ground with a thud. Her wail came long and loud.

"I'm so sorry." Forest scooped her up before Paige got to her.

Piper lunged toward Paige, crying and glaring at Forest like he pushed her off the swing on purpose.

"There, there. You're okay." Paige cuddled her. "Remember how you have to hold onto the chains tightly?"

Piper hiccupped, nodding against her shoulder.

"Is she okay?" Forest asked.

"She's fine. She's a toughie like me."

His eyebrows rose like he doubted that. "Sorry if I pushed her too hard."

"If she notices something shiny or pretty, she lets go. It's happened before. It'll happen again." Paige sat down on the porch, holding Piper, but the girl's meltdown had reduced to sniffles.

Paige nodded for Forest to join them. A tad close for comfort, his thigh brushed hers as he sat down. A lightning bolt wouldn't have shocked her more than the sensation that sizzled through her, but she didn't have time to mull over her reaction.

"Piper"—she took a breath—"I want to tell you something. Forest is your … your daddy."

"Hey, princess."

"Can you say 'Daddy?'"

Piper stared at Forest with a puzzled look. Was it too big of an idea for her to fathom?

"Just try," she coaxed. "Daddy."

Piper hid her face against Paige's chest.

"It's okay." Forest shrugged. "Thanks for trying."

"She's only two."

"I know." He pressed his lips together. Was he stopping them from trembling or from saying something unkind? Finally, he said, "If I'd been here all along, she'd understand I'm her dad."

Yep. That blame rested on Paige's shoulders.

"Come on, Piper, let's put on a movie." She rarely used videos for babysitting, but this would have to be one of those times. She and Forest needed to talk.

While Paige set up a cartoon on the TV, Forest remained in the kitchen.

Dreading the conversation to come, she reentered the kitchen and faced his grief-stricken expression. He scrubbed the arm of his jacket over his face, and something tore in her heart.

"She's amazing," he whispered. "So much like …"

"You?"

"Like my sister's kids, too. Blondies all."

"My aunt has mentioned her hair. 'Where'd she get the blond hair, Paige?'" She mimicked Aunt Callie's voice.

"You should have told me," he said hoarsely.

"I know. I'm sorry, now, that I didn't. I figured if you wanted to be involved in my life, you'd come looking for me."

She decided to go for broke. "Even when I sent the divorce papers, I partly hoped you'd decline to sign them. That you'd come back to me."

"You did?"

"I pushed for answers the only way I could without begging you to leave Elinore and come home."

"Oh, Paige." He covered his face with his hands. "What a mess we've made."

She glanced at the ceiling, controlling her urge to weep as Piper did earlier. "Why didn't you come back after you made sure Elinore was okay?"

The sound of children's laughter reached her from the cartoon playing in the living room.

"Why didn't you contact me before filing for divorce?"

He was the one who left and didn't call. What was she supposed to think when her groom took off, rushing back to his ex? "Rehashing what each of us did or didn't do won't get us anywhere. What's done is done. We should focus on Piper."

"Seeing her, realizing she's my daughter … the thought of walking away is more than I can stomach." He took a deep breath, then exhaled slowly. "I've missed you, Paige. Haven't dated. Haven't sought a distraction in anyone else." A vulnerable-looking smile crossed his mouth. "Haven't you missed me at all?"

What could she say to that? Miss him? She couldn't confess the things she'd written about him in her journal. How she imagined kissing him, dreamed of being in his arms, dancing in the street over such a man loving her. Her face flushed hot.

In all this time, he hadn't dated? Why not? He was handsome. Had a great personality. A breathtaking smile. Plenty of ladies would have gone out with him.

"I should go."

Was he upset that she didn't answer his question?

He strode toward the living room, then paused. "We both need time to think. Thank you for letting me spend time with Piper." He told Piper goodbye on his way out.

Paige was left with unsettled feelings. He hadn't dated anyone? Not even Elinore?

Thirty-seven

Paisley set her napkin on her empty plate and gazed across the makeshift table, meeting her husband's baby blues. Dinner on the veranda beneath the stars, although the forecast called for rain tonight, had been delightful. They'd dressed up for their date, even though they were staying home. She wore a snug-fitting navy dress, a set of pearls, and heeled sandals. Judah wore a light blue button-up shirt and a navy tie that matched her dress.

"Care to dance?" He extended his hand toward her.

"Yes, I would. Thank you."

He led her to the far side of the pavers. The area wasn't spacious, but they had danced on their veranda in the past. The ocean waves rolling in and out created perfect background music.

"You look beautiful." He kissed her cheek, sending shivers up her neck.

"Thanks. You look dashing yourself."

"Why, thank you, lovely lady." Positioning her right hand in his, his other hand sliding around her waist, he drew her closer. "Love you, Pais," he whispered near her ear as they swayed to the nautical music.

"Love you, too."

They moved languidly across the pavers, almost as one, in tune to each other's movements. After a while, Judah tipped her back like dancing couples sometimes did at the end of a song in the movies. She appreciated this time of being alone together and her feeling more normal, finally.

He brought her to a standing position, never breaking eye contact. His lips brushed hers with butterfly softness. The wind swirled around them, reminding her it would get blustery soon, and according to the weather report, rain was on its way. Judah's kiss deepened and Paisley snuggled against the warmth of his body, at home in his arms.

He left a trail of kisses from the corner of her lips, across her cheek, and down her neck, being so gentle with her. She stared up at the few remaining stars and a childhood rhyme came to mind. *I wish I may, I wish I might, have the wish I wish tonight.*

She wished she and Judah would have a beautiful life together. A lasting romance. And she hoped they'd have a family. A breath caught in her throat as he led her into another slow dance. She wanted a child who looked like Piper with dark hair. A daughter who she might occasionally see Misty Gale in.

"Is something wrong?"

He must have felt her tightening up.

"Nothing's wrong." Exhaling, she let go of the thoughts as best she could. *Lord, help us heal,* she silently prayed the words she thought many times over the last few days. She wanted tonight to be special, the start of something wonderful and right with Judah. A new beginning for them.

He'd been kind and caring toward her all evening. Yet, something concerned her about the cautious way he treated her. As if he were being China-cup delicate with her. She wasn't fragile. Yes, she needed inner healing. But she was doing much better physically—didn't the doctor say so?—and getting stronger, every day. She wanted, no, she needed, for tonight to be more than Judah tiptoeing around her. She needed them back as a real couple. Whole.

Did she dare do something to force him to view her as an independent, strong woman who wanted intimacy with him as much as he wanted it? That she'd eagerly anticipated tonight, too?

An impish idea came to mind, and she stepped out of his embrace. She grabbed hold of his tie and tugged him forward. "Come with me, Mister."

He broke into a wide smile. "Where are you taking me?"

"Remove your shoes." She slipped out of her sandals and felt the roughness of the pavers beneath her bare feet. "Hurry up. Take them off." She tugged on his tie again.

"Okay, okay." He laughed, sounding nervous. "Give me a second." Good thing he wore slip-on dress shoes, but he had to bend over and peel off his socks.

"You might want to roll up your pant legs, too."

"Thanks for the warning." He gazed at her like he wondered what in the world she planned to do, but his eyes sparkled as he rolled up his pants.

The wind blew off the ocean like usual, and they trudged through their sandy beach in front of the cottage, her leading him by his tie. "Hurry up, slowpoke."

"Yes, ma'am. What do you have up your sleeve, Mrs. Grant?" He said, "Mrs. Grant," like a caress.

Tingles shot up her middle. She kept leading him, walking through the mud squishing between her toes, then into the water until their ankles were submerged in the waves rolling in. Then their shins.

Standing in knee-deep water swishing around them, she faced him beneath the light of the moon peeking out around a dark cloud. She let go of his tie and ran her palms up his smooth shirt, feeling his pounding heart, staring into his dreamy blue eyes. She clasped her hands behind his neck. "Remind you of anything?"

He wrapped his arms around her as a wave sloshed against them. "Our second wedding?"

"Mmhmm. I never want us to forget it."

"I won't. I promise," he whispered huskily.

He moved in to kiss her, but she held up one finger over his mouth, stopping him. She smiled, hoping he saw in her sparkling eyes how much she wanted their playfulness, romancing, and their lovemaking, later.

"I need you to recognize that I'm okay."

Judah nodded, still staring into her eyes.

"I'm not a China doll."

"I didn't think you were, Pais." A puzzled look crossed his face as he smoothed his hands across her cheeks, pushing her hair back, tangling his fingers in her long strands.

"I want everything tonight holds for us." Paisley kissed the corner of his lips softly.

"Me too."

Slowly, she planted more kisses across his freshly shaved cheek. Heard his soft groan.

"But"—she pushed her fingertips against his chest,

moving with the sway of the sea buffeting her—"I want you to love me for who I am today."

"Okay." He still wore a befuddled expression.

Taking a step back into the cold surf, she grinned, imagining what she'd do next to prove to him that she was Paisley Rose Grant, a healthy woman. A wildly-in-love-with-her-husband wife. A lady who didn't want her husband gazing at her like some broken kid.

"I love you so much, Judah." She faced the waves.

"Pais?"

With her hands raised as if she were about to fly downhill on a roller coaster, she ran farther into the sea. Cold water splashed against her thighs, then her waist. Laughing, gasping a little, she shivered, and her teeth chattered, but she didn't focus on the chilling temps. Her attention was on her and Judah rediscovering each other as a couple and having some fun with flirting.

Suddenly, he stood beside her, picking her up, laughing, twirling her in the waves. And she kissed him deeply, momentously, sealing—she hoped—the truth in his heart that she was ready to be his wife in every way.

They kissed hungrily, passionately, clinging to each other, all the way back to the seashore.

"I c-can't b-believe you d-did—"

She pressed her lips against his, deepening the kiss, silencing him.

The wind sliced against them, but she was numb to anything but the heat of the kisses they exchanged all the way up the beach. All the way to their cottage.

All the way into their bedroom, where she dropped her shoes and gently kicked the door closed behind them.

Thirty-eight

The next morning, with his freshly-made blueprints spread across a table in the project house, Judah pointed out his plans for the kitchen to James Weston, his father-in-law's neighbor. Mom had told him she wanted a center island with a butcher block. Callie requested white shiplap for the walls. Kathleen asked for plenty of storage space since the three women planned to merge cooking utensils. They each had preferences he'd incorporated into the simple drawings.

If there was any hope of accelerating the project, he needed to hire more workers. James, a godsend, had volunteered his time, but this massive remodel required laborers who could do hard work every day. Was the older gentleman up to doing strenuous activities?

"You figure on gutting the whole thing?" Sniffing, James peered at the blueprints through his reading glasses.

"Yep. That's the plan."

"That'll take more muscle than I have." James eyed him skeptically.

"Lots of work and a large sledgehammer will do the trick," Judah said jokingly.

"Okay, then." The older man fingered his glasses up onto this head. "Where do you want me to start?"

"Why don't you check through the cupboards and make sure the ladies didn't put any stuff in them? Then we'll shimmy the fridge and stove out of the way so I can smash the cupboards." He looked forward to that part. Chip Gaines made demolition look easy on TV.

Since Paisley was going by Bert's diner today to apply for work, Judah had asked her to post a job listing for him on the community bulletin board. In the wake of Hurricane Blaine, there must be some locals in need of extra work. He checked the volume on his cell so he wouldn't miss any calls.

When Paisley kissed him goodbye this morning, lingering in his arms, she teasingly asked if he wanted her to join his crew. Her whispered words and the way she nuzzled his earlobe tempted him to forget work altogether. Grinning, he told her he wouldn't get anything accomplished if she were one of his employees.

He sighed at the remembrance of her sleeping in his arms last night, so thankful for their date and what they were sharing as a married couple, finally. He chuckled over the image of her leading him into the water by his tie. And all that followed afterward. *Thank You, God. I'm grateful You've worked such a healing miracle in our lives.*

Callie bustled in through the front door, grocery bags in hand, and came to a stop, glaring at Judah, then James. "What are you two doing here?"

"I'm going to tear out the kitchen cupboards." Judah lifted his sledgehammer.

Her jaw dropped. "Not today. Not now!"

"Yes, today. Yes, now."

"Good morning, Callie." James's voice turned pudding soft. "Nice to see you."

"James. Why, pray tell, are you here?"

"Helping Judah. We've got the muscles for the job." James flexed his arm.

Judah chuckled.

Callie, seemingly flustered by his comment, or simply by James's presence, turned red. "I didn't know you were starting today. I made plans already. Important plans."

"What do you mean?" Judah asked.

"I have a meeting here in a few minutes."

"I'm sorry to cause a scheduling conflict." Nothing he could do about that now. "As you know, we're on a tight schedule. If you ladies want to be able to move in soon—"

"We do. I get it. Fine." She trudged across the room.

"Why don't you meet at Bert's?" James trailed her through the empty living room. "Isn't that where you and Maggie usually meet to gab about everything under the sun?"

Judah chuckled at the man's boldness. Or was it provocation?

"I'll have you know, we are meeting for more important matters than gabbing." Callie's voice swelled. "Town matters that don't concern you!" Her footsteps thudded up the stairs.

"Well, I'll be." James reentered the kitchen, pocketing his reading glasses. "I bet she and those gal friends are up to their usual troublemaking."

"Oh, well. Let's move the fridge to the outer wall." Hopefully, James could handle moderate manual labor. Judah checked his phone. No calls yet.

An hour later, the sledgehammer had done its worst. Fragmented chunks of wood lay scattered across the kitchen. Dust filled the room.

Mom, Kathleen, Maggie, Miss Patty, and Sue Taylor had all marched through the entryway, coughing and commenting on the mess, the noise, and the musty smell of sawdust before continuing through the living room and up the stairs. Even Paige breezed through and waved. Why was his sister-in-law involved in this meeting about who knew what?

"I told you they were up to mischief." James smirked.

All Judah's loud pounding and the crashing sounds of wood hitting the floor had to have annoyed Callie and the rest of the ladies. But he'd been asked to tackle this job quickly, and that's what he planned to do.

The next person who showed up on the property surprised him too. He and James were hauling armloads of smashed wood pieces and hurling them into a big pile in the front yard when Forest exited his white rental car.

"I heard you could use some help."

"That's the truth. You interested?" What would Paige say if he hired Forest? Judah dropped his load, making a clattering sound, then shook his hand. "Did you know Paige is here?"

"Saw her car out front." Forest whistled as his gaze traveled over the old house. "Paisley put up an ad in the diner. Since I've decided to stick around Basalt Bay, I thought I could lend a hand here on a part-time basis until I finish up the case, if that's okay. After that, I can work full time, if you still need the help." He pulled a pair of brand-new-looking gloves from his pockets and slipped them on.

James rubbed his hands together. "We're not getting anything done standing around gabbing like those yakity-yaks upstairs."

"Glad to have you help out, Forest." The rest—his involvement with Paige and Piper—was up to him and Paige to work out. Not Judah's concern.

For the remainder of the morning, the trio hauled armloads of broken wood outside and finished the kitchen demolition. Judah and Forest shuffled the fridge and oven onto the porch to be hauled to the dump later. Hopefully, the floorboards would support their weight.

Finally, the women traipsed back through the kitchen, one by one, and exited the front door. Each person paused to peruse the room or comment about their progress. Paige and Forest stared at each other without speaking.

"You made enough racket to break our eardrums," Callie grouched.

"But look at this room, will you?" Kathleen smiled brightly. "You've gotten so much accomplished. Good work, gentlemen."

"Thank you." Judah nodded at her.

"It's looking great, Son. I knew you could do this." Mom strolled through the open space. "I can't wait to see how it turns out."

"Judah?" Paige appealed to him with large brown eyes that reminded him of Paisley's. "Could I speak with you?"

"Sure thing." He met Forest's concerned gaze, then followed his sister-in-law outside. "What's up?" He stood opposite her near the pile of discarded wood.

"Why is he here? Did you hire him?" She crossed her arms, glaring at him.

"Forest offered to help." Hadn't he guessed this might be a sore spot for her?

"Why isn't he leaving town if he's done gathering evidence?"

"You would know the answer to that better than me." He shuffled his shoulders a couple of times.

"Meaning?"

"My guess is he wants to be around his daughter. You, too."

"Did he say anything?"

"No."

"I don't want him here."

"Why not?" He held up his hands, palms out. "Sorry. Not my business."

"No, it isn't, but I asked you to come out here." She dug the toe of her black canvas shoe into the dirt. "Don't get involved, okay? You shouldn't have hired him. I mean it, Judah." She trudged to her car without glancing back.

"Sorry."

He heaved a sigh and returned to the house. In the kitchen, he picked up a hammer, ready to pound nails and expend some energy. "We have work to do. Who's with me?"

"Count me in." James raised his hand.

"You still want my help?" Forest stood by the door as if ready to leave.

"You're welcome to keep working if you have the time. You and Paige have your own stuff to work out."

"Okay, thanks. I have one question."

"Shoot."

"Know of any places for rent? I made a mistake in leaving her before." Forest shrugged. "Staying here, trying to make amends, working it out the best I can is what I hope to do."

"Sounds like a good starting place."

"Yeah." If only Paige would agree.

Thirty-nine

*After only a few days of wedded bliss, Paige knew
she loved Forest more than any other person on the
planet. Their fairytale honeymoon was just the
beginning of a beautiful life together.*

On her way home from the meeting Aunt Callie invited
her to, and still feeling frustrated about Forest working with
Judah—since when was he a carpenter?—Paige parked in front
of her old art gallery. There was something she'd put off doing.
Something she still needed to do. She exited her car and stood
outside the building where she'd been so proud for people to
come and enjoy the talents of local artists, including her own
work. The art gallery had been her dream-come-true before the
hurricanes, and Edward Grant, ruined everything.

"Goodbye." She patted the door like she might have
petted a dog for the last time. The gesture was symbolic, saying

goodbye and letting the gallery go. But why did it have to hurt so badly?

Maybe releasing this dream was about more than letting a building go. It was like it represented all the dreams in her life she'd let go of—her marriage, being a prolific artist, owning her own business. That made the farewell even more bittersweet.

She would have done anything to get the old place repaired and functional again. Too bad Edward undercut her chances of succeeding because of his greediness. What would happen to it now with him locked up?

Tears moistened her eyes, and she squeezed her eyelids shut. None of that. Feeling sorry for herself wouldn't help anything.

"Why, if it isn't Paige Cedars."

Mia's shrill voice tightened Paige's already taut nerves.

Gulping, she faced the other woman. "Hello, Mia."

"What are you doing on Edward's property?" She rattled the doorknob and glared at Paige as if she might have caused some damage. "You're not trespassing again, are you?"

Again? "No one owns the sidewalk. Besides, how does this concern you?"

"As Edward's personal assistant, if it involves him, it involves me. We wouldn't want Deputy Brian to have to put you in jail with Craig, now, would we?" She snickered. "On second thought, just imagine being locked up in a cell with all that male energy. Whoa, baby." She made a low wolf whistle.

Paige stifled a groan. "I'm sure it's an awful experience for him." She still felt terrible for her part in his capture.

"No doubt. Still." Mia lifted her chin. "Can I give you a little girl-to-girl advice? Edward has plans for this building, so you should stay away from it. Don't be discussing his dealings with you or your sister with anyone, either. I'd hate for anything … unfortunate … to happen."

Was she threatening Paige?

"Who are you to tell me anything? Are you the one who wrote—"

"What's this I hear about you and that yummy detective?" Mia cut into her question. "I can see why he's such a temptation. Lucy said you two had enough sparks at Bert's to set the place on fire."

No way was she commenting on that. "Goodbye, Mia." Gritting her teeth, Paige strode to her car and slid behind the steering wheel.

Mia followed and grabbed ahold of the door handle, hindering Paige from closing it. "One might surmise you and Forest had a dirty little affair to hide. But I understand. I couldn't take my eyes off him during my interview, either." Her fake eyelashes fluttered. "You don't have a claim on him, do you?"

"I do not."

"Excellent." Mia released the handle and scurried down the sidewalk, her fancy high heels clicking double-time.

Paige slammed the door and gunned the engine. Mia was going too far. Bossing Paige around. Acting flirty about Craig. Now, Forest?

Back at her house, Paige flopped down on the couch, her words that she didn't have a claim on Forest taunting her. Now, Mia would probably go right after him. But why should Paige care?

Because it was Mia Till, that's why!

Flinging her arm over her face, she pictured the way Forest had looked at the project house with dust covering his brows and nose. How he gazed tenderly at her. Why was he sticking around Basalt Bay? Because of Piper? That was a great reason, right?

However, before he knew anything about having a daughter, didn't he say he cared for Paige? And wasn't she the one who said if a man loved her like Judah loved Paisley, she'd sing and dance in the street? But that was before she told Forest they were finished. And before she watched him get wrecked and broken about being a dad and not knowing. That mental replay still churned in her mind, troubling her, making her feel guilty.

If she were being honest with herself, she wished he were staying in town because of her, because of what they shared three years ago. Because he wanted her back. Not that she'd tell him that. And their two-week marriage wasn't some "dirty little affair" like Mia said, either.

Someone knocked at the front door and Paige jumped up. Still nervous after the warnings she'd received, she opened the door just enough to peer out with the chain fastened.

Bess Grant stood on the porch, dressed in a gold turtleneck sweater and black slacks, smiling at her. "Hello, Paige."

"Oh, hi."

Why was Judah's mom here? Quickly unlatching the lock, she yanked the door open.

"I hope you don't mind me popping in like this," Bess said. "I wanted to discuss something with you earlier, but I thought we should talk by ourselves."

"Of course, come in." Paige stepped back. "Welcome. Have a seat."

Bess sat down on the recliner, gazing around the room. "What a charming home you have."

"Thank you. Can I get you something? Tea? Water?"

"Just a chat, if you don't mind."

"Absolutely." Paige dropped onto the couch, clasping her hands, trying not to look as nervous as she felt. What was this unexpected visit from Bess Grant about?

"You're probably wondering why I've barged in on you like this." Bess pulled a folded piece of paper from her large handbag. "I've been talking with my accountant about the gallery."

"Oh?"

"You see, Edward failed to sign all the necessary paperwork to proceed with ownership of the building. Considering his current circumstances"—Bess did a brief eye-roll—"I am in the dubious predicament of having to sign them for him."

"Oh." Paige sagged against the back of the couch. For a moment, she thought Bess meant something else. That Edward couldn't get the building because he failed to sign the papers.

"Or I might just refute it altogether." Bess chuckled lightly. "The man is in jail."

"What do you mean?"

"It was nice having an art gallery in town." Bess smoothed her free hand over the golden fabric at her neckline. "What might be done about restoring it?"

"Restoring it?" Excitement darted through Paige. "Are you serious?"

"It was such a great resource for the community. Don't you think so?"

"Yes! I loved having the gallery available for local artists to display their work. And for tourists and locals to enjoy it." Was Bess implying there might be a way for the gallery to reopen? Heart hammering, Paige willed herself to stay calm, cool, and collected. Yeah, right. The thought of having a gallery again pulsated inspiration and hope through her, especially considering she just told it goodbye.

"Did you want to give it up?" Bess set the piece of paper in her lap.

"Not at all. It was taken from me quite abruptly by ... well, you know." Paige shrugged. "I enjoyed my business before the hurricanes hit."

"I thought so." Bess nodded. "What would you say to us working together in a partnership for the good of the community and the enhancement of the arts in Basalt Bay?"

"That sounds amazing!" Paige wanted to jump up and down and squeal with joy. "But what exactly are you suggesting?"

"Here's my idea." Bess scooted forward in the chair. "How would it be if you and I, and one other interested party, partnered together and got the gallery up and going again?"

"Do you mean it?"

"I do." Bess passed the folded piece of paper to her. "Read this and tell me what you think."

Paige clasped the official-looking document and read out loud, "'I authorize Paige Cedars to resume control of the building formally called the Basalt Bay Art Gallery and Coffee Shop.' Bess! This is amazing!" It was signed by Bess and notarized by Geoffrey Carnegie, the postmaster. "How—? I don't know what to—"

Another name on the document leaped out at her. Below Bess's name, Forest Harper's signature was written in his bold script. Why was Forest involved in this?

"What do you say?" Bess asked softly.

"What does he ... I mean ... is Forest the other partner?" How could that work? Was he going to be involved in every area of her life now?

"The three of us would be equal co-owners, if you're okay with the arrangement." Bess placed her palm on her chest. "I don't know what's transpired between you two, and it's none of my business, but he seems like such a nice guy."

"He is." Sigh. Could Paige handle not only figuring out how to co-parent with Forest, but becoming co-owners in a business with him, too? Could she accept such generosity from him? Was he doing this out of a sense of obligation because of Piper? That dug at her pride.

Although, to say no simply because of his involvement was unthinkable. Opening the gallery again would be a great opportunity for her and other local artists. A benefit for the community too. "What would I have to do? I refunded the artists after the hurricane damage, but there are some remaining funds from the insurance money that could go into repairs."

"Excellent. The day-to-day workings will be up to you. The three of us—you, me, and Forest—will form a board." Bess clasped her hands in her lap. "Can you create a game plan for getting the gallery functional as soon as possible?"

"Yes, certainly." Tonight. Immediately.

"Wonderful. Two hurricanes hit our city and ruined a lot of things we cherished and valued. I believe if we keep working together, we'll get Basalt Bay back to its old self." A sad look crossed Bess's face. "I'm sorry for my ex-husband's takeover of your building. I remember the day you and Paisley came up to the house. How horrible he treated you both."

"That wasn't your fault. And this offer is so generous of you ... and Forest." Saying his name, she gulped.

"I'm righting a wrong. Sometimes we must do that." She smiled kindly. Yet her words dug a trench in Paige's heart. Had Judah told his mom about Paige and Forest's past? "You're my son's sister-in-law, so you're a part of my family, too." Bess stood and hugged Paige, an embrace she gladly returned.

"This may sound funny, but earlier I stopped by the gallery and told it goodbye." Paige chuckled. "Now my brain's whirling with possibilities."

"Good. I'm sure there will be plenty of hurdles to cross."

"No doubt. But I can't thank you enough."

"Your grand opening will be all the thanks I need." Bess moved to the door. "How about meeting me tomorrow at the bank and we'll get your signature on the paperwork?"

"Okay. Thank you."

After Bess left, Paige sank onto the couch, reading the notice and the signatures again. Why was Forest doing this?

"I'm righting a wrong," Bess said. Any chance she meant Paige should go and do likewise?

Forty

*Two days after arriving in Basalt Bay, Forest
received an emergency call from Elinore's mother—
Elinore had been in a head-on collision and might
not make it. He had to leave immediately and go
to her.*

Forest sat down in the same booth at the back of Bert's diner where he met Paige a week ago. This morning he received a cryptic text from Paige asking him to meet her here. Did Bess inform her that he'd be a partner in her gallery? Was she upset about his interference?

He sighed, dreading Paige being angry with him again.

When he'd overheard Judah and Bess discussing Edward's takeover of businesses in town while the owners were down on their luck, including Paige's gallery and coffee shop, he felt an urge to help. Maybe God was nudging him to be generous and supportive of her. Maybe Forest wanted to get on Paige's good side, too. Even if he didn't understand what prompted her to not tell him about Piper, he wanted to do his part to make amends. With his involvement in Edward's case nearing an end, he felt the freedom to make a few changes in his life—taking the job with Judah, investing in the art gallery, and relocating here.

He liked his job as a detective, but he wanted more in life too. He wanted Paige and Piper, a family, if only he could convince Paige of that.

Paisley hustled over to his table carrying a glass coffee container. "Hey, Forest. Want some coffee?"

"Yes, please. You got the job. How's it going?"

"Great. This was my first job back in the day." She tipped over a coffee cup and filled it. "Cream?"

"Black."

"You got it." She leaned down closer as if trying to speak without anyone hearing her. "Did you mean to sit back here at the k—?" Her face reddened. "I mean, do you want me to find you another seat near the front of the diner?"

"No, that's okay." Recalling what the other server called this booth, a kissing booth, his cheeks warmed. Gave him hope too. Paige knew the table's nickname. "Paige told me to meet her here, so I'll stay."

"All right." She smiled wider. "I spoke to Judah for the first time right here at this booth."

"Really?"

"Yep. I was sixteen. I'll be back to take your order in a few." She scurried away, filling other customers' cups with coffee.

The door jangled. Paige entered the diner, met his gaze, even smiled in his direction. Her smile alone could set his heart on fire.

As she crossed the room, a sense of awe hit him that the pretty woman heading his way had once been his wife, and that she was the mother of his daughter. Was Paige here for friendly reasons? Or did she ask for this meeting because she was upset with him for contributing to the gallery, or for his work at the project house, or because he arrested Craig?

She said hello to a few people. Waved at her sister.

He stood, unclear whether nervousness or chivalry dictated his actions. "Paige."

"Hello, Forest." She sat down on the seat across from him.

He sat back down, gazing at her, taking in her smiling lips.

Paisley followed with a cup and the container of coffee again. "Hey, Paige."

"Morning."

Paisley didn't ask if her sister wanted coffee or creamer. Just filled the cup, slid it toward her, and dropped two individual creamers on the table beside the cup.

"Thanks."

Before scurrying away, Paisley dished Forest a warning look. What? Treat Paige nice, or he'd have to deal with her? Treating Paige "nice" was all he had in mind.

Paige prepped her coffee and took a couple of sips. Then gave him a long stare—one he didn't break contact with—before dropping her gaze to the mug she cradled between her hands.

"Why did you want us to meet here at the kissing booth?" He couldn't resist mentioning the term in a teasing tone.

"I didn't mean anything—"

"I know. Sorry. I couldn't help myself." Although, he enjoyed seeing her blush. "Seriously, what did you want to talk with me about?"

"Bess stopped by my house yesterday." She ran her finger around the rim of the cup. "I signed papers this morning. Why'd you do it? Why stick your neck out for me like that?"

"I'd do anything for you. And Piper." He cleared his throat. "I have some savings and want to help."

"That was really thoughtful of you." She studied him, and he tried not to squirm. "What I'm wondering is … what, um, do you expect in return? In exchange for your generosity, I mean."

What was she talking about? Oh, did she mean— "Hey, listen, I don't have any ulterior motives, if that's what you're getting at. You're my ex-wife, my daughter's mother, and I'm willing to pitch in and help where I can."

Her cheeks hued a cute pink. He didn't dare glance at her mouth. No allowing his thoughts to roam in romantic directions, either. Too many things remained unsaid between them for him to dare cross that line in the sand.

"I'm sorry, but I had to ask." She sighed. "Getting my gallery back means the world to me. Thank you for doing this, Forest."

He gulped at hearing his name said so softly on her lips. "Sure."

"And the job with Judah? A carpenter, huh?" So she was here, partially, because of that.

"It's how I worked my way through college. Odd jobs with a crew building a subdivision." He took a swallow of his coffee. "If Basalt's going to be my home, I want to help out here, too."

"Your home?"

"I plan to be near Piper. Watching her grow up." He'd tell her he wanted to be near her too, would never leave her again, but he doubted she wanted to hear that, yet. "I'm sorry for threatening you about custody. That was just a bad reaction."

A startled look crossed her face. "You're not going through with it?"

"Not if we can work out something amicably. If I'm living in town, I can see her regularly, huh?"

"Certainly. That's great news."

Yet she looked nervous, nibbling on her lower lip, which meant he was gazing at her mouth. She was so lovely—delicate, yet strong; introverted, yet outgoing. How could she have such contradictions? Maybe that's what attracted him to her. And he *was* still drawn to her. Still wanted her for his wife.

Paisley stopped at their table, notepad in hand. "What can I get for you guys?"

"Nothing."

"This is fine." They spoke at once.

"Okay." Paisley stuffed the pad of paper in her apron, eyeing them. "Need more coffee?"

"No." Forest twirled his empty cup between his fingers.

"No, thanks." Paige shoved her cup toward the center of the table.

"All right, then." Paisley strode to the next table.

Why did Paige choose this noisy diner to talk, anyway? Especially with her sister checking on them every few minutes. "What would you say to us getting out of here? Would you take a beach walk with me?"

"Because I'm such a fan of the beach?" She gave him a wry expression.

"Might be more private to talk."

"I guess." She didn't sound enthused.

Sighing, he stood and dropped a twenty on the table.

A few minutes later, after a silent walk to the seashore, they paused in front of City Beach. The ever-present wind greeted them, but it felt refreshing.

"You don't seem to mind the tumultuous waves like before. You told me you didn't love the ocean."

"That was before Piper. I don't want her growing up with a dread of the sea as I did."

"And now?" He pointed toward the waves barreling up the sand. "This doesn't bother you?"

"Sometimes it still does. I'm working on it." She groaned. "I owe you an apology, Forest. Yet, it's so difficult for me to do."

He understood what she meant about apologizing being difficult. Weren't his own failings in their past something he owed her an apology about, yet struggled to find the words to say, to mean? Typical of blame. Both parties condemning the other person, yet not knowing how to make things right.

"We both made mistakes." He met her gaze.

"I know that."

He chuckled at her bluntness.

"However, I am sorry for not telling you about Piper." Her voice softened but not to where he couldn't hear her. "Because of my anger, and jealousy, I caused you to miss out on her birth and babyhood. I justified my actions based on your abandonment, but that was wrong of me." Her smile wobbled. "You'll make our girl a great daddy. She's lucky to have you as her father."

"Thanks. That means a lot." Paige's words tugged on his heart, soothing and healing. That she wouldn't stand in the way of him being a father to Piper was a relief. Maybe it meant they could work out some of the other things between them, too. His eyes misted up. Wretched tears.

The way Paige crossed her arms around her middle, as if protecting herself, revealed her uncertainty or worry. Forest wanted to reassure her, to tell her all was forgiven and forgotten, to take her in his arms and make her realize they were still right for each other. But those things would take time and more healing.

He had things to confess too. Things that stuck in his throat. *Lord, help me to be honest and have Your grace living in me.*

He took a breath, released it. "I'm sorry for the pain I caused you, too. For leaving as I did. Not stepping up when I should have." The words, the pain, tore loose from his heart, washing away some of his grudges. "In leaving you, I made a terrible error in judgment. I knew it as soon as I drove away. But I felt guilty for Elinore's accident, too. I was troubled that what I told her in the last phone call may have been the cause of it."

"Oh, Forest, I never thought of that."

He nodded, unable to speak for a few moments. "Even though you and I had that awful fight, I should have returned and tried to work things out with you. We promised each other a lifetime of love."

"I know." A tear dripped down her cheek and she brushed it away.

He gazed deeply into her eyes, trying to read if she were sad because of their mutual hurts or if, maybe, he'd find a shred of love left inside her for him. He took a chance at her rejecting him and gently drew her into his arms, hugging her like a friend. She trembled, not pulling away, and a mix of protectiveness and longing came over him.

She stepped back. "Anyhow, that's what I needed to say, why I asked you to meet with me, so we could speak honestly about the past. And to tell you how grateful I am for your help with the gallery. Thank you. Your financial backing and support is truly remarkable."

"You're welcome." Their gazes snagged. "Is there … is there any chance you can forgive me?" He felt the anguish of the question all the way to his toes. Was a second chance possible for them? Or was it already too late?

"I'm trying. Honestly, I am."

"That's good."

If she knew God's love the way he'd come to know His love, they could pray together, sharing in their faith, and asking Him to help them both with forgiveness and grace. Forest would have to keep praying about that by himself.

"I said this before, but I still love you." He was taking a risk, exposing his vulnerable feelings, and possibly severing all hope of a romantic future together, but he had to tell her how he felt.

"How can you say that after three years with no communication?" She stared at him, one eyebrow lifted. "I still care for you. But love? I'm not sure we truly loved each other before."

"Paige, I was crazy about you." He'd like to pull her into his arms and kiss her to convince her of his feelings. What would she say if he did?

She started walking again, and he matched his stride to hers.

"We were infatuated with each other, attracted, lustful, even." She shook her head doubtfully. "But love?"

"If we weren't in love, I don't know what love is." He linked her arm, drawing her to a stop. "Please, can we talk about this?"

"What good will come of talking? We've both apologized."

She pulled away from his loose hold. "Let's focus on you and Piper spending time together. That's what's important."

"And that's all?" The knife of unrequited love turned over in his gut. "You don't want anything to happen romantically between us?"

She stared at him for the longest time as if she were trying to figure out something. "When I picture your kisses"—her cheeks turned a beautiful rosy color—"I long for them like a dream I never want to awaken from."

Her poetic tone stirred his senses.

"When I remember how we cherished each other for those two weeks, I turn weak at the knees, almost heartsick with the wonder and the loss of it."

Her brutal honesty tore up his emotional fortress.

"Can't we try again?"

"I don't think so. Too much pain lies between us."

"Even when you've imagined kissing me?"

"Even then."

A great sadness filled him that seemed to match hers. He'd prayed and hoped for a different outcome. Wasn't willing to give up. "I'd love the chance to be a real family, to be Piper's dad. But to be your husband again would be an honor beyond anything I can imagine."

A shadow crossed her face as gray as the clouds hanging low over the ocean. "Looks like we're in for a storm. We should get back." Not meeting his gaze, she trudged toward town, sending up billows of gritty sand in her wake.

He let her go. Her heart seemed walled up. And he had no one to blame but himself.

Forty-one

With a pry bar and muscle power, Judah hacked away at the lower portions of Sheetrock around the perimeter of the kitchen where flooding from the hurricanes had damaged it. Forest and James were prying up rotten floorboards on the porch. Considering Maggie's recent injury when she tripped on the stairs Judah made at Paul's, and the accident Callie had with a damaged rocking chair, he didn't want to take any chances on the ladies or their guests stepping through aged wood and hurting themselves.

As he worked, an image of the card Pastor Sagle gave him a few days ago flashed through his thoughts like an unwanted neon sign. He'd tucked it in his Bible—out of sight, out of mind. Why did he have to think of the card now? Was the Holy Spirit reminding him it was time to pray for his dad?

He sighed.

Lord, You know this is a tough subject for me. But everyone deserves grace and mercy. Even Edward Grant. Even my—

"Hey, Judah." Forest leaned through the front door wiping sawdust off his face. "We've got company. Mia Till's here."

"Aw, man. What does she want?"

"Who knows? I told her she couldn't enter until we replaced the wood on the porch."

"Good for you."

"Can you step outside and talk to her? I can't hold her back much longer."

"Be right there."

"Oh, Judah, there you are." Mia's heels clomped across the floorboards straight toward him. "Aren't you a sight for sore eyes?"

"How did you—?" Forest stared dumbfoundedly at her.

"You didn't expect me to wait in the rain, did you?" She grinned up at him. "My word, you are handsome with all that dust in your hair. Makes a girl just want to run her fingers through it. Too bad Paige let you go."

Forest's face hued a brilliant red. "I told you—"

"You're sweet, but I won't be ignored."

Judah felt bad for his coworker's discomfort, but he was relieved Mia had someone other than him to sink her claws into. He finished yanking out the board, which broke into several pieces, creating a white dust cloud.

Mia coughed. "Do you have to do that while I'm standing right here?" She waved the air with her manicured fingers. "Stop, will you? It's important that I speak to you."

"Should have waited outside like Forest told you to do."

As soon as Judah stood up, she wrapped her arms around his waist, hugging him, and stroking his back. He peeled her fingers away from him, disturbed by her proximity, strong perfumed scent, and her roaming fingers.

"If you hadn't noticed, I'm busy, Mia."

"Doing carpentry work? Judah Grant, you're better than this." She scowled at the gutted kitchen.

"It suits me." Better than he would have imagined.

"I came here to talk with you. Can't you spare me a few minutes?" She cast a glowering look toward Forest. "If you don't mind, this is a private conversation."

"Be nice to my workers," Judah told her.

"I'll be nice all right." She finger-waved at Forest. "Talk with you in a minute, hon."

Grimacing, Forest lunged out the door. Judah bit back a chuckle. Mia certainly had a way of wrapping her tentacles around a man. At least Forest was single, unless he and Paige had reconciled. By the gloomy look on his face when he arrived this morning, the discussion Paisley said happened at Bert's yesterday wasn't a romantic one.

Judah knew firsthand how hard reconciliation could be. He might have some words of advice for Forest. But however good his intentions might be, unwanted advice wouldn't help anyone.

"Are you going to stop staring into space and listen to me?" Mia huffed.

He dusted off his jeans and flannel shirt, which stirred up more dust, making Mia hack again. "So, what's the problem?"

"First"—she ticked her right index finger against her left pinkie—"Craig wants to see you, today. Why he imagines I'm his messenger, I have no idea." She leaned toward Judah, her lips parting in a wide smile. "I knew you two good-looking men had to be brothers. I saw the resemblance all along."

Sure she did. However, the genetics of their possible brotherhood remained a mystery.

"What else?" Judah wanted to get this over with.

"Your father wants you sworn in as mayor immediately. This stalling and"—she lifted her hands toward the bare walls—"pretending to be a builder must stop."

"Tell him 'no thanks.' I happen to enjoy this 'pretending.'" He set his hand on her shoulder and nudged her toward the door. "Thanks for stopping by. Sorry you wasted your time driving out here."

"But your father expects—"

"I don't care what he expects. I'm working, so if you'll excuse me."

She glared at him, all iterations of flirtation gone. "If only you knew what awaits you if you don't do what he says."

Was that a threat? He clenched his jaw. "Be careful on your way out."

"You didn't hear my third point."

"Don't care to, either." Picking up the pry bar, he knelt and slammed it against the Sheetrock, sending particles bursting into the air.

"Judah, stop, and listen."

He held the tool midair. He'd give her three seconds.

"There's news buzzing around town about Paige and that detective." She smoothed her palm over his shoulder. He sloughed it off. "It'd be a shame for everyone to hear what she's been up to with him."

"Leave it be, will you?" He rammed the pry bar against the wall, taking out some of his frustration on the board.

"One other thing." She nearly shouted in his ear. "Your mother plans to reopen the art gallery with Paige. Her doing that without Edward's approval is going to cause trouble."

Fury zinged through him. "Forest!"

"Yeah, boss?" He leaned in through the doorway, eyeing Mia like he might a snake.

"Escort Miss Till safely off the property, will you?"

"That won't be necessary." She glowered.

"Come on, Miss Till. I'll help you through the maze of broken boards." Forest grimaced at Judah as if saying, *"Thanks a lot."*

"Fine." Mia linked her arms with Forest's, stroking his biceps, her eyes sparkling up at him. "You're so strong. You don't seem like Paige's type at all."

Forest cast another grimace toward Judah then led Mia out the door.

Forty-two

Outside Craig's jail cell, Judah couldn't help remembering his own lock-up in this chamber a little over a month ago. Even though that had been only for a couple of hours, he felt empathy for the man who appeared as miserable as Judah had felt.

Edward wasn't in the other cell. Since Judah called ahead to make an appointment, maybe Deputy Brian had moved him into the interrogation room.

"Thanks for coming by." Craig thrust his hands over his dark hair. "Sorry I had to send Mia. She can be intense."

"That's putting it mildly."

Craig chuckled, his unshaven face pale. "I hoped it wouldn't come to this. Locked in here with nothing but time to reconsider my whole life."

"Sorry, man." Witnessing his previous friend, the man who intervened on Paisley's behalf, caged and looking at his wit's end, tore at Judah, even though they'd had their difficulties too. "What did you need to speak with me about?"

"I thought we should get a few things aired before they haul me to another facility." Craig's shoulders slumped. "Hopefully, I won't end up in the same courtyard in prison as Edward."

"Will it come to that?"

"If I don't yield the information Deputy Brian and the detective are pursuing, the deputy says I'll be accused of what Edward is accused of."

"Do you still feel loyalty to the mayor?"

"Big Daddy-o?" He snorted. "No, but I'll be in trouble if Edward reneges on his oath of silence." Craig stared hard at the ceiling corner as if checking for surveillance. "Mia's been snooping around, too. Seems to be doing whatever Edward tells her to do. Considering our possible family connection, and our history with the Cedars' girls, I wanted to warn you to watch out for both. All three, actually."

Adrenaline shot up Judah's spine. "Are you saying they're in danger?"

"If things don't go Edward's way, namely him getting released, there will be consequences," Craig spoke in a gravelly whisper. "He's making plans, although I can't say what exactly. Townspeople have been traipsing in and out of here. Something's going on."

"You think Mia's involved?" She was a flirty manipulator, but engaged in illegal activities? Goodnight. She was a receptionist. Not a mastermind criminal.

"She's up to her eyeballs in something."

Judah blew out a breath. How could he protect his wife, sister-in-law, and niece? "What is Edward after, other than his freedom?"

Craig grasped the bars with both hands. "Get me out, and we can protect them together. You said you'd speak up for me."

"So I have. Deputy Brian took my statement."

"Not good enough." The whites of Craig's eyes were so big they seemed to glow. "You have connections with the detective, right?"

Did he know about Paige and Forest? "I'll talk to him if that will help."

"You do that." Craig thrust his hand through the gap between the bars and clutched Judah's arm. "The confinement is driving me crazy. Edward's prattle is killing me."

Judah jerked free of the man's grip. "I'm sorry for the situation you're in, but I'm not the law. I said I'd explain how you helped with Paisley's escape, and I did. When you go to court, I'll testify on your behalf. What else can I do?"

"Get me out of here." He sounded desperate. "I'll do anything to keep Paige and Piper safe."

"Is bail possible?" Judah didn't have extra money to offer, but he could speak to a bondsman.

Craig shook his head. "They say I'm a flight risk, but I won't run. Not with so much at stake."

"What about Mia? What's going on with her?"

"Just don't let Paisley out of your sight." Dropping to the edge of the cot, elbows on his knees, Craig pressed his thumbs against his forehead. "I wish I'd never heard of Edward Grant. If you were mayor, you could get me out."

Judah groaned. "I can't believe you're still following his directives." That's what was going on, right? Edward probably told Craig to pressure Judah into accepting the position. "If you called me in here for that, it's a waste of time." He strode to the door, knuckles raised toward the window.

"Wait. You hear about Mike Linfield?"

"What about him?"

"Fired. Gone." Craig clicked his fingers. "Just like that."

"Why? I spoke with him three days ago."

"That's what happens when you cross Edward." Craig's dark look said he had personal experience with that. "C.L. is in charge of C-MER now."

"C.L.? I saw him the day I spoke with Mike about the peninsula." Judah's old boss was out on his ear, and the mystery guy digging through the files in Mia's desk was in charge? Weird. Troubling, even. But not Judah's concern.

"One other thing. Mia took a hair sample."

"You let her?" Judah groaned.

"Not 'let.' Has she touched you recently?"

"Yeah." She hugged him at the project house earlier today.

Craig yanked a strand of hair from his head, winced, and extended it through the bars. "Find out for yourself, will you?"

Judah traipsed back to Craig and clasped the hair sample. Forest would know how to get a DNA test done quickly.

"I'm serious about you watching out for the women. Don't take any chances."

Were they in real danger? Or was this just a ruse for Craig to claim a Get-Out-of-Jail-Free card?

Forty-three

Heartsick, Paige awaited Forest's return, her mind churning with scenarios of him getting back together with Elinore. After their two-week honeymoon, how could he just walk out on her the way he did?

Paige didn't know why Judah texted her to come out to the cottage, but as she pulled into his driveway, the vehicle already parked there made her want to turn around. Forest? Why was he here? He wasn't invited to family gatherings. She exited the car and trudged to the backside of the house, grumbling about him butting his nose into her business.

"Paige." Paisley rushed over and hugged her.

"Hey." She wanted to demand to know why Forest was here, but it was hard to do that with him sitting on the patio wearing a grim look, staring back at her.

"The reason I asked you here"—Judah swayed his hands out, encompassing all of them—"is because Craig is concerned that Paige and Paisley might be in danger. Piper, too."

"What?" Paige's gaze crashed with her sister's. Paisley had already gone through a horrifying ordeal. Paige was threatened twice, three times counting what Mia said yesterday. Now Craig was warning her too?

"Craig thinks Edward is stirring up folks about something. Hard to say what's real. That's why I asked Forest to join us." Judah crossed his arms. "While Edward might be blowing off steam, sending meaningless messages through Craig and Mia, what if he has another diabolical scheme planned?"

Paisley covered her face with her hands and groaned.

Paige's stomach muscles clenched. Would Edward try to harm Piper? Was this what Mia's warning had been about?

"Seriously, what can he do from his jail cell?" Judah glanced at the sky as if asking the heavens. "It's probably nothing for us to be concerned about. Still, I felt we should talk it over."

"I think—" Forest bit his lip. "Sorry. I can't comment on an ongoing case."

Paige glared at him. She and their daughter might be in danger, and he couldn't comment? Fine. She faced Judah, her back to Forest. "Why would Craig warn us if it's nothing?"

"Because he wants to get out of the slammer badly."

"Why did you go and talk with him?" Paisley asked quietly.

"Mia showed up at the job site today."

Paisley sighed. "What did the troublemaker want this time?"

"She said Craig needed to talk to me." Judah paced across a small section of pavers, stroking the back of his hand over his forehead. "Get this, he warned me to be wary of her. It's a three-ring circus—Edward, Mia, Craig. I don't know which one to believe."

"I trust Craig more than the other two." Paige met Forest's gaze with a bit of defiance. He was the reason Craig was in jail. Even if Craig knew something bad was happening on the night he rescued Paisley, he'd never let harm come to Piper. "Mia warned me not to tell anyone about Edward's dealings with me or Paisley. She said she'd hate for anything 'unfortunate' to happen."

"What?" Forest shot to his feet. "Why didn't you tell me?"

"Because it's Mia. If she told me the town was on fire, I wouldn't believe her. She's hardly a credible threat." Although, seeing Forest worked up, shaking his head like she'd made a terrible mistake, tremors raced through her. "Do you think she's the one who sent me the note?"

Forest shrugged but didn't answer.

"What note?" Paisley linked her arm with Paige's. "Are you okay?"

"Yeah, but someone sent me a threatening message. Freaked me out. I told Deputy Brian and Forest about it, even though the warning said I shouldn't." She stole another glance at Forest. He gazed back at her with a gentler, but pensive, look. "Mia won't come after Piper, will she?"

"No, that's not going to happen," he said in a determined tone. "I won't let it."

At least he was sticking up for Piper, maybe sticking up for her, too. But what could he do? What could any of them do if Edward were ordering people around from his cell, and they were obeying him?

"Can't you just arrest Mia?" Paisley squinted toward Forest.

"On what grounds?"

"Threatening my sister. Being a ... nuisance." She cringed.

A small smile crossed Forest's mouth. "I wish it were that easy. While I don't like what Mia said, there are conditions criminal threats are weighed against. Did she threaten you with great bodily harm? Was it vague, or clear and immediate? Was Paige in sustained fear for her life? Then there's Mia's First Amendment Rights."

Paisley groaned. "What about our rights?"

"Exactly. You have rights, too."

Paige would like to stay and discuss things more, but she wanted to get back to Dad's and pick up Piper. Then remain behind locked doors for the rest of her life—or until she felt safe again. Before she left, she decided to say one more thing in Craig's defense. "I'd appreciate it if Craig were watching out for Piper and me. He protected us from Edward before. I'm sure he would do so again."

Forest moaned. "What if he and Mia are in this together?" He stared at her with his own look of defiance.

"What do you mean?"

"I'm not at liberty to say anything about the case. But let's say, hypothetically, Edward coerced Mia into doing something." He stroked his chin. "What if she needed Craig's help?"

"That would explain his urgent need to get out of jail." Judah whistled. "I should have seen that coming."

"Is that what's happening?" Paige took a few steps away, ready to run for her car. "Are Craig and Mia working together for Edward?" She couldn't believe it of Craig.

"Just a possibility. If I had enough evidence for a warrant, I'd—" Forest clamped his mouth shut.

"I still trust Craig." Paige lifted her chin. He wasn't perfect, but he'd been a loyal friend to her. "Maybe one of us could talk to Deputy Brian on his behalf?" She'd do that herself if it would make a difference.

"There is one thing. If he were to make a statement against Edward"—Forest's gaze remained locked on Paige's—"I'd put in a request for bail."

"You'd do that?" Now, why did her voice have to sound so breathy when she spoke to him?

"I would."

His soft gaze seemed to say he'd do anything for her. Or was that wishful thinking? She did appreciate his kinder attitude toward Craig.

"What should we do now?" Paisley asked, drawing Paige's attention to her.

"If Mia is carrying instructions to townsfolk who might consider it their duty to obey the mayor, that's where the pipeline needs to stop." Forest's gaze shuffled between each of them. "I can ask Deputy Brian to suspend visitation to the jail. Or I'll speak to the regional director about it."

"It's worth a shot." Judah nodded.

"If the town had a new mayor, not Judah," Paisley said, "Edward's control would be limited, or nonexistent, right?"

"That's right," Forest answered.

"We are talking about Edward." Judah slid his arm over Paisley's shoulder. "He has a way of getting his demands heard."

Paige recalled what Aunt Callie and her group of women's activists had been discussing. Some of the ladies were vehement about replacing Mayor Grant permanently.

"I don't want us to live in fear," Judah said. "But I'm recommending that neither of you ladies go out at night, or alone during the day for a while."

"But I have to work." Paisley stepped out from beneath his arm. "I told Bert I'm available for all shifts."

"That's fine, sweetheart, but I'll accompany you for a few days. We're sticking together like glue, you and me."

At least Paisley had someone willing to risk everything to take care of her, to be there for her. While Paige had—? She met Forest's gaze. Whatever she once thought she had, she didn't now.

Forty-four

*After Forest knew Elinore would recover from
her accident, he planned to return to Paige.
However, nursing his wounds over their argument,
and still smoothing things out with Elinore's
family, he stayed away too long.*

After the meeting at Judah's house yesterday, Forest tried
convincing Craig to make a statement against Edward and to
renounce his involvement in the man's unlawful actions. If he
could prove to the District Attorney that Craig was willing to
cooperate, things might go easier on him. Despite Forest's
compelling reasons, the prisoner refused to comment or write
another report.

Which made Forest question his integrity even more.
Although people he respected—Judah, Paisley, Bess, and
Paige—had written in their statements about Craig sticking out
his neck to rescue Paisley, Forest had doubts. Craig knew
Edward wanted him to do something illegal that night, and he
went along with it. If Craig refused to turn on Edward now, he

didn't stand a chance of a lighter sentence. Would Paige blame Forest for that, too?

He'd also requested a halt to Edward's visitation privileges. Visitation rights could be suspended for any or no reason, but Deputy Brian acted nervous about enforcing it. Finally, after he and Forest discussed it at length, he agreed to a temporary isolation for the prisoners.

Today, Forest was keeping a sharp eye on Paige and Piper. No one was coming close enough to his family to hurt them or to threaten them. That's why he was sitting in his car before seven a.m., using his binoculars. He scanned Paige's front door, her yard, the carport, her neighbors' yards, and back to the front of her house.

The door opened. Paige stepped onto the porch wearing a large shirt with colorful paint splatters on it, frowning right at him. Uh-oh. It looked like she wasn't pleased to find him here. By the way she marched across the short yard toward him, she had some choice words to say.

Forest lowered his binoculars and opened his window. "Good morning."

"What are you doing out here?"

"Ensuring your safety." He deepened his voice. "Doing my job."

"Since when is sitting outside my house with binoculars doing your job?"

"Your safety matters to me. As does our daughter's."

Paige's strong words, yesterday, about Craig being trustworthy, and how he'd protect her and Piper, had gotten to Forest. He wanted her to see that he was here to faithfully protect her, too. He wasn't here in the past the way he wished he would have been. That was changing now.

Paige waved at a woman picking up a newspaper across the street before giving Forest a dark glare. "Why don't you come inside instead of sitting here spying on me and my neighbors?"

"You wouldn't mind?"

"I mind plenty, but it would be less conspicuous. Two neighbors already called to inform me a strange man was sitting in a car outside my house." She scratched at a smudge of paint on her fingernail. "Are you trying to get the locals to gossip about us? I've had enough of people talking about me. I don't want any more of it."

"I'm sorry. That wasn't my plan."

"Piper will be awake in a few minutes. You can read her stories while I clean up, if you want." She stomped back toward the house, muttering, "Then you can leave."

Forest exited the car and followed her, but he was going to make one thing clear—he wasn't leaving. Never again.

At the next house, curtains jerked together as if someone had been watching him, or them. In another window, a woman peered out and glared at him. Curious neighbors? Or were they the mayor's eyes and ears, too?

Ugh. Now he was being paranoid. Soon he'd be envisioning the whole town involved in a conspiracy to get Edward out of jail and back into office. Surely, that wasn't the case.

Forest opened Paige's front door, uncertain whether he should have knocked. He slipped inside the living room, locking the door behind him, then stood by the entryway.

When Paige didn't return, he crossed over to look at the pictures on the hearth he saw the other day. Peering at each one, he smiled at the baby photos—Piper with Paige, Piper with her grandfather, the three of them in a cozy pose. If he hadn't been absent during Piper's babyhood, there'd be a picture of him and her on the mantle also. Since he was thirty-six, was she the only child he'd have? And he missed out?

A hot iron pressed against his spirit, burning him with regrets. Anger boiled to the surface like it often did whenever he pondered the secret Paige kept from him. She should have told him. Should have—

He covered his face with his hands and let out a subdued groan. Sometimes forgiveness was difficult. Tender feelings hit him at the strangest moments. He had to let it go, but how? As a follower of Christ, he knew to beware of bitterness. He was supposed to forgive seventy times seven, right?

Mistakes weren't foreign to him, either. Didn't he walk away from his new bride? Wasn't he the one who stayed away too long, the one who didn't reach out and keep communication going between them? He needed to remember that and pray some more, seeking God's help with forgiving Paige and letting the past go. *Lord*—

"What's wrong?" Paige entered the room, bouncing Piper on her hip.

He shook his head, not ready to explain.

Paige was so beautiful, not only as a gorgeous woman he'd loved, but as a mom who looked adorable with a kid in her arms. Softer, gentler, somehow.

He waved at Piper. "Good morning, princess."

She pointed at him, jabbering and laughing.

"That's right," Paige said as if she understood her. "He's your daddy. Say 'Daddy.'"

Barely breathing, he focused on his daughter's face.

"Daddy," Paige coaxed again.

"*Daeee.*" Piper squealed and clapped.

Joy raced through his veins, exploding endorphins in his brain. Tears made it difficult to see.

"Yes, that's right. Daddy," Paige reiterated.

"*Daeee.*"

Forest crossed the room, wanting to embrace them both. Instead, he held out his arms toward Piper. Laughing, shrieking, she propelled herself into his embrace. He caught her and held her close. His daughter. He and Paige had a daughter. Oh, the wonder and amazement of it.

"Thank you," he mouthed to Paige. Some of the knotted-up frustration and unforgiveness he'd still been dealing with melted from his heart. He kissed Piper's cheek. "Hey, princess."

"How about some breakfast?" Paige asked.

"Would love some."

Although the circumstances weren't ideal, he was grateful for this time of getting to know Piper. And being with Paige, too. Even with the threats, and the chasm of past hurts, a thread of hope bound him to these ladies. Since Paige encouraged Piper to call him Daddy, and asked him to join them inside the house, maybe she'd accept him into her life on some level, too.

If so, thank You, Lord. Forest's prayers were being answered.

While Paige cooked breakfast, he entertained Piper by looking through some books with her at the kitchen table. What Paige was making smelled fantastic. His stomach growled.

Other than Piper's babbling, with the occasional word he understood, the room was quiet while they ate. He longed for a quick fix to remedy the awkwardness between him and Paige. In time, he prayed that would get better.

"This is great. Hits the spot." He held up a forkful of pancakes. "Thanks."

"Sure." Paige smiled.

After breakfast, they rinsed their plates and filled the dish-washer as if they'd shared the task many times. He enjoyed them being like a family, feeling as if he belonged, but there were things they needed to discuss, too.

"Any chance we could talk?" He asked Paige when their daughter danced into the living room.

"Okay. Wait here." She followed Piper out of the room.

A few minutes later, the cartoon video played. Children's songs. Piper laughing. Happy sounds reached him.

Paige returned and stood by the sink, leaning against the counter, arms crossed. He remained near the table, respecting the space her stiff body language dictated.

"Did you find out anything about Craig's release?"

Too bad her first question centered around another man.

"It depends on what he's willing to testify about. Do you still care for him?" That was an abrupt segue, but it was fore-most on his mind.

"It isn't any of your business, Forest."

"Right." Clenching his jaw, he kept himself from telling her it certainly was his business. They could tap dance around past mistakes, even chatting about Craig or Elinore, but he was done skirting the real issue. "Okay, then. Do you still have feelings for me?"

"Forest—"

"I still have feelings for you." He decided to lay it on the table. "I said it before, and I mean it, I'm working on getting over what happened between us, the same as you, but I do love you." He stepped closer, letting her have the safe space she needed, but he hoped to assure her that he was interested in more if she was.

"But I ... how can you—"

"I'm here for you, Paige. Not only to protect you, although I'm here for that too. But also, for if you ever discover you care for me in the way I care for you." He drew in a long breath, staring into her wary gaze. "I'll always be Piper's dad, but if I could have one other wish, I'd choose to be married to you again."

"What?"

He'd obviously taken her by surprise which might work in his favor. Or not.

"There's too much water under the bridge for us to just waltz back to where we were before." She parked one fist on her hip.

"I know." Forest's heart sank into his ribs.

"However"—she sighed—"I haven't forgotten the good things that happened between us." She linked her hands in front of her waist, a less intimidating pose. "I've even journaled about that part of our lives." She blushed as if embarrassed by the admission.

He'd pay a lot of money to read those journal entries. If she had written things about him, that must be a good sign. Maybe she wanted more between them, too.

"I've wondered what our lives might have been like if we stayed married," she said.

"Me too." He stepped close enough to take her hands gently in his, smoothing his fingers over hers. "Is there any scenario where you can see us trying again? I'm not saying this instant, but in the future. I'm going to stay right here in Basalt Bay, near you and Piper."

"You mean quit being a detective and becoming a handyman?" She had a teasing glint in her eyes.

"If that's what it takes, yes."

Their gazes held for a few moments.

She stepped back, disengaging his hands from hers. "Would you care to hang out with me this afternoon?"

Her change in topic surprised him, but he answered, "Yes! Absolutely. What did you have in mind?"

"Talking. Facing the past."

"Oh." A band tightened around his chest.

Any chance they could skip talking about the past and leap right into the let's-get-married-again part? What would she say if he threw that on the table?

Forty-five

Decisions were often made with the slightest impulse yet could take years to undo. If Forest listened to the cry of his heart, he'd get in his car and drive to Basalt Bay, back into the arms of the woman he loved.

Forest walked out of Paige's house and came to a standstill, gawking at the VW Jetta. Thick black letters had been spray painted across the side of the white vehicle—"Get out of town, or else!"

"What in the world? I can't believe it."

"What is it?" Paige asked from where she carried Piper and locked the door, obviously not seeing what he was looking at.

"Some crook vandalized my rental car." Every muscle in his body tightening, he dashed across the yard, perusing the block as he ran. On the other side of the vehicle, "Get off the case!" blared from the metal surface. "This is nuts."

Leaning down, he peered through the open passenger window that had previously been closed and the door locked. Every instinct for self-preservation and for keeping Paige and Piper safe surged through him, running ice-cold then burning hot. The glove compartment stood agape, papers strewn about, his weapon gone. He blew out a breath. While this could be a juvenile prank, it reeked of someone getting more brazen in their warnings. More dangerous.

Did any of Paige's neighbors observe this destruction? Forest peered at the houses where people had been watching him earlier. No fluttering curtains. No eyeballs glared back at him now.

"Oh, Forest, I'm so sorry." Paige followed him, carrying Piper. "How terrible! Who would do this to your car?"

"That's what I want to know." He yanked out his cell. "I have to make some calls. Can you wait inside the house?" He didn't want her out in the open. Her and Piper's safety came first. He checked up and down the street but didn't see anything out of the ordinary.

"How about if I drop off Piper at Necia's while you're making your calls?"

"I'd rather walk with you to your friend's place."

"It's only three houses down." She squinted at him as if she thought he was overreacting.

"All right. Come straight back, okay?"

"I will."

He touched Piper's cheek. "Bye, princess."

His daughter grinned, melting his heart. How could he best keep her and her mom protected?

Who was behind these threats? Mia? Based on her ditsy,

flirtatious mannerisms, he doubted it. Was it someone else following Edward's directives?

He gripped his cell phone, watching Paige like a hawk until she turned into a walkway down the block. Then he tapped the icon connecting him with Brian. "Forest, here. We have a problem." He filled the lawman in on the details of the crime.

"Why didn't you have your weapon with you?"

"I was in a house where there's a child."

"Ah. You're at Paige's." The deputy made a disgruntled sound.

"Didn't I mention that?"

"Nope."

"I was surveilling her property, but"—he realized this might sound like a private escapade instead of a work-related mission—"I went inside, had breakfast."

A weighty silence followed.

"Want me to send photos of the vehicle, or are you coming over?"

"Shoot me some photos. Don't touch anything," the deputy said curtly. "I'll get the crime-lab to dust for prints."

"Will do." Something caught his eye. "Wait. There's a piece of paper tucked into the front seat." He reached through the window.

"Don't touch—"

"Too late." He grimaced and tried not to handle anything but the paper.

Brian sighed. "What does it say?"

Forest unfolded the sheet and read the words written in block letters, "'Stop butting into things that aren't your business. Nobody wants you here. Get out of town, or you'll regret the day you stepped foot in Basalt Bay. I'm watching you. Paige and the kid, too.'" On alert, he stared intently at the location where Paige had turned in. He should have gone with her. Was someone observing her now?

"I have to go."

"I'll be there in a few."

Forest disconnected the call and sprinted down the sidewalk. Before he reached Paige's friend's walkway, Paige strode toward him, her eyes wide.

"What's going on?"

"I need to talk with you."

"Yeah, that's why I dropped off Piper."

"No, I mean—" He lifted the paper he still held in his hand. "Come on." His hand at her back, he drew her toward her house and the vandalized car.

"Are we still going for a walk on the beach?"

"Possibly." He tried to keep his voice calm. No need to worry her more than his defaced car sitting outside her house probably did. "Deputy Brian is on his way. There's been a development."

"Oh?"

He was tempted not to tell her. However, she needed to hear the truth so she wouldn't be cavalier and refuse his proposed protection detail. Now there was a threat against him, too. His remaining safe was essential to keeping her and Piper protected.

Keeping an eye on the bushes across the street, he stopped in her yard and read the note to her.

"Someone's watching us?" She met his gaze tensely, then she, too, peered across the street. "Should I go back and get Piper?"

"In a few minutes. Let's take a short walk. Then we'll get her together."

Her gaze flickered toward the car. "Any chance someone's warning you to stay away from me? This happened outside my house."

Her meaning hit him. "Like Craig's behind this? Warning me away from you?"

"No. I shouldn't have said that." She shook her head. "He wouldn't make a threat about Piper, or allow anyone else to, either."

Pondering her defense of Craig, he slipped the note into his pocket for safekeeping. "I have to stay with you tonight."

"What are you talking about?"

"I'm sticking to you and Piper like glue just like Judah told Paisley." His tight smile felt lopsided.

"Yeah, but they're married. We aren't."

He'd like to change that fact. Would, if she'd accept his proposal.

"They don't have to worry about the neighbors gossiping about them." Paige met his gaze with a panicked look. "Tongues are probably wagging over you being in my house already."

"Can't be helped."

"Want to bet?" Paige waved at a woman carrying a garbage bag toward the back of her house. The woman frowned in their direction. "You don't know what I've put up with in this town of gossips—between my mother's odd behavior, my sister getting into trouble, my brother leaving town suddenly, then me turning up single and pregnant."

He gulped at her passionate speech. "I'm sorry about that. And I'm sorry my involvement in the case may bring more trouble to your doorstep, but with your permission, I'd like to crash on your couch. I want to be close to you should someone try to enter your house."

Her jaw dropped. The fight in her seemed to wilt. "You think that might happen?"

"I hope not. But if you despise the idea of me being in the house overnight, I'll run a stakeout from the car."

"That would be worse! Your sitting in a vandalized car outside my house all night will be more fodder for the gossip mill." She groaned. "Wait until Aunt Callie hears about this. What if I stayed at my dad's?"

"If it makes you feel safer, great. But I'd still sit in my car there, too. Non-negotiable."

She stared at him without speaking for about fifteen seconds. Then, "Fine. Stay on the couch. Make my life miserable." She stomped toward the house and spoke over her shoulder, "I'll call Necia and tell her to keep Piper indoors. That'll give us time to talk."

Oh, yeah, they were going to talk. He doubted she'd like what he had to say.

Forty-six

Two months after their wedding day, Paige realized she'd missed her monthly cycle for the second time. A pregnancy test confirmed her suspicions. Sweeping her hasty marriage under the rug wasn't going to be as easy as she thought.

Paige walked silently beside Forest along the sandy seashore at City Beach, maintaining a space between her and the tide rolling in, and between her and him. How would she survive his presence in her home and keep her heart intact? Now she had to adjust to not only co-parenting with him, but being business partners *and* sharing house space?

Groan.

Even with the tension between them due to the threatening note and the car vandalism, and him being the person who arrested her friend, walking next to him made her pulse hammer double-time. She imagined them holding hands, sitting on the beach and her leaning into him, kissing him like she did in her dreams. She had blatantly denied her attraction to him, even told herself she didn't care for him, but every cell in her body seemed to know better.

She paused and scanned her cell for texts. After explaining about the damage done to Forest's car, Paige had told Necia to text her if she saw anything suspicious. Hopefully, no texts meant everything was okay. Still, Paige was in a hurry to get back and take Piper home. But was home safe? Did she need Forest staying with her like he suggested?

The wind swept against her, taking her breath away. Sand flecks got in her eyes. She pulled up her sweatshirt hood for protection, glad for the distraction from thoughts of what her hand would feel like in Forest's, what her mouth moving softly against his mouth would be like.

Just stop, already.

All the talk of threats and danger, and the possibility of Forest staying with her, must be at the center of her mixed-up thoughts. Not romance. Not love.

"Maybe we'd better stick to the tree line," Forest said.

"Good idea." She traipsed ahead of him toward a log near the trees.

She sat sideways on the driftwood with her back to the sea and the wind. He straddled the bench-like log, facing her.

"Basalt Bay is an amazing place. So beautiful." Forest sighed. "I could get used to the idea of living here for the rest of my life."

Why did he have to say things like that, getting her hopes up only to be dashed when he left town? Once, she believed his promises when he asked her to marry him and live with him forever. Considering how that turned out, how abandoned she felt in the aftermath, it was hard to imagine him staying committed to anything, or anyone, for the long haul.

Besides, she needed to focus on what she had to say to him, the honest things that remained to be said between them. Nothing else. Nothing more.

How could she start? *Forest, I'm so sorry*— Or *I wish things had been*—

"This is difficult." She expelled a breath.

"What is?"

"Dredging up the past."

"I'm sorry for my part in it," he said in a hoarse whisper. "It's hard for me too. I didn't mean for my leaving you to check on Elinore to last weeks, as it did." He glanced in both directions as if keeping a continual watch. "I should have called. Reached out and assured you of my intent to come home again, even if I thought I needed some space, too."

"Why didn't you call?"

"I was a fool." He met her gaze. "Hurt. Prideful. Too caught up in what was going on in Portland."

"And you loved Elinore."

"Not in the way you mean." A shadow crossed his face, either by a cloud blocking out the sun or from some deep emotion. "I cared for her as a family friend, almost like a sister."

That's what he'd told her before, but the explanation fell short of satisfaction when she needed the complete truth now.

"If you only cared for her as a friend, why wouldn't you have returned to me, your wife?" Ire rose in her. If they were going to stay in the same house, this needed to be addressed. "If you cared for her platonically or as a sister, why wouldn't you have come back to me as soon as you assured yourself of her welfare?"

"Well, I—"

"Did you sit beside her in the hospital room? Holding her hand? Laughing and talking about old times?" With each question, each swell of frothing emotion, Paige's voice rose. "Did you fall for her again?"

"Paige, no. I'm telling you it wasn't like that. I never loved her as I loved you." Yet his face hued wine-colored. What wasn't he telling her? Was the way he kept scanning the beach a means of protecting her or was he avoiding her gaze?

"If there's any hope of reconciliation, even for us to be friends, you'd better come clean and say what needs to be said." A second more of this and she'd stomp back home, lock the door, and let him sleep in his defaced car.

"Okay." He exhaled. "You know I didn't break things off properly with Elinore before I went to the conference in Vegas, before I met you, although I tried repeatedly."

"Yes."

"So when you and I fell in love, I thought it would be a perfect explanation for Elinore and our families to accept that the engagement was truly off."

"You used me?"

"No." He leaned in closer to her, gazing right into her eyes now. "But I'm trying to be completely honest here."

He clasped her hands loosely, but she withdrew them from him. She wasn't in any mood for hand-holding.

"I loved you. I meant what I said in our vows."

"But?" Part of her didn't want his excuses. However, the other part of her needed to hear every word he had to say if she were ever to look him in the eye without doubts and heart-ache plaguing her. "Did you lie to me about your feelings when I agreed to marry you?"

"Absolutely not." He raked his fingers through his hair. "But I shouldn't have proposed until I talked to Elinore in person and ended things once and for all. I got swept up in our romance in Vegas. I don't regret that, but I regret how it affected Elinore. How my leaving affected you, even after all these years."

"And you."

"Yep. Me too." He sighed. "I didn't care for her like a future wife. However, my concern for her, and my guilt, propelled me back to Portland to be there during her surgery. To face the music with our families afterward." He touched the back of Paige's hand, smoothing his palm over her knuckles. "What about you? Why did you divorce me so quickly? Why not give us a chance to make up before ending it? Was it Craig?"

"No. Not that." She was tempted to jerk her hand away to show her lack of feelings for him. But the brushing of his fingers across her skin, the ticklish sensation, felt soothing, mesmerizing.

"I thought it was over. That you went back to your first love."

"You were my first true love."

"*First true love. First true love,*" danced through her thoughts.

"Over the last few years, I've traveled and worked, keeping myself busy to hide from the fact my heart was broken." His eyes moistened. "That I missed you terribly, longed for you and what we had for such a short time. Those feelings never left me. I still want you. And what we shared as a married couple."

She gulped, trying to stifle the nostalgia and longings his vulnerable-sounding words created. They'd both lost so much, not only her.

"Will you allow me to try to win you back? I can't promise I'll succeed, but will you let me try? Please?"

Whoa. He just leaped way ahead of her emotionally. Scrambling to figure out the past, forgiveness and acceptance had to come first. And here he nearly proposed. How was she supposed to react to that? Yes, she was attracted to him. Yes, she wished for the past to mesh easier with the present. But—

His gaze darted to her lips, her eyes, her lips again. With him looking at her so sweetly, rational thinking became difficult. She imagined how they acted toward each other in her dreams. The passionate kisses. The tender way he held her. What would it be like to have his very real, soft lips caressing hers again? To know the strength of his arms, the gentleness of his love like she once did? To be undeniably sure of it?

Even if she gave him another chance—was she actually considering it?—would she always question if he came back only because of Piper? Of course, there was the other thing she hadn't forgotten. Thinking of *"Sweet dreams, Elinore,"* cooled her ardor right down.

She scooted back, putting the kibosh on any ideas of kissing, reconciling, or second chances. She needed more time to figure out her feelings, and to find out if she could trust Forest again.

Forty-seven

Forest gripped the divorce papers, his hands shaking. Why had he been such an idiot in leaving Paige that day? Did she think his marrying her had been an act? That he hadn't cared for her at all?

Still keeping a watch on both sides of the beach, Forest stood and motioned for Paige to walk with him back toward town. If he kept sitting on the driftwood, facing her, he'd wind up pulling her into his arms and kissing her with all the passion he'd been feeling since he first saw her nine days ago. By her guarded expression, that wouldn't go over well.

The topic he hadn't broached yet made his heart pound a loud drumbeat in his ears. Would he be making another stupid blunder by proposing too soon?

It was difficult for him to stop thinking about the vandalized car back at Paige's house and the note he'd turned in to Deputy

Brian. "Or else," taunted him. Or else what? What extreme thing might someone do to get him to back off the case? The words, "I'm watching you. Paige and the kid, too," riled him. How dare someone threaten his ex-wife and daughter! How could he keep Paige and Piper safe other than to stay in their house with them? He glanced up the beach as he'd been doing every few minutes.

Wait. Was someone hiding in the bushes up ahead? Watching them? It looked like a woman. Or— Now, he didn't see anyone. Was that just his imagination?

Still, the sensation of being watched didn't leave him. He tried to shake off the premonition of danger, or of someone stalking them. He and Paige needed this time to reconnect, to spend a few minutes together. Maybe then, if they walked and talked, she'd be more open to his idea. Or at least, not hate him for suggesting it.

Holding out his hand toward her, he decided to take another chance at pushing things a little between them. At first, she hesitated as if she wouldn't take his hand, but then sliding her palm against his, she linked their fingers together.

His world realigned. A deep sigh rumbled through him. If holding Paige's hand felt this great, what would kissing her be like? First things first. Winning back her trust in him was at the top of his list—way before making out with her. Although, that would be nice, too.

"What are you expecting, Forest?"

He gulped at her unexpected question. Good thing she couldn't read his mind.

A few responses leaped into his thoughts. A second chance at love. Marriage with the woman he wanted to cherish for the rest of his life. The chance to be around Piper every day.

Keeping them safe—he couldn't deny the compelling urge that drove him to be willing to take risks, even to ask her to marry him again.

Instead of answering out loud, he drew her into his arms and held her a moment, taking another risk of rejection. This wasn't too intrusive, was it? "Will you let me be here with you like I wasn't before?"

"Forest, can't we just keep talking and see where this goes?" She leaned back and gazed up at him, blinking slowly.

"I know where I want it to go." He wanted to kiss her, despite his personal lecture on what should come first. Staring into Paige's eyes, feeling the magnetic pull between them, as strong as the day he met her, and her trembling in his arms, was more than he could take in and not do something. "Is asking for the chance to prove myself too much?"

Please, God, let her find it in her heart to forgive me. Let us have this chance at a future together, despite my need to rush things again. Help her understand. Keep her and Piper safe.

"No, but why come to Basalt Bay and ask for another chance three years after us breaking up?"

"You are my reason, Paige." He stroked his fingers down the side of her face, sparks pinging in his chest. "You and Piper are the reasons I plan to make Basalt Bay my home."

She pushed out of his embrace. "And if you tire of us, what then?"

That was a punch in the gut. But he had to reassure her of his honesty and sincerity. "I will never tire of you, Paige. I will never leave you or Piper, either. You have my word."

When she didn't say anything, he set his arm lightly over her shoulder, turning her to face the sea. "Look at those amazing waves rolling up the shore." He nodded toward the incoming tide, the water crashing against the rocks and bursting white foam into the air. "They keep returning, never giving up, never stopping. Steady as a rock. Faithful. True. That's like I want to be for you and Piper." He met her gaze. "I know I failed you in the past, but I'm here to stay. If you're in Basalt Bay, that's where my home is, where my heart is, from this day forward."

"I'd like to believe that."

"I want you to believe it. You can trust me, baby," he said, daring to use an endearment. He whisked back some long strands of her hair, loving the silky feel of it between his fingers, hoping for a way to reach her heart, to connect on some deeper emotional level. Then, not giving in to the urge to check the beach, focusing completely on her, he asked, "Would it be okay if I kissed you?"

Her eyes widened. "Oh, I, um, haven't agreed to anything." Yet she stroked the chest of his jacket like she was considering his request. She met his gaze, her dark eyes shining like glistening chocolate.

He didn't break eye contact with her as he leaned in slowly, giving her all the time in the world to pull away if she wanted to. What he still needed to ask her swirled in his thoughts, but he didn't say anything, didn't want anything ruining their first kiss this time around.

"I am sorry for hurting you by not telling you about Piper," she whispered, her soft breath caressing his lips.

"I know. I'm sorry for how I hurt you."

She took the last step between them, embracing him like a friend instead of meeting his lips. Not exactly what he hoped for, but surely it was a step toward trust. He hugged her back.

"I may have misrepresented myself by saying I wasn't attracted to you, Forest." She chuckled, gazing at him. "Honestly, I have missed you. Missed what we had. This."

If anything was an invitation, that was. Smiling, feeling the heat of a thousand candles of hope, he gently brushed his lips against hers, taking it slowly despite the sparks shooting through him.

"I may have missed that too."

Her half-teasing, half-flirting got to him.

"Yeah? And this?" Pressing his lips against hers more fully, exploring her soft mouth, he maintained a distance between their bodies, but kept kissing her.

When she didn't pull back, but leaned into him, smoothing her hands behind his neck and playing with his hair, he held her closer and kissed her with every ounce of the fireworks exploding in his brain. "Oh, Paige," he whispered against her cheek. "Will you marry me again?"

She shoved away from him. "W-what?"

He gulped. Too soon?

"What did you say? We can't—"

"I'm sorry. I should have ... waited."

"I'll say." She huffed. "Forest, you courted me fast and furiously in Vegas. Is this the same thing? I fall for you, and you walk away like it's nothing?"

"Of course not." Brutal disappointment hit him. They'd moved two steps forward in apologizing and in that whopper of a kiss. Now they were backtracking lightning fast. By the abhorrent look on her face, she thought he was pursuing her for a fling. "I'm serious about a lifelong relationship with you, not a whimsical dalliance to stir up what we had before."

"Do you m-mean that?"

"Yes."

Her gaze met his with such longing, he almost reached for her again, wanting more of her kisses. But if he did, wouldn't that validate her concerns? If she thought his kisses were too soon, she'd think his proposal preposterous. Considering her reaction, he had to agree. Although not completely.

"You don't want me staying at your house because of the possibility of scandalous rumors, right?"

"Right." She crossed her arms tightly over her middle. "I have to protect my heart, too. Forest, a relationship between us would have to be taken slowly this time. Carefully."

"I see." Sighing, he did a quick scan of the beach. Then met her gaze again. "Hear me out, okay? If we were to get married, 'slowly' continuing what we started three years ago, that would resolve your worries about gossip. And"—he rushed on—"as your husband, I would be able to stay close to you, and Piper, for security reasons." He couldn't leave it at that. "We both know we have enough chemistry to light the house on fire." His smile didn't elicit one from her. "C'mon, Paige, please? Give me a chance to make things right. To build a family together."

She gnawed on her lower lip. "Pick up where we left off, huh?"

"Something like that." He gulped at her icy glare. What could he say to make her believe he had her best interests at heart?

Forty-eight

Forest wished he could roll time back to their wedding day. Return to the mistakes he made in the days following, so he could fix them. Second chances were rare, but if he ever got one, he'd cherish Paige with everything in him.

Forest stretched, groaning at the kink in his neck. Between being on alert for any signs of trouble, his thoughts churning over the rejected marriage proposal, and the lumpy couch he was resting on, that was one rough night's sleep. A sound from the kitchen made every muscle in his body tense. Who was that? An intruder?

A soft light glowed in there. Might be Paige, but he'd better check. With cat-like agility, he pushed off the sofa cushions and tiptoed across the carpet barefooted. He should have grabbed an object to use as a weapon, a book or a vase, if it was needed. Clenching his fists, he eased around the corner, ready to pounce, slugging, or kicking, whichever came first.

Instead of running into a prowler, he staggered at the tranquil scene of Paige painting beneath the light coming from above the sink. Her back to him, she worked on a gorgeous picture of the lighthouse where he followed her last week.

Wow. This woman had talent.

A rush of air left his lungs. His shoulders heaved, relaxing, as the muscles in his body let go of tension. Leaning against the wall between the living room and kitchen, he watched her. The movement of the paintbrush grasped between her finger-tips was beautiful to observe. She dipped the brush into a glob of paint, then whisked it back and forth against the palette, blending, twirling it in graceful movements.

He was captivated by her absorption in her art. Watching the woman he'd loved for so long, his mouth went dry. Heat spread across his chest, reminding him of their kisses yesterday. If only he had his cell phone—where was it?—he'd snap a couple of shots to capture the moment. He never wanted to forget her like this.

As if sensing his gaze upon her, Paige glanced over her shoulder. "Oh, it's you. Give a girl a warning, why don't you?"

"Sorry, I didn't mean to startle you." He'd like every morning to begin like this, being here with her, watching her painting. If she didn't mind, he'd step forward and slip his arms around her. Kiss her good morning. "It's beautiful." He nodded toward the picture. "Is this one for the gallery opening?" If so, he'd buy it.

"Thanks. And yes." She set the paintbrush in a jar of water, wiping her hands on a cloth. "Want some coffee?"

Her question surprised him, since last night she hardly spoke to him other than to ask a couple of questions about the gallery remodeling.

"Sure, but I don't want to interrupt what you're doing."

"I could use another cup." She turned toward the coffee-maker. "Sorry if I awakened you. This is my normal painting routine before Piper gets up."

"You didn't wake me." He rubbed the sore muscles along his neck and shoulders. "I sleep lightly when I'm on duty."

"Right. Duty."

Was that disappointment in her voice? Did she wish he were staying here for something more than obligation, even though she said no to marrying him?

Probably not. Just wishful thinking.

After he used the bathroom, scrubbing toothpaste over his teeth with his finger, and smoothing out his wild-looking hair, he returned to the kitchen. Paige sat at the table with her coffee mug gripped between her hands. Another mug was near the chair opposite her, so he sat down there. He liked this domestic scene—drinking coffee together, chatting about their upcoming day, exchanging glances. He wouldn't mind this every day.

But before anything could happen between them, he had to find a way to prove to her that he was here to stay. That he'd never again leave her as he did before. How to convince her to take a chance on him, on them, was a mystery he'd like to unravel. In his line of work, it was his task to uncover truths. Perhaps, figuring out how to reach Paige's heart would be his greatest investigative challenge yet.

"I've been considering your proposal while I was painting," she said quietly.

"You have?" He clutched his mug without taking a sip.

"Throughout the night, too, since I couldn't sleep."

"And?"

"I kept thinking ... I don't know ... what if I agreed?" She chuckled a nervous-sounding laugh. "What if we just went ahead and got married again?"

"Wait. Do you mean it?" He shot up and was on his knee by her chair a second later, holding her hand. "Paige, baby—"

"Rushing into marriage still seems foolhardy. Boy, does it ever." She gave him one of her serious glances. "But you're planning to sleep on my couch to protect Piper and me indefinitely, right?"

"Yes, I am."

"If we were married, the neighbors would be less likely to stir up tales about us."

"True." Although her lackluster explanation sounded more like a business deal than the loving declaration he wished for. "Is that all?" He loosened his hold on her hand. "You don't want anything more happening between us?" What if he reminded her how much he cared for her with another toe-curling kiss?

"It would give us time to sort through our feelings and get reacquainted, slowly." She tugged her hand away. "Apparently, Piper and I need your protection." She cringed as if she hated admitting that.

He swallowed with difficulty. He'd hoped for so much more.

"Oh, uh, I think I made a mistake." Her face flushed. "I meant to say in name only. What if we got married in name only?"

"What?" He rocked on his heels and stood. "Paige, I want to marry you for real. I want to be your husband."

"We married so fast before." She stood also, her expression wary. "Putting our desires above getting to know each other."

"I wanted to marry you for more than—"

"But if you'd lived here in Basalt Bay, we would have dated and learned more about each other first."

"I knew you and loved you." He drew her left hand to his lips, kissing the place where her wedding ring used to sit. "I want to be married to you and stay close to you for the rest of my life. Yes, I need to protect you and Piper, but I want to be your husband, too. A real part of this family."

"That sounds good. Honest, it does. But we need time to mend before we're ready for anything else." She pressed her lips together as if stopping them from trembling. "At least, I do."

Within a minute's time, she offered him the world, then snatched it away. But he wouldn't give up. What would it take to remind her of everything good they'd experienced as a couple? To show her how much he loved her still?

"Paige, you are the love of my life. That's how I felt three years ago. It's how I feel now." Gazing into her eyes, he slid his fingers over her cheeks, caressing her soft skin. "Will you marry me again, baby?"

"I will," she said without hesitation. "But until we build trust and truly get to know each other, we'll have to sleep in separate spaces."

"A marriage of convenience." Disappointment nearly choked him.

"Temporarily, yes."

Forest sighed. Wasn't a marriage of convenience with Paige better than no marriage at all?

Lord, is this arrangement even right for us to consider?

"Would you be willing to marry me knowing we'll have to wait for love and normal married things?" she asked.

"I already love you."

"I know you love what we shared in the past. It was amazing." She lifted one shoulder. "What about how we feel now?"

"I love you now."

She sighed.

Obviously, he hadn't convinced her. Maybe he'd have to show her, starting with a commitment he wouldn't fail at. Starting with stepping up and becoming her husband and their daughter's father like he should have been all along. Taking a deep breath, he clasped both of Paige's hands. "Okay, yes. I will marry you, resuming our vows from three years ago to stay married for the rest of our lives." He paused. "However, I have an addendum to add to this in-name-only marriage proposal.'"

"What is it?"

"I left you before, causing this rift, this lack of trust, between us." He tapped the center of his chest. "I take the blame for that."

"We both made some bad decisions."

He gazed into her eyes, still wanting to take her in his arms like he did on the beach. "I love you, for real. So, when we marry, it won't be pretending or in name only for me. It'll be with all my heart." Lowering his lips toward hers, he whispered as if stating his vows, "I, Forest Harper, love you, Paige Cedars, 'til death do us part."

Then he kissed her with all the emotions he had in him, hugging her closely, hoping she'd soon want more for them than a temporary marriage of convenience, too.

Forty-nine

Judah sat at a corner table near the front of Bert's diner, watching Paisley work, for the second day in a row. The owner had been staring glumly at him for the last hour. Probably due to Judah taking up a booth for two days without ordering much more than coffee. Maybe he'd eat a burger today.

He picked up his phone to check his emails, focusing on the screen, and saw movement out of the corner of his eye. Mia slid onto the seat opposite him. Ugh. What did she want?

"Hey, Judah." She grinned at him in her typical flirtatious way.

"Hello," he said without inflection, trying to make it obvious he wasn't interested in whatever game she was playing. He checked the door between the kitchen and the dining area. What would Paisley say when she saw Mia sitting at his table?

Mia clicked her fingers toward Lucy who was carrying a coffee carafe.

The redheaded server rushed over and dropped a cup on the table. "Hey, Mia." She poured the dark steaming liquid, glancing back and forth between them. "What are you up to today?"

"Nothing much." Mia winked at Judah. "Just hanging out with this handsome dude."

"Oh." Lucy nodded and grinned at Judah.

Just great. Now she'd probably race into the kitchen and blab some lie about him and Mia to Paisley.

Mia sipped her coffee, her eyes sparkling at him.

What was she doing here? Wasn't she partially the reason he sat here in Bert's, thanks to her messages from Edward?

Forest had informed him about the rental car being vandalized outside of Paige's, and about the warnings he received. Even a threat aimed at Paige and Piper. Was Edward behind those? Was Mia involved?

Paisley rushed across the diner, scowling.

Oh, man. Judah's shoulders tightened.

"Mia, how nice to see you," she said in a high voice. Not wearing her apron, she dropped onto the seat next to Judah, bumping against his side.

"Hey, sweetheart." He kissed her cheek and slid his arm over her shoulder. Sighed. He liked this—him and Paisley portraying a unified front toward Mia—although he felt tension rippling across her neck and shoulders.

Mia set down her mug with a clunk. "I came here to inform you of what Eddie told me before the detective stopped me from visiting him. Your dad doesn't like what's happening in his town."

"What's new?"

"This time it's serious." She waved at someone across the diner.

"Just say what you have to say, then go." Paisley squinted at Mia. "You've caused all the trouble you're going to cause us."

If looks could kill, Mia's glare would have done Paisley in. "Listen, honey, you don't know the trouble I could cause, if I wanted to."

"Hey," Judah barked. "That's enough."

"And don't call me 'honey.'" Paisley jabbed her finger at Mia. "Or I'll have Bert toss you out."

"He wouldn't dare. Didn't you hear he took out a construction loan in the local bank where, you guessed it, Edward is a shareholder?" Mia grinned like she made a game-winning point. Then frowned at Judah. "Eddie says step up and do what you should have been doing already. Otherwise, chaos is coming like you wouldn't believe."

Judah leaned toward her, frustration churning in his veins. "Let him give me his worst, I won't budge."

Mia huffed. "I thought you and your dad were playing a game of cat and mouse. That you'd come around eventually."

"It's not a game to me." Judah thumped the table with his index finger. "Don't you ever threaten me or my wife again!"

"Fine." Mia stretched her red lips over her teeth. "Don't blame me when the world falls apart at your feet. I'm just looking out for you like a good friend should." She brushed her fingertips against his arm.

Paisley clamped her hand around Mia's wrist. "Keep your hands off my husband."

Mia disengaged her hold. "Eddie was right. You are low class."

"Don't say that!" Judah felt like throwing her out of the diner himself, but he needed answers. "Did you send Paige a threatening note? Did you spray paint a message on Forest's car?"

"Don't be ridiculous." Mia stood and dropped a couple of bills on the table. "If I did something so sinister, wouldn't you see the truth in my eyes?" She leaned down and batted her lashes, her orbs glistening right at him. "Watch out for C.L., though. His agenda is different than Edward's."

"What's that got to do with me?"

"C.L.'s in charge at C-MER. He asked for your file. That means something." Blowing air kisses toward Judah, Mia sashayed toward the door.

"Good riddance." Paisley groaned. "I bet she wrote the note, sent the text, vandalized the car, everything. Deputy Brian should arrest her."

"Yet she denied it to my face."

"You believe her?" Paisley stood abruptly. "I have to get back to work."

"Wait. I'm sorry for what she said about my dad."

"Nothing I haven't heard before." She marched back to the kitchen.

Groaning, Judah ran his hands through his hair. Then he sent Forest a text telling him what Mia said.

After thirty minutes of watching his wife performing server duties without glancing once in his direction, he had to do something. As soon as she finished taking an older gentleman's order and headed toward the kitchen, Judah followed her.

He didn't get far into Bert's culinary domain before the owner stopped him, hands extended. "Whoa, there, Sonny. Employees only in my kitchen."

"Sorry, Bert." He met Paisley's miserable-looking gaze. "I need to speak to my wife."

"Now, Sonny—"

"What's wrong?" Paisley asked. "Did something happen?"

"No, but we need to talk."

"She already took her break." Bert twisted the ends of his mustache. "Can't it wait until her shift is over?"

Judah wouldn't make it more difficult for Paisley by insisting she speak with him. Waiting for her shift to end would be hard but doable. How she felt mattered most to him. "Pais?"

"Two minutes, Bert?" She made an imploring expression toward her boss. "I'll stay late to make up for it."

"Fine."

"Thanks." Holding out his hand to Paisley and smiling at her, Judah hoped she recognized his attempt at an olive branch. When she clasped his hand, he sighed.

"I'm so sorry," he said as soon as they were outside. "I didn't mean to stick up for Mia over you, or over your opinion."

"I'm sorry I got offended." She hugged him, and he hugged her back. Then she tapped his chest with her finger. "However, I've warned you about her before."

"I know. She stirs the pot everywhere she goes. But criminal stuff? Crazy flirtatious behavior is more her style."

"Even so, I'm wary of her. You should be too."

"I am, believe me." He linked their pinkies. "I don't want anything coming between us. That was our first disagreement since we got married again."

"All because of Mia. Can't let that happen."

"Huh-uh." He leaned in to kiss her—their first makeup kiss, too.

Unfortunately, Bert rapped on the glass door and made a show of tapping his watch.

"Time's up." Paisley sighed. "Thanks for this. I needed it."

"Me too." Not willing to let the moment pass, and even though Bert still scowled at them, Judah kissed his wife softly. "Love you, sweetheart."

"Love you too. I have to get back to work."

"Okay." He let her go, glad he followed the impulse to not let things go unsaid between them. That's the way he hoped the rest of their marriage went. Always seeking out each other. Always believing the best in one another, no matter what happened in the future.

Fifty

For months, Forest couldn't get over the idea that he'd made a dreadful mistake in signing those divorce papers. Yet he didn't know how to undo what he did.

On his way to the police station, Forest mulled over what marrying Paige again meant to him. Today was the day he'd longed for during the three years he was away from her. The day he finally got to make things right. An answer to his prayers.

He was thankful she'd agreed to marry him. Yet, they weren't getting married for the exact reasons he hoped for. Still, he was making a commitment to Paige that would last, this time. He'd make sure of it. God was working in his life, too. *He'd* help them work out stuff in their marriage. And, hopefully, soon Paige would trust in the Lord also. That was a matter of daily prayer for Forest.

The kidnapping case, and the threats, still weighed heavily upon him. The need to protect Paige and Piper strummed through his veins. Even now, he wanted to be with them around the clock. That feeling wasn't going away until every shred of evidence against Edward, and whoever was helping him perpetrate his crimes, was discovered.

Ever since hearing of Mia's threat at the diner yesterday, something Forest previously noticed in the hospital video but hadn't zoomed in on kept replaying through his thoughts. Just a hunch. But sometimes his hunches unlocked hidden mysteries in a case. He'd learned to listen to his gut instincts.

Tomorrow, a dispatcher from Regional was arriving to pick up his reports and all the evidence. This would be his last chance to double-check everything. He didn't have much time since he was meeting Paige back at the house in an hour, and he didn't want her to be there alone. Then they'd drive to Florence and say their vows before a judge.

Vows. A tightening in his throat reminded him that he hadn't kept his promises to her last time. He let Paige go without trying hard enough to fix things between them. This time their marriage would be a top priority over his job, his life goals, and over every other woman on the planet. Other than Piper. He grinned at the thought of his daughter. Hopefully, he and Paige would have a couple more kids just like her.

As he strode into the deputy's office, he told himself to focus on the case for a few minutes. Then he'd let it go for the rest of the day and concentrate on making a beautiful memory with Paige. The start of their happily ever after. He wished his family—Mom, Dad, and his sister, Teal—were here to celebrate with him. Maybe after he and Paige had a chance to work out the realities of their marriage, they could do a mock wedding ceremony or a reception so both of their families could meet and celebrate with them.

"Morning," Forest said to Deputy Brian, who sat at his desk drinking coffee. "I need to see the video evidence."

"Again?"

"Yeah. Something's bothering me. Might be nothing, but I have to check."

"Fine." Brian strode to the safe. A few minutes later, he brought up the video on his computer.

Leaning over, squinting at the screen, Forest peered at the slightly blurry video of Edward forcing Paisley down a deserted hospital hallway in North Bend. The resolution was far from clear, but why were the halls empty? Where were the nurses and technicians that would normally be in a hospital hallway during that time of day?

"Play it again, will you? And double the size."

The deputy messed with the computer mouse.

"There. Freeze it!"

The frame stopped too late.

"Go back a second."

Grumbling, Brian moved the mouse again.

"That's it. See that shadow?" He pointed at the screen.

Both men peered toward the monitor.

"What are you seeing that I'm not?" Brian asked.

"Right there. In the doorway." Forest tapped the screen, excitement pounding through him. His hunch was right. "Check out the reflection in the glass. What do you see?"

Brian stroked his chin. "A short woman? Can't tell for sure."

"Exactly. That's what I see, too." Biting his lip, Forest kept his gaze on what he suspected was a light-haired woman wearing a medical mask. "Did she witness the crime? If so, why didn't she come forward? Was she Edward's accomplice? Did she clear the hallway for him?"

"Beats me. You're the detective."

Both men leaned down again, staring at the less-than-stellar image of a person seen only through the window's reflection. Not great evidence. Still, it was something.

"Short, blond, wavy hair, heavily made-up eyes," Forest assessed the person. "Remind you of anyone?"

"Are you implying it's Mia Till?" Brian scoffed and stared hard at the screen. "Considering the poor quality of the video, that's unlikely."

"Maybe."

Was Brian sticking up for the woman? Or stating the obvious?

"Regional should be able to fine-tune the image clarity. Then we'll know for certain."

This might be the break Forest had been searching for since he came to Basalt Bay two weeks ago. Or, if they couldn't verify the woman's identity, it might be nothing. Still, he'd check the hospital employment records. Show the picture around the facility.

"You want me to get some backup here, then you and I could escort this video to the regional office in my squad car?" Brian asked.

Delay the wedding ceremony for the case? Paige might already be back at the house waiting for him. Forest was committed to discovering the truth about the woman in the reflection, but he wouldn't put it before marrying Paige.

He planned to interrogate Mia too. Just not today. "Tomorrow will be soon enough."

Brian stared hard at him as if questioning Forest's dedication to the job. But the other man didn't know he was about to get married.

While the deputy returned the flash drive to the safe, Forest perused the second monitor on the desk that showed surveillance of the station's two jail cells. In one cell, Edward paced, his mouth moving rapidly as if he were shouting. In the other cell, Craig sat on a cot, his hands pressed against his ears.

When Brian returned to his desk, Forest asked, "Can you turn up the volume on this conversation?"

"Yep. Fair warning, since the lockdown on visitors, Edward has been more belligerent than ever." Brian made a couple of mouse clicks.

"I told you to keep her quiet," Edward said sharply. "I told you she'd cause trouble. Was I right? Huh, was I?"

Who was he talking about? Mia? Paige?

"But, no, you wouldn't listen to me. Judah never listens, either. No one does. Other than—" He mumbled something indistinguishable.

Forest squatted down to observe Edward's mannerisms on the screen—jerky body movements, thrusting his hands through his hair, eyes wide like golf balls, teeth showing as he bit off his words.

"Are you listening to me?" Edward yelled and jabbed his finger in the direction of Craig's cell, even though the two men couldn't see each other. "Do you see the trouble you two have caused?"

You two. Who else was Edward referring to? His accomplice?

"Just stop talking, will you? I'm sick to death of it." Craig flopped down on the cot, his gaze aimed toward the ceiling.

"I'd do anything to get away from your obnoxious voice. Your crazy lies."

Hmm. He was willing to do anything? Even turning against Edward?

"You should have done what I said." Edward clenched his hand into a fist. "Then none of this would have happened. We'd be free."

"Why would I do anything to help you?" Craig scowled.

"We both know why. Need me to spell it out?" Edward peered into the camera, eerily staring right at Forest. "Then everyone will know the truth about who committed the crime."

Was the ex-mayor blaming someone else for his misdeeds? Someone Craig knew about? Or was Edward implying that Craig had been in on his wrongdoings all along?

Forest's fact-finding mission for the Grant case was nearly at an end, that's what Sheriff Morris wanted, what Forest wanted too, but it seemed it just got a little more twisted and stirred up again.

Fifty-one

*Six months pregnant, Paige finally told her father
about the baby. He didn't act surprised, so maybe
she hadn't hidden it, after all. During her final
trimester, she planned to call Forest, but something
kept her from doing so.*

Driving to the project house, questions and worries
whirled in Paige's mind. Why was she getting married to Forest
on the sly again? Embracing the man she fell for, divorced,
then couldn't get over, as if she loved him all along, when she
was still so unsure? Were they about to make the worst mistake
ever? Or was it possible this leap into the unknown might bring
them into a genuine relationship, eventually?

She thought of Aunt Callie's analogy of jumping off a rock
into the water. How she said Paige had missed out on something
spectacular by never having done that. Was this her leap of
faith?

She dreamed of kissing Forest again last night. Not any blasé kiss, either. One of those heart-throbbing, hot-faced, knock-your-socks-off kisses that felt so passionate you might die from it. Even now, her heart nearly went into palpitations just imagining the amorous kiss.

Sighing, she unclasped Piper from the car seat and made her way down the trail to Bess and Aunt Callie's project house. She called earlier and asked Paisley if she'd watch Piper here while Paige and Forest went on a date.

Getting married could be classified as a date, right? Her chuckle bordered on giddiness. She'd better control her laughter and be careful inside the house, or the truth might come spilling out at some unsuspecting moment.

If she confided in Paisley and Judah about what she and Forest planned to do, then she'd have to tell Aunt Callie. Her aunt would demand an invitation to the ceremony. Paige didn't want that. Didn't want fanfare over what might be only a fake marriage. She dreaded disappointing anyone, too.

Then there were her wishy-washy feelings toward Forest. One minute, her thoughts were full of his tender kisses. A second later, "Sweet dreams, Elinore," played through her mind like a dark omen. Would those hurtful words ever disappear from her memory?

"Paige, hello!" Paisley met her on the porch with a wide grin. "Hey, Piper. Want to look at some books with me?" She held out her hands.

Piper wrapped her arms tightly around Paige's neck.

"Remember Auntie Paisley?" Paige jostled Piper, hoping for an easy transition without tears. She thought this would be the safest place for her daughter to stay while she and Forest were away for a couple of hours, especially with all the people here. "Auntie Paisley," she prompted.

"*Peezee?*"

"That's right."

Piper loosened her hold on Paige's neck, stealing glances at Paisley.

Laughing, chattering about a squirrel in a tree, Paisley scooped up Piper. She bounced her and galloped the way Judah usually did as she brought her into the house. By Piper's giggling, she was thrilled with the activity.

Relieved to avoid a tantrum, Paige followed with her backpack.

Judah and Bess, who were leaning over blueprints on the butcher-block island in the kitchen, greeted her in normal tones as if this were an ordinary day. Nothing special. Not a wedding day. If only they knew.

"Do you have a date planned for the gallery opening yet?" Bess smiled. "No pressure. I'm just eager to start our new venture."

"Not yet, but soon. Forest and I have been ... distracted with the threats and all." Again, they had no idea.

"Oh, right." Bess ran her hand over Judah's arm. "Things have slowed down here as well."

"I'm making up for lost time today." Judah held up a hammer.

Happy sounds from the living room reached Paige. Paisley was talking to Piper about the ocean and whales. Piper jabbered back to her. Paige should make a quick exit while all was peaceful.

She and Forest had gone in separate directions this morning. While she was delivering Piper to Paisley, he was checking in with Deputy Brian. He might already be back at the house, waiting for her to join him. Waiting for her to take this monumental step with him.

Aunt Callie shuffled into the room. "I thought I heard your voice." She walked over and gave Paige a hug. It was unusual for Aunt Callie to be so affectionate.

Did she suspect Paige was up to something? Did she look guilty?

"What are you and Forest up to today?" Aunt Callie asked with a sparkle in her eyes.

"Uh, well, um, er." Paige nearly choked.

"I recognize that look on your face."

"You do?" Paige coughed.

"It's the look of love, my dear, the look of love." She patted Paige's cheek.

Gulp.

Footsteps sounded across the porch and the front door opened. Paige tensed, but when James Weston entered and tipped his derby hat in their direction, she relaxed. Why was she so on edge today?

"Morning, folks. Callie." His voice turned soft and squishy sounding.

Aunt Callie's face flushed.

Hmm. Someone else in the room might have the "look of love," too.

"James." Aunt Callie bustled into the kitchen. "Want some coffee?"

"Yes, ma'am." He followed her.

"I should be going." Paige moved toward the door. "Call if Piper has any problems, okay?"

"Will do. You guys enjoy yourselves." Judah winked.

Her face heated up. She cleared her throat. Did he notice her discomfort? If so, he probably thought she was embarrassed about going on a first date with Forest.

If Judah were aware of their wedding plans, would he try to intervene? Perhaps tell them they were making a huge mistake? Or, believing in grace and second chances the way he did, would he shake their hands and offer them his sincere congratulations?

Fifty-two

Paige stood facing Forest in front of Judge Baker, a short-haired, fiftyish female judge who wore a navy robe at the Florence Courthouse. She didn't like the burden of another secret, and she didn't know if she was making the right decision in agreeing to this quick marriage. However, not having to make explanations to Dad, Aunt Callie, and Paisley, no fancy prepping, and no wedding dress hunt made it easier. A relief, even.

She'd dug out her old wedding ring and washed it in liquid detergent, put on a little more makeup than usual, and wore her dark gray sleeveless dress—the same one she'd worn three years ago—and pearls. That was the extent of her wedding day preparations.

Tomorrow, she'd explain her reasons for marrying Forest so promptly and secretively to her family. Hopefully, they'd understand and support her. Still, she would have liked Paisley to be in attendance as her matron of honor, the way Paige had been maid of honor in her beach wedding, and for her dad to give her away.

All the other stuff—being a wife again, living with Forest, co-parenting, and doing everything she could to keep her and Piper safe—would have to be faced too.

Forest caressed her cheek. "You okay?"

She nodded, glad he couldn't read her uncertain thoughts.

Thanks to him getting the three-day waiting period for a marriage license waved by the county clerk, they were here today. Two of the judge's clerks stood to the side of the room, serving as their witnesses—a woman who appeared to be in her mid-thirties, and a twentyish man in dark-rimmed glasses.

"You look great in that dress." Forest smiled at her. "It's the same one, isn't it?"

"Yes." She was glad he noticed.

"Do you, Forest Harper, promise yourself to Paige Cedars? To love and cherish her all the days of your lives?" Judge Baker asked, a sober expression on her face.

"I do." Forest clasped both of Paige's hands. "I will always love you. You have my word."

Heat infused her neck, her face. Did the judge notice how much she was blushing?

"Do you, Paige Cedars, promise yourself to Forest Harper? To love and cherish him all the days of your lives?"

There was the part about love she struggled with. Three years ago, she was certain she loved Forest and that he loved her. But since their breakup, she doubted love, or the longevity of it.

She appreciated how Forest wanted to be with Piper as a daddy. The way he was putting his career on hold, backed her gallery, and was determined to protect her and Piper were all noble and good things.

Love came in different forms, didn't it? Maybe she would never experience the fireworks she once did, except in her dreams. That didn't mean zero love resided in her heart. Maybe it just needed rekindling. Those kisses with him on the beach, two days ago, had been amazing. When he took her hand in his and gazed into her eyes, it seemed as if they belonged together.

Maybe she loved him more than she realized.

"Paige?" he whispered, a note of panic in his voice.

"Oh, I do."

He squeezed her hands.

"By the power vested in me by the state of Oregon"—Judge Baker swayed her hand toward them—"I pronounce you husband and wife."

Just like that, and the same as before, they were married without inviting anyone, without telling anyone. The last time they rushed back to their hotel room eager to experience the intimate joys of married life. This time they'd go home to separate rooms but, at least, back to the same house.

"You may kiss the bride." The judge chuckled and nudged Forest's arm.

"Oh, yes, ma'am." He gazed at Paige, lifting an eyebrow as if asking her permission.

She shrugged. A little kiss would be okay.

Gazing warmly at her, he drew her into his arms and snuggled her against his chest as if they had all the time in the world. She didn't step back or tell him to slow down or remind him this was going to be a fake marriage. Instead, she gazed into his eyes. Today, his irises weren't gray-green. Not jade colored, either, like he was feeling emotional or romantic.

Instead, their hue was the most beautiful shade of forest green, perhaps the truest color of all. Was this the hue of love she saw in his eyes?

"You are the most important person in my life," he whispered near her ear. "I want you with me more than anything. For all time. For real." He kissed her cheek.

Oh. Was he going to kiss her only on the cheek at their wedding? Disappointment flooded her. She started to step back, to disengage from his arms, but he pulled her closer again as if he didn't notice her withdrawal.

"I promise to stand by you," he continued, "to protect you, to be your partner 'til death do us part."

His gaze intertwining with hers, his lips brushed her mouth lightly, teasingly. He deepened the kiss and the intensity of his lips exploring hers. Dormant sparklers ignited within her, startling her. He kept kissing her, and she kissed him back, unaware of anything but him.

Forest ...

Breathless, she met his gaze, a smile of awe widening her tingling lips. If she said anything, she might blurt out that she did, in fact, love him. If she wasn't careful, she might tell him she didn't want to sleep in separate rooms, after all. Whose silly idea was that?

Air, she needed a deep guzzle of air, then her brain fog would clear. They were going to take their time and become friends again before romancing each other, right? She had to learn to trust him before she gave her heart, her whole self, to him. Which meant no more kissing like *that*, for goodness' sake.

Judge Baker shook their hands and congratulated them.

Forest linked his and Paige's fingers together, grinning broadly, and led them outside into the rainy stormy day. Even with the cold fall winds blustering about them, she felt warm because of the tender gazes emanating from the man she pledged herself to again—and the heated kiss they shared.

Forest paused on the sidewalk and took her in his arms again. "Mrs. Harper, there's only one thing left for us to do."

"Oh? What's that?"

Still holding her, he smoothed his fingers down her cheek, tangling them in her hair. Then his lips met hers in the sweetest, most delicate kiss she ever knew. All those times she tried to remember what kissing him had been like, she never pictured one this searching, this gentle, this ... intimate. And it was just a kiss. But a passionate one that said while he might be staying in the living room tonight, if she wanted more, whenever she wanted more, he'd be ready and waiting.

"I'm yours, baby. With every speck of vulnerability and strength I have, I am yours for the rest of my life."

She gulped and gulped again.

"What shall we do now?" he asked.

"I don't know." She hadn't thought ahead to what they'd do after they exchanged vows. "Drive back to Basalt Bay? Go to our house?" Although, with the romantic way she was feeling after his kisses, that might be dangerous.

A mischievous look crossed his face. "Let's get some food and talk first. Get to know each other."

"And then?"

"Then we'll live together as husband and wife, Forest and Paige Harper, forever." He sealed the promise with another soft kiss.

Oh, my. She'd better rein in her racing heart, and her tender thoughts toward her husband, or this marriage of convenience was going to get real much sooner than she imagined.

Watch for more about the Grant and Cedars families coming in Fall 2021:

Port of *Return*

Restored 6

They failed at marriage before, but this time, Forest wants to convince Paige he's in their relationship for keeps. Will protecting her and Piper prove his sincerity? Stepping up as a father? Or will more of the kisses he's sure she likes make all the difference?

If you would like to be one of the first to hear about Mary's new releases and upcoming projects, sign up for her newsletter—and receive the free pdf "Rekindle Your Romance! 50+ Date Night Ideas for Married Couples." Check it out here:

www.maryehanks.com/gift

A special thanks to everyone who helped with this book!

Paula McGrew ~ Thank you so much for helping with this project! I appreciate your diligence and thoughtfulness as you work through my stories, word by word. Thank you for your encouragement, too. You are a treasure!

Suzanne Williams ~ Thank you for another lovely cover design! I appreciate your talent and helpfulness so much.

Kellie Griffin, Mary Acuff, Beth McDonald, Joanna Brown, and Jason Hanks ~ Thank you for beta reading another book in this series! I love your enthusiasm for the story and the characters. I appreciate all the heartwarming comments and the critiques, too! God bless you for encouraging me, and guiding me, in my writer's journey.

My family—Jason, Daniel, Philip, Deborah, Shem, & Traci— who hear tidbits of my writing progress and cheer me on. Thank you!

The Lord who gives me creative ideas—*Thank You*!

(This is a work of fiction. Any mistakes are my own. ~meh)

Books by Mary Hanks

Restored Series

Ocean of Regret

Sea of Rescue

Bay of Refuge

Tide of Resolve

Waves of Reason

Port of Return (Fall '21)

Second Chance Series

Winter's Past

April's Storm

Summer's Dream

Autumn's Break

Season's Flame

Marriage Encouragement

Thoughts of You (A Marriage Journal)

maryehanks.com

About Mary Hanks

Mary Hanks loves stories about marriage restoration. She believes there's something inspiring about couples clinging to each other, working through their problems, and depending on God for a beautiful rest of their lives together—and those are the types of stories she likes to write. Mary and Jason have been married for forty-plus years, and they know firsthand what it means to get a second chance with each other, and with God. That has been her inspiration in writing the Second Chance series and the Restored series.

Besides writing and reading, Mary likes to garden, do artsy stuff, go on adventures with Jason, and meet her four adult kids for coffee or breakfast.

Connect with Mary by signing up for her newsletter at

www.maryehanks.com

"Like" her Facebook Author page:

www.facebook.com/MaryEHanksAuthor

maryehanks.com

Made in the USA
Middletown, DE
09 November 2022

14497041R00196